MW01610309

My friend, my 'little sister', and mother
of my 'pretend child'.

Joaquin

Joaquin Barrientos

THE FACE IN
THE MIRROR

Limited Special Edition. No. 7 of 25 Paperbacks

Joaquin Barrientos resides in London, Ontario, with his wife, Julie; and their two cats. Ever since he became fascinated with ghosts at an early age, he has become obsessed with all things horror, despite having an intense fear of the dark. When he isn't reading horror novels or watching slasher films, he and his wife can be found travelling around the world, one country at a time.

For Julie, the love of my life; and Hector, my brother and unofficial creative partner.

Joaquin Barrientos

THE FACE IN THE MIRROR

AUSTIN MACAULEY PUBLISHERS™

LONDON • CAMBRIDGE • NEW YORK • SHARJAH

A CIP catalogue record for this title is available from the British Library.

ISBN 9781528903172 (Paperback)
ISBN 9781528903189 (E-Book)

www.austinmacauley.com

First Published (2019)
Austin Macauley Publishers Ltd
25 Canada Square
Canary Wharf
London
E14 5LQ

Thank you first off to Austin Macauley Publishers for taking a chance on an unknown author, who will now see his name on a published book. You have made my lifelong dream a reality and I'm eternally grateful.

Thank you to my brother Hector, who, through seemingly random conversations, helps me come up with story idea after story idea. One day, we will write that comic together and become the next Joe Hill and Gabriel Rodriguez. Six years ago, this story started out as a comic you and I were planning on writing together. You had asked me to write the back story after we were inspired by the way Stephen King and Scott Snyder collaborated on *American Vampire*. But once you read what I had, you told me to run with my story and forget about the comic. Thank you for reading my story six years ago and for reading the countless others I continue to send you.

Thank you to Carmen, Ana, Juan, my mother and my father, who constantly support me and love me.

Thank you to the substitute teacher I had in my first week of Grade 9 English, who accused me of plagiarism when I wrote an original short horror story. You thinking that my work in the ninth grade was strong enough to be mistaken with that of a real author inspired me to pursue this dream, as did that A+ you gave me.

Thank you to Nick Cutter and Stephen King, whose novels *The Troop* and *Carrie* helped me finally figure out how to lay out this story when I was stuck figuring out how to make it all work. Stephen King, you taught me that not every thriller needs blood and gore to make it work. And Nick Cutter, you taught me that it's okay to make a story and the characters Canadian, not every story needs to be set in NYC, LA or Boston.

Lastly, thank you to my wife, Julie, who used to find the mistakes in my university essays and made me fix them myself so I would learn how to not make them again. My writing style became legible thanks to you. And an even bigger thank you to you for turning me into a reader when we first moved in together, I would never have been able to finish all of those books without you first encouraging me to pick up The Hunger Games to read when I was 'bored at work'. Two hundred books later, my Goodreads account and I thank you. I love you and couldn't have done this without you.

Table of Contents

Prologue

From the pages of the Middlesex Community News

Tragedy Strikes at Middlesex County Hospital

By: Pat Foley – Middlesex Community News
Monday, November 16, 2015

Middlesex County Hospital, located on the outskirts of Thamesville, has long been regarded as one of the provincial leaders in innovative health care for patients with mental illnesses. Today, however, the hospital's award-winning Mental Health program is not the receiver of praise but rather of mass criticism following an incident from this past weekend.

A resident who had been admitted to the hospital just one year ago was recently transferred into the hospital's Mental Health Recovery Complex, where they were looking to transition patients back to independent living before they are finally released. Sources tell us that the patient was being considered for release and was in a counselling session to determine if she was indeed prepared to leave the hospital's care. During the session, however, the patient grew aggravated and attacked the attending counsellor, before finally taking her own life.

Sources state that the counsellor who was conducting the session suffered potentially fatal wounds; however, no more information has been released to their status.

The on-site living complex where the patient had been residing at the time of the incident was recently introduced as part of the hospital's new Adult Mental Health Program. This portion of the program in particular had brought the hospital high praise from the medical and social services community alike.

13

Katelyn Thomas, head of the hospital's Adult Mental Health Program explained to us the purpose of the hospital's on-site living complex. "The living complexes are meant to be an on-site transitional housing program that assists patients who are being released from intensive mental health care back into the community. This program keeps the patients on hospital grounds where they have easy access to counselling, social supports and medical supervision. The program also benefits them as it prepares them in adjusting back to an independent living. Once the medical staff and highly trained counsellors agree that the patient is ready to be reintegrated into society, we have our social services team assist them in finding safe and affordable housing. So far we have seen the recidivism rate of patients with mental health issues decrease significantly. It's the lowest it's been in decades."

When asked how a patient in the final stages of being released from this therapeutic program could relapse so suddenly to the point of suicide and violence, Ms. Thomas replied: "Patients can relapse at any moment in time. Whether it's a day into counselling or ten years. We advise all of our patients about immediate supports they can access if they are ever in crisis. We have the numbers of each crisis centre and the mental health line in each individual living unit and we have staff on call 24/7 who service the complex. We put in as many safeguards as we can to support our clients. From what we understand of this situation, the client was receiving constant counselling and had shown signs of improvement. It was as much a shock to us as it was to everyone else."

The hospital will have a lot of questions to answer surrounding these tragic events and one can't help but wonder how this affects the living complex and the funding the program was receiving annually from the province.

When asked about the condition of the staff who responded to the situation, Ms. Thomas told us: "We are doing the best to support everyone involved. The staff is speaking with counsellors, and we have offered the same thing to the patients who knew the deceased. We are working very hard to get everyone onto the road of recovery."

The hospital staff is still in the process of contacting the family of the patient and of the counsellor who was attacked. Until they have been notified, we cannot release the names of either party.

For more details, visit our website at www.middlesexCN.ca

From the pages of The Thamesville Gazette

Fire Erupts in Old South
By: Denise Herrera, Thamesville Gazette
Monday, May 30, 2016

The oldest housing district in Thamesville, better known to residents as Old South, was hit with a monstrous house fire last night that completely destroyed the home at 1124 Lorne Street. The fire department was contacted shortly after large plumes of black smoke were seen across the street, at which point the majority of the interior damage had already been done. The fire department stated that the roof of the house collapsed only minutes after their arrival and that the house, along with its contents, were unsalvageable.

Investigators stated that the source of the fire was arson, which was started by the resident who actually owned the home. Police managed to apprehend the resident, Crista Sunderland, immediately as she was reported to be standing outside the house, screaming hysterically and in fact confessing that she had started the fire.

Neighbours informed us that Crista was always incredibly quiet and always kept to herself. One neighbour stated that she seemed like a well-adjusted individual who you'd sooner forget lived there by how much she kept to herself. Another neighbour said that she never caused trouble of any kind and that she was always respectful of noise. It came as a shock to the community when they witnessed her outside of her home, confessing to its destruction.

When asked what had caused her to light her own house on fire, Crista would not answer.

She simply kept shouting that she had started the fire.

Thamesville Fire Marshall, Lawrence Chan, stated that the amount of damage to the home was significant and that sorting through the debris was going to take a substantial amount of work. Chan then went on to state that the surrounding homes also experienced significant smoke damage that will require immediate repairs.

Police have not stated whether anyone else was in the household as they are still investigating the scene and so far have been unable to get any further details from Crista.

Crista remains in police custody and sources state that she will be taken to Middlesex County Hospital, where she will be transferred to the Psychiatric Ward where she will be psychologically assessed to determine if she is fit for trial.

More updates to follow.

For more details, visit our website at www.thamesvillegazette.ca/news.

Part 1

Chapter 1
June 2016 – Jack

The first thing I did that morning when I pulled into work was throw my car door open and vomit all over the parking lot.

Some of it splashed back into the car and onto my feet——this only made me feel even sicker, which resulted in me throwing up even more. My head was pounding as the thought of standing made my head spin. I was surprised I was able to drive to work with a hangover this bad, but I impressed myself when I did manage to arrive here without incident. But that was when my stomach decided to expel the gin and beer I had mixed the night before. I wasn't sure I'd be able to stand up from my car when I heard the voices of the other staff in the parking lot——they weren't even trying to hide their voices or their pointing. Everyone was watching the disaster that was Jack Fletcher.

After a few deep breaths to make sure that I had my stomach under control, I stumbled from my car and made my way into the office. The walk from my car to my office left me feeling completely wiped out. The room had begun to spin and I was sure I was about to throw up again so I bent over and put my head between my legs. And without realizing it, I had fallen asleep.

It was the whispers that had woken me up. If it had only been one or two of them outside my office whispering, I wouldn't have even noticed. But when the entire office is whispering about you, well that makes it awfully difficult to ignore.

They had all seen me stroll into the office with yesterday's shirt, an unshaven face and flaky hair with unwashed hair gel still lingering inside. My hair was thick and often refused to stay down unless I poured an entire bottle of product into it, and whenever I forgot to wash it out the next morning, it would turn into a pile of dry white flakes. This morning I had realized I had run out of hair gel so I resorted to the oldest trick a boy's mother teaches him. I licked my hand, then patted the top of my hair in an attempt to flatten it. It was incredibly unsuccessful.

My hair was the least of my concerns—my eyes were being carried by two dark heavy bags that highlighted the fact that my eyes were more red than white. They were bloodshot, tired and screamed hangover. I had tried downing an entire pot of coffee before leaving for work and buying another cup on the way in an attempt to wake myself up, but when I pulled into the parking lot, I caught my reflection in the rear-view mirror and saw that it hadn't worked. My hangover was apparent for everyone to see, but to be honest they had all come to expect it by this point.

I'd been demoted to essentially a paper pusher ever since I had come back from my 'voluntary leave of absence', otherwise known as my forced workplace suspension. It was easier saying voluntary leave of absence than it was to say 'the allotted time I'm allowed to remain on payroll before they revoke my Social Workers License and fire me officially'. The hospital had distributed my clients amongst the other case workers and had me doing menial and pointless clerical work.

File this. Fax that. Call this client. Cancel with that client. Organize these folders. Shred those ones. Hate your life.

I had fought to get back some of my clients but Katelyn made sure that wasn't an option.

Katelyn had originally been my biggest advocate and supporter during my time here at the hospital. I was the youngest practicing social worker the hospital had ever hired, which in turn meant the least experienced. The hospital board had been hearing consistent negative feedback about their existing staff of so-called mental health professionals for years, namely that they were often out of touch with clients, cranky and burnt out.

They were mostly a group of older, bitter and unfriendly women who had become social workers in the 1970s when all it took was a two year college diploma and no life experience whatsoever. I had two undergrads, years of volunteering in low-income neighborhoods and had to pay an exorbitant amount of yearly fees to the Ontario College of Social Workers just to keep my status. Yet to them, I was an entitled and privileged recent grad who never had to work for things like they did. Try to understand that.

Katelyn had been the youngest social worker on staff before me, and upon completing her second degree in non-profit management, she was promoted to the head of the Adult Mental Health Program that was looking to reinvent itself. The board hired her on the promise that she would take the outdated and out-of-touch program and reinvent it with new methods of counselling, new community initiatives and most of all, new and compassionate counsellors. She was looking at social workers, psychiatrists and child psychiatrists who were only a few years out of school who hadn't yet been hit with burn out, and who had experience working in the community with actual clients. Her hope was that this could bring a new perspective and method of practice to the incredibly outdated mental health program the hospital was looking to rebuild.

Katelyn's first act as new Program Director was to hire me. For a time it proved to be a solid gamble on her part as I exceeded expectations and set the bar of how the hospital's counsellors should interact with clients. For a time I was her best hire.

Today, however, I was considered her worst hire and her biggest mistake.

When I had started working, my ability to connect with the clients and build a solid rapport was a thing of beauty. Other case workers often complained about the noise and laughter coming from my appointments and those that didn't complain would slam their doors in protest.

I had been incredibly successful in breaking down the most difficult clients and helping them reach more of their goals than other caseworkers could even dream about. In the time it took someone else to make any sort of progress with a single client, I had made progress with five.

I had eventually accumulated the largest caseload of all the counsellors, and yet somehow I was still managing it better than the other staff who had half of what I was handling. My clients dropped by the office just to visit me and chat or even to bring me a coffee. They refused to speak with other staff and would always ask for me by name. I wasn't only successful in managing the most clients but also in closing out the most amount of files. My success rate of closing client files from our services was the highest in the entire hospital for 21 consecutive months.

There wasn't any client I wasn't willing to work with. Mental health, addictions, victims of abuse, clients recently released from incarceration and PTSD were all clients I could handle. More often than not I sought out the most challenging ones, just so I could prove to myself and the other case workers that I was that good.

I was confident. I was successful. I was slowly moving up to the top of my field.

Then Gwen's name came across my desk. And everything changed.

Gwen left me broken, miserable and depressed. The clicking and clacking noises that the other staff often heard coming from my bag wasn't a pack of tic-tacs. It was the numerous pill bottles I had filled with anti-anxiety and anti-depressant medication ever since my encounter with Gwen. My hands shook uncontrollably without these pills, but what was worse than the shaking were the dreams. Without the sleeping pills the doctor hesitantly prescribed me, I wouldn't sleep due to the incredibly vivid and anxiety-inducing dreams I so frequently experienced.

Well, not dreams. These were nightmares.

Nightmares about Gwen.

My mind wandered to the most recent nightmare I had experienced about Gwen, and how vivid the whole thing had been. She was sitting in the chair across from me, downing a tall glass of water before smashing it and lunging at me. I shook the vividness of the dream out of my head, and quickly came out of my mental fog, which had distracted me from noticing Katelyn who was standing at my door, calling for my attention.

"Jack," Katelyn near shouted with the angriest motherly tone anyone had ever heard from someone who wasn't my mother. I could tell from her tone that this wasn't the first time she had called my name, and that she wasn't happy about it.

I wiped the sleep from my eyes and tried to look casual in my chair as I pretended to look at my computer screen that was so obviously not on. Judging from the frustration in her face, I had failed in appearing busy.

"Katelyn. What can I do for you?" I said with a forced smile on my face as I pretended to turn away from my computer that very clearly didn't have any work being done on it.

"Do you not have enough to do?" she said in that same angry motherly tone. My brain told me to leave it alone and apologize. But my mouth betrayed me.

"Actually no. If I had some clients to work with, I might be able to—"

"Ha!" The volume of her laugh hurt my head. "You're serious? You want to have this discussion again? Because I'd be more than happy to have a full lengthy discussion about this again." I cringed away at her booming voice. The pounding in my head was bad enough, but her yelling only made it that much worse. I moved my eyes away from her and back to my computer, this time saying the sensible thing.

"I'm sorry, Katelyn, no you're right. I have lots to do."

"Then let's see you get back to it." She looked overhead and upon noticing that I had kept the office lights off, she flicked the light switch back to on and stomped behind me and opened the blinds. It was a cloudy and grey day outside, so the dramatic effect of having the sun's light flood into the room was lost. But it didn't stop her from making a production of the entire thing. She looked at my blank screen and scoffed loudly and dramatically so I could hear that I had been caught pretending to do work. She stormed out of the room and I heard her shout at the other staff that if anyone needed more work, then she had plenty for them to do. The whispering stopped and everyone rushed back to where they were supposed to be.

I turned back to my computer and actually turned it on this time. I fished out my iPod from my pocket and threw my battered, cheap headphones into my ears in an attempt to drown out the very poor attempt at whispering that my co-workers started up again after Katelyn had left. Due to the pounding headache, I couldn't shake. I felt that my usual 'wake up' playlist, which consisted mostly of hard rock from the 1990s, would be a bit much for me this morning. I instead chose to go with an easy listening playlist of 'Classics' that I only listened to on rare occasion and hit shuffle.

'Hey, Jude.'

"Goddamn it!"

I kept intending to delete that song from my iPod, but every time I went to do it, I found I couldn't do it. It was Amy's favourite song in the world, even though as I pointed out, it was the most overdone song in the world.

Well when a song is that good, of course it's overdone! Now put the song on your iPod because I'm your wife, and you love me, and I asked you to.

It was the first song she played every single time we got into the car, and once we were married I never went a day without hearing it. Once I tried skipping it and she took offence; so she downloaded it onto my phone and made it the ringtone that played every single time she called me. I changed it about a thousand times, but every single time I got a call from her the song would come back onto my phone. It was the Frankenstein of songs; no matter how much I tried to get rid of it, she would find a way to get it back into my life.

Eventually, I gave up and I told her if she loved it this much I'd let her listen to it as much as she wanted. The next morning when my alarm came on, the song came blaring out of my phone. She woke up giggling and I woke up groaning as that song had invaded every aspect of my life.

I winced at the memory of listening to the song with her and immediately hit the skip track button on the playlist. Simon and Garfunkel's 'Sound of Silence' came on and helped snap me out of my momentary mental paralysis. In classic Amy fashion, she had monopolized my thoughts for an extended period of time. I tried to ignore these invasive thoughts as I hummed along to the new song selection.

I turned my music up as loud as I could bear it so I could drown out the whispers of everyone in the office but it made no difference—I knew what everyone would be saying without me having to listen to a word. Everyone knew that it was only a matter of time before I was fired.

The hospital had tried to fire me but had been unsuccessful since I hadn't technically violated any company policy. My Union Rep fought them pretty hard on that point and in the end, he saved my job and my bank account by having the hospital cover the cost of my medication and counselling.

When the arbitration was done, however, he told me that it was only a temporary fix. The Professional College of Social Workers was looking to investigate the incident and all signs pointed to my membership being revoked permanently.

Without a practicing license, I wasn't eligible to continue working at the hospital. So they wouldn't be firing me for my behaviour, they'd be firing me for lack of a license. Which the Union told me was 100% permissible and there was nothing they would be able to do in that scenario. I asked him what my options were to try to appeal with the Ontario College of Social Workers, but he had only shrugged and told me he only deals with hospital regulations. He told me I would have to hire my own lawyer since he wasn't a lawyer and any legal counsel the hospital had only covered themselves.

In the meantime, however, the hospital had to guarantee me work until the investigation with the college was over; however, it could be any work they assigned me to. It didn't have to be directly related to my previous position; it simply had to be work. Thus my menial clerical tasks.

The clerical work I was being assigned was essentially a death sentence. It was traditionally the hospital's practice to distribute the caseload of anyone on their way out of the organization to all of the other staff while giving the departing employee clerical work. Your intakes were all cancelled and your schedule was blocked out before your end date so you could clean up your last few remaining clients. When your last day finally came, you'd be left with no clients and no work left to do. Normally the departing counsellor didn't mind since it gave them a day to clean out their office. Unfortunately, however, this mirrored my daily work situation. I had been left with no clients, no intakes, no appointments and no hopes whatsoever of keeping my job.

Not that it much mattered anyways; with no clients I had no interest in the work they had assigned to me. I would be fired from my job of doing nothing, which would result in me being at home, doing nothing. The day I had made that realization was the first day I had come in hung-over. It was incredibly obvious and everyone in the office smelled the stench of alcohol coming off of me immediately, but I quickly noticed that there were no consequences. It was the first time I had ever come in hung-over since being an active counsellor basically made it impossible to ever come in less than 100%. If you came in for a day of client meetings hung-over, it was torture.

You couldn't sleep, yawn or show any disinterest in your counselling sessions when someone is pouring their heart out to you. You have to keep incredibly detailed client notes, which can be horrible when you're trying not to throw up whatever greasy late night food you had the night before. You are assigned to counselling rooms that are surrounded by staff, so rushing out of an appointment to go throw up would be seen by everyone. It was the worst way to spend your day here, but now, it's how I spent every day.

I was pulled from my day dream when I heard a faint song coming from the tattered and worn leather shoulder bag hanging off the back of my door. That workbag hadn't carried anything important in it for the past few months and yet I still brought it to work every day. I didn't even carry a lunch in it. All it carried was old memos, a notepad with drawings I made in meetings when I was bored and a crushed granola bar from a brand that went out of business years ago.

The only real purpose of the bag was simply to carry my phone, which I often avoided looking at the morning after a hard night of drinking. More often than not I wiped all of my messages the night of a binge so I could forget anything I sent. But on nights like last night, I knew that no amount of erased messages would help me in forgetting what happened, because the call the next morning was going to remind me. For that reason I had tucked my phone into the bottom of my bag and had hoped that I would be able to avoid looking at it all day.

Unfortunately, the ringing continued and the person wasn't giving up any time soon so I stumbled over. I had no interest in talking to anyone on the phone that morning, but if it was who I thought it was, I knew she wouldn't give up.

I clumsily rifled through my bag until I felt the various cracks in the screen from the numerous times I drunkenly dropped it. I grabbed the phone out of my bag and squinted to make out the name coming in on the caller display. The name on the screen was faint but the song I had assigned to this person's ringtone was unmistakable.

'For well you know that it's a fool who plays it cool. By making his world a little colder.'

I felt sick to my stomach, not from the hangover but from the dread of the conversation I was about to have. The light of the screen continued to light up as the phone continued ringing. My finger moved to the swipe to answer icon and I held my breath as I read the screen one more time.

Incoming Call: Amy.

"Shit."

I swiped right. "Hello?"

Chapter 2
June 2016 – Jack

"Are you fucking serious?"

"Look before you start, Ames, I don't remember calling you. I told you before if you see my name pop up, just ignore it. Delete the voicemail and just forget it. It'll save us both a lot of trouble and embarrassment." I had never spoken to her like this when we were together. I would've blindly apologized and hope her anger would subside after a few hours. Now I challenged her authority every chance I could find.

"No, you don't get to just absolve yourself of all responsibility by saying you were drunk. You're fucking naïve if you think that's all it takes." She always did have the mouth of an angel.

"Well can you tell me what I did before you—"

"No, you're going to have sit there and listen. You don't get to rush this! You call me"—I groaned for the incoming lecture, but she kept talking without acknowledging it—"and I ignored your first nine calls but finally picked up on the tenth! Then you tell me you're on your way over! I was scared to fucking death! I was ready to call the police!"

I sighed and threw my head back in my chair. I shut my eyes and just waited for her lecture to be over. I knew she was in the right, but I could not have cared less at this point.

When we first started dating, a simple apology would kill off any argument. But by the end, Amy had found it necessary to lecture me on everything I did wrong. My simply apologizing often didn't do enough to rectify the situation. I had to be explained why it was wrong of me, what I needed to learn from it and how I could avoid it in the future. She never lectured me like this when we first began dating, which you would have thought she would.

Namely because Amy had been my TA who ran our weekly seminars and who at the time was aptly named 'The Ice Queen'.

Students in their last year of the Social Work program would always warn the incoming classes about The Ice Queen. At the time, she was the youngest TA at the university and had been guaranteed a job as a professor when she graduated.

When I met Amy, I had already completed my undergrad and was now working through my second degree, this one in Social Work. I was the oldest student in the program and only two years younger than her.

A bit about Amy. She had been offered a position with the university while she was still completing her Master's in Social Work. She had turned them down initially and chose to work with various non-profit organizations before the university wore her down and she took a part-time position with them. She was only in her late twenties at the time.

The only thing more astounding than her drive and intelligence was her beauty. She was tall and slender with pale porcelain skin and straight shoulder-length auburn hair. She wore thick-rimmed glasses that complimented her subtle green eyes perfectly. Every male student had a crush on her, until they met her and she went from being beautiful to terrifying.

Amy was incredibly critical of the social work field and that's what drew me to her originally. The empty and 'enlightened' statements my classmates uttered throughout class discussions would often earn praise from the other professors, which in turn had the negative impact of inflating their egos. The professor, who had been the worst for this, was the professor Amy had been assigned to that semester. During our lectures, the professor would invite these kind of meaningless and hollow statements, and it seemed that no one besides me ever noticed Amy with her arms crossed and rolling her eyes at every statement.

When it came time for our weekly seminars, the professors wouldn't attend and would leave the facilitation up to their TAs. Which, this semester, was Amy. She would work diligently on breaking those egos the professor had only days before inflated and she made examples out of anyone, whenever she could.

There was one incident with my classmate Jasmyn, who I absolutely hated. Jasmyn was always quick to raise her hand and point out how her vast experience in the social services qualified her to judge the rest of us, and how anyone who did not share her social views was ignorant.

She referenced her two months' worth of experience working with the homeless on a daily basis, and frequently told us all that until we did the same, we had no idea what these people were struggling with. She criticized us for being privileged and ignorant to the horrors of the streets—even though she carried her notebooks in an authentic Louis Viton bag. She wore fair trade bracelets and only drank fair trade coffee, which really complimented her Lulu Lemon Hoodie and Yoga Pants. Her outfits alone cost more than my laptop.

She made empty statements such as "we need to support those with mental health" with no sort of follow up or concrete plan. But still, this would receive a round of applause from the class and a nod of approval from the other professors.

She tried this exact statement in Amy's seminar and while waiting for the nod of approval, Amy remained stone-faced and challenged her.

"How?"

The students who were waiting to applaud her stopped dead in their tracks. Jasmyn who had been waiting for Amy's praise was taken aback.

"What do you mean?"

"You said we should support individuals with mental health. Tell me how do you support individuals with mental health?"

Jasmyn had started to turn red, her chest was turning blotchy and her face was growing a darker shade by the second. She began to stumble over her words. It was evident no one had ever challenged her or bothered to ask her what her grand plan of rescue actually was.

"Well, I mean... I. Well I mean, talk to them and support them and help them when they need it?"

"You have a client with paranoid schizophrenia who has been known to be violent and is currently homeless. You want to talk to them? Pat them on the back and tell them that it's going to be okay?"

"Well yeah... I mean no not like that—just like supports!"

Amy's expression didn't change, but no one noticed because no one was looking at her. They were all looking at Jasmyn who was becoming visibly upset. Her empty knowledge and hollow words were being revealed and she didn't know how to handle it.

"So by supports do you mean medication?" Amy said in what was very much a trap.

Without hesitation, Jasmyn took the bait.

"Well yeah! That would work!"

"Do you realize that the majority of individuals with severe mental health don't have access to family doctors and those that do,

29

often can't afford the medication you're speaking about? So if they can't afford it, then how can we support them?"

"Oh! I didn't mean. I mean those who can afford it—"

"What about those who can't?"

Jasmyn's eyes were welling with tears. People in the room were incredibly uncomfortable and you could tell no one was willing to jump in to save their one-time hero.

Jasmyn's ego had been built by years of people telling her what a great person she was. Amy had just destroyed that ego in just a matter of two minutes. That was the moment I fell in love with her. So I thought I'd jump in. Not to help Jasmyn, but to help myself impress Amy.

"Funding."

Amy turned to me. "Sorry, what was that Mr.?"

"Fletcher."

"Mr. Fletcher. What were you saying?"

Every pair of eyes shot towards me, all except for Jasmyn who was wiping at the corners of her eyes now that no one was looking at her.

"I was saying that we need to look at funding opportunities. A lot of organizations are already supporting individuals with severe mental health issues but a lot of them are grossly understaffed or underfunded. One thing we can do is look at funding opportunities for these programs through say something like community initiative projects or introduction of new programs. The province usually sponsors new programs for existing organizations which in turn creates new positions within those organizations. Clients are already familiar with these organizations so they can continue going where they're already comfortable but now they have better supports. More funding means better supports for clients."

I stopped speaking when I saw the stunned look on everyone's face. I was usually the student who hung out in the back corner and kept his hand down and his mouth shut. No one had any idea I had that sitting in my back pocket.

Amy held her stone face on me for a few seconds before she smiled for the first time that semester.

"Interesting point, Mr. Fletcher. Brilliant point in fact." She moved on with the discussion and at the end of the seminar, Jasmyn scurried out and her posse of followers scurried after her. I lingered behind so I could speak with Amy. She was facing the white board and wiping away her notes when I approached.

"Hi, Professor Ryan?"

"It's just Amy, I'm not a professor yet." She turned around and her eyes lit up "Oh! Yes! Mr. Fletcher, thank you for staying behind. I was going to ask you to anyways but you've saved me the trouble. I just wanted to tell you, it's refreshing having someone in my class who actually understands the reality of this field."

"It's equally nice having a professor who isn't babying us when we need to be challenged."

"I'm not a professor," she repeated a little more sternly, but still there was an air of affection in her words.

"Right, my bad." I looked down at my feet to try to hide my smile. "I'm just so glad that someone finally put her in her place."

"When you say 'her', you mean your classmate Jasmyn?"

I smirked and shrugged my shoulders sarcastically; it was clear who I meant. At this we both began laughing and for a brief moment we locked eyes and I could immediately tell that my infatuation with her was not one sided.

The encouragement she gave me that day turned me into a completely different student. I began sitting at the front of each of my classes and was raising my hand in every discussion. I successfully challenged Jasmyn on just about every point she would make and soon her posse of blind followers started abandoning her. It wasn't long after that that my professors began approaching me about writing letters of recommendations for me. I had Amy to thank for all of it.

After writing my final exam, I went to her office to thank her for everything she had done for me that year. I told her about a job interview I had already secured with a not-for-profit organization specializing in assisting low income families secure housing. She extended her hand in congratulations and when I held it, our hands remained holding for longer than was necessary. In a split second I had decided to gamble, and I pulled her into me and planted my mouth on hers. Her chest pressed against mine and I felt her kissing me back. I had fantasized about this all year and was in disbelief for the first few seconds that this was happening, but seconds turned into minutes and when we finally separated, I was out of breath. I knew immediately that she was the only person I ever wanted to kiss.

We immediately began a relationship and within a year we had already moved in together. Our relationship was filled with laughter, deep discussions, a little bit of yelling and a lot of great sex. We agreed on so many things related to our field, and even everything outside of it. We both knew how to turn off our brains from work at the end of the day so we could simply enjoy each other's company. We read the same books, loved the same movies and even had the same hobbies.

Within two years I had proposed. And within three years we had purchased our first home. While my salary at the non-profit wasn't exactly high, Amy had finished her Master's and had started her own private practice which had taken off quicker than expected, all while also commuting to the university where she was taking courses towards her PhD. She was also still teaching part-time at the university and was continuously being offered a full-time role. She never resented my lack of high earnings or my moderate success. If anything, she valued it—she was competitive and having more success than me actually made her happy.

When the hospital posted the Social Worker position, Amy was incredibly encouraging. She helped me prep my resume, write the cover letter and even helped me prepare for the interview.

The day they called me with the job offer, she took out the $300 bottle of wine we had received as a wedding gift and decided this was an appropriate time to drink it and celebrate. I had told her that we should drink it on a night to celebrate something for the both of us, but she waved my protests away.

"I want to celebrate you. I love you." She kissed me gently on the mouth before she turned away from me with the bottle and popped it open before I could stop her.

After finishing the entire bottle, we had passionate, slightly drunken sex that night and slightly hung-over sex the morning after. Everything was going perfectly and I couldn't believe how well life was going for me.

Tears began to form in my eyes as I reminisced about life with Amy. My hand went to rub at my eyes before the tears had time to form and that's when I realized. My eyes were closed, and I had begun drifting off to sleep.

My eyes stayed shut a little bit longer than I intended and I was startled awake by her voice shouting at me.

"Are you fucking kidding me? Did you fall asleep? I'm talking to you!"

I inhaled deeply which gave me away immediately. It was my signature noise from waking up and Amy had picked up on it the first month we lived together.

"Jesus Christ! I can't even keep your attention for two goddamn seconds!"

"I'm sorry, I didn't mean to, Ames. What were you saying?" I took a deep drink from my now lukewarm coffee and sat up in an attempt to be fully alert. The phone sat in silence for a few seconds. It was her favourite trick when we argued—sit in silence so I could reflect on the fact that I just lost the argument. What would often be a few seconds of silence for her, felt like an eternity for me.

"Amy?" I could hear her sniffling on the other side. "Ames, I'm sorry, I—" The day she left me was the first time I had ever seen her cry. I didn't realize it until that very moment that I had never seen Amy cry. It takes a special kind of fuck up to make 'The Ice Queen' cry.

She continued sniffling on the other end of the phone and made sure I could hear it. She wanted to hear how upset I had made her.

"Call me again and I'm calling the cops. I don't give a shit if it's sober or a goddamn pocket dial. You don't call me again, understand?"

"Sure, of course, whatever you say." I knew I was going to call her again, and I knew she wouldn't ever call the police.

The line dropped and it took me a moment before I realized she had hung up on me. I tossed the phone into one of my drawers and put a stack of blank paper on top of it. I began organizing the files I was going to be inputting into the computer that morning and tried to grab enough that would see me through to lunch, where I could hopefully take a nap in my car.

I reached for my now cold coffee and planned on downing the rest of it. Right before I could drink any of it, the lid popped off the paper cup and coffee spilled all down the front of my shirt.

I didn't even react—I just sighed in defeat.

What a wonderful way to start my day!

Chapter 3
June 2016 – Jack

Katelyn's e-mail had come at the end of the day yesterday. I had managed to avoid her and keep my head down after she had scolded me in the morning. I had even been able to hide the sleep lines on my face when I came back from lunch, which was impressive since my face was covered in them. So when I received her e-mail, which read: "Come see me first thing tomorrow morning", I was a little more than nervous. My mind began racing over the events of the day as I tried to think of anything I would have done that would have resulted in a private meeting with Katelyn, first thing in the morning.

Normally, I don't mind admitting when I've messed up at work or when my performance is suffering; in fact, I'm always quicker to point it out than Katelyn is. But I thought back to yesterday and thought it was actually one of my better days. I thought maybe she had heard something from the college and that this meeting was to tell me my license was being revoked.

The thought made me drink myself into a blackout as an unhealthy form of preparation. Unfortunately, my hangover was outweighed by the small panic attack I experienced the morning of my meeting with Katelyn, which resulted in my taking a double dosage of my anxiety medication. This was something my doctor very much insisted I not do, but I disregarded that warning the first week after she had prescribed it to me.

Since I had returned to work, I had been anticipating the inevitable which had resulted in my lack of caring about the job or my own mental state. When I knew that I would be fired once my license was revoked, I lost all motivation to do a good job or even care about my work.

Nothing had been able to motivate me, until now. Now that I had a meeting scheduled and now that my 'being fired' was becoming a reality, I had snapped out of my state of near mental paralysis and had found myself panicking about life outside of the hospital. I realized I actually love what I do as a career, and I didn't want to throw it all away just because of one mistake.

A mistake called Gwen.

I didn't want to give up so easily. I would argue with the decision, I would go to the union, I would go hire my own lawyer. I would do anything to stay at the hospital and rebuild my now-broken reputation.

Using my newfound determination, I went to work focused for the first time in months. The unwelcome feeling of anxiety overrode my hangover, but in a strange way it helped bring some clarity to my head. After composing myself that morning, I threw my blankets off and rushed off to my once forgotten morning routine.

I shaved, showered and looked a bit like my former self, the beloved Social Worker with the incredibly successful and beautiful wife. I pulled out a clean pair of ironed chinos from the bottom of my drawer and threw the same pair of dirty jeans I had been wearing all week into the dirty laundry hamper. I put on the light blue dress shirt Amy had bought me for Christmas that I never wore. I always thought it looked over the top professional for my office. It was the kind of shirt a manager would wear, and I was certainly no manager. I paired my shirt with my navy blue cardigan and admired myself in the mirror. For the first time in a long time I looked presentable.

I looked like the man Amy had once loved.

That morning when I walked into the office, I noticed a few eyes linger on me. It would only be a few more seconds until the whispers started but I didn't care. I had to keep my cool and stay calm so my meeting with Katelyn went well. If I didn't play my cards right at that meeting, then they'd have a lot more to whisper about.

Continuing to ignore everyone, I walked to my office and dropped my empty bag off on my desk before I made my way to her office. The door was shut and I could see she was in mid conversation with one of the doctors. Her eyes met mine and she gave me the slightest of head nods, acknowledging me and telling me to wait a second. I nodded back and stepped away from the door so I wouldn't be in her line of sight anymore. I began wiping away the nervous sweat from my palms against my pant leg, hoping that they wouldn't leave a visible mark. I began nervously clicking the pen I held in my hand and had anyone been around me, I'm sure they would've yelled at this annoying nervous habit of mine.

The door swung open and out stepped a familiar face that I immediately recognized. It was Doctor Wyatt, one of the board members that oversaw the Adult Mental Health program and one of the board members who tried to have me fired at my hearing. I wanted to hate him, but it was nearly impossible to hate a man who's appearance made me chuckle every time I saw him. I always thought that he looked like a general from the civil war. He had a thick, well-groomed mustache that took up half of his face. His hair had an old military flat top look that complimented the strong lines of his hardened face. His entire appearance made you want to salute, grab your musket and follow him into battle.

He walked past me and acknowledged me with a quick polite smile before realizing who I was—suddenly the warm grandfather-like smile disappeared and the civil war commander re-emerged. I was used to this cold greeting around the hospital by now and so the look of utter disdain did nothing to phase me. I simply rolled my eyes and turned towards Katelyn's office where she was waiting patiently for me.

"Have a seat," she gestured to the chair across from her. I sat down and maintained a straight back with proper posture. I was trying to look attentive and professional, instead of looking like a slacker sitting in the back corner of a classroom. The last thing I needed Katelyn to do was to tell me to sit up straight and pay attention.

When I looked across at Katelyn, I saw that she was holding a blank expression which made her mood almost impossible to read.

As a Social Worker, one of your biggest tools is the ability to read people. You have to use empathy to gauge the emotions of the person in order to try to meet them at their level. Don't be an 11 when they're a 6, and don't be a 6 when they're an 11. The most practiced of counsellors could use this, not only in their professional practice but also in their day-to-day lives. It was a technique I excelled in, but it was one that I was struggling to use on Katelyn as she was keeping her face as stoic as possible, perhaps with the intention of throwing me off.

Katelyn didn't seem upset, angry or sad. I couldn't approach this conversation the way I had planned on my drive to work. I had anticipated an aggressive tongue lashing from her and had my guard up just in case, but she remained in silence and it was making me feel ill at ease. It was giving her all the power, and I couldn't afford that if I was going to save my job. I watched her face, trying to study it and suddenly I saw that she seemed to have a look of reluctance on her face, as if she was about to tell me something she really didn't want to.

I was being fired. Without question. So I jumped into a defense.

"Katelyn, I honestly think it would be a mistake to fi——"

"We're giving you a client." She had cut me off with her stern and commanding tone. I was thrown off by the interruption but also with what she had said. Of all the things I was expecting her to say, that was not one of them. I sat stunned for a few seconds, trying to find words and finding myself getting incredibly flustered. I had walked into this meeting expecting to lose my job and now I'm finding that they may keep me? Permanently?

"What about the College's Disciplinary Committee? Have they contacted you?" She shook her head and tossed a file folder at me.

"No. But we need you in the meantime. Our caseloads are getting unmanageable, and this client has proven to be quite difficult. She won't speak to any female counsellors but any of the male counsellors who meet with her are often met with sarcasm and resistance. Now getting reluctant clients to open up was the thing you were best at, so I've made the recommendation to Dr. Wyatt that you meet with her. Her name is Crista Sunderland and she was admitted recently when they found her hysterical outside of her home. She had just finished burning it to the ground."

I picked up the file and skimmed through the pages. I wasn't reading any of it; I just wanted to confirm that this was a real file. I felt my throat open up which I only ever felt right before I had a sudden urge to cry. I hadn't realized how much I missed counselling until this second.

"I've put a lot of my reputation on the line by telling them you would be able to work with this girl, Jack. Don't make me regret it." I could tell by the way she went back to her paperwork that this conversation was over. I tucked the file under my arm and showed myself out silently. I was in such a state of shock that I didn't bother thanking her for the opportunity or for sticking her neck out for me——I was too busy trying to process what was happening. It had been eight months since I last had a client; I was beginning to think I'd never have one again.

On top of the file was a post-it which read: 'appointment @ 10am', so I rushed back to my office to prepare for the meeting but also to try to calm myself. My excitement was filling me with adrenaline and I needed to calm it down before I met with the first new client I had been assigned in months.

I wanted to call Amy, and tell her the good news. I wanted her to tell me she was proud of me and that she knew I would get a client again. I wanted her to tell me that she loved me and missed me and wanted the best for me.

But I knew that a call to Amy wasn't an option anymore. Part of me thought I could tempt fate and try her phone just once, but another part of me thought I just missed having a person to call when I had news. I listened to the sensible part of my brain and avoided calling her. Besides, I had more important things to be doing right now than talking on the phone.

I had a client to prepare for.

I

Dear Christopher,

Twins. Can you believe it, Christopher, we're going to have twins! I didn't even know that twins ran in my family but the doctor said there was no mistaking it, we're going to have twins! She doesn't know the sex yet but we'll find that out soon enough.

I couldn't help but get ahead of myself. I started looking at twin outfits for boys and twin outfits for girls. I don't know which ones were cuter. There were the twin cowboy pajamas for boys that I nearly died over, but there was also the twin sheep pajamas for the girls. I wanted to buy both sets for our babies but I know you'd just get annoyed with me if I did that since I can be so impulsive.

I did look at twin cribs and twin strollers, however, since those are all unisex. I know it's too early, but when I laid my eyes on the two cribs that attach in the middle, I swear I felt some kicks. Our babies were excited about the idea of sleeping beside each other, I swear! Can you believe that they're already best friends?

I know I know, I'm getting excited when I should be staying calm. But I just can't believe that we're going to be having two small people enter our lives. I had always wanted to have a large family, I just didn't think our family would grow so large overnight. I'm getting giddy again, but I just can't calm down. I love them already.

You're going to be such a great father. I just know it. Do you remember last year when we were visiting Jill and Matthew after they had Glenna? I had always loved you, but I didn't know how much I loved you until I saw you holding Glenna in your arms. You were so happy and you had no idea that we were all watching you. You just held her and couldn't stop staring into her face. I swear the entire time your faces were just inches apart. The look you had in your eyes when you looked at that baby was a look of pure unfiltered love. I was so happy that day and I knew that you were going to make the best father.

I started picturing you playing with our future children that day; they would climb all over you while you juggled with them in your arms. Two would wrap themselves around your legs while you carried two more in your arms and one would be clung to your back as you walked through the house. They would all laugh and call me over to watch this tangle of limbs and you would begin to chase me with all of our children throughout the house. Then they would catch me and start planting kisses all over me, while we all wrestled on the ground. Then we'd all cuddle on the couch and put on a movie for us all to watch and we'd all be covered in blankets. The kids would all nod off to sleep and you and I would stay awake, admiring our family.

Now that fantasy is going to become a reality. We're going to be gifted with two small children. I can't wait to see you hold them. I can't wait to see the look on your face when you look down into their tiny little eyes and see how much they love you.

I thought that if they were boys, we would name them Gerald and Charles after your uncle and my father. And if they're girls, I thought about Crista and Jane after my mother and your mother.

I can just picture the children's blocks that spell out both of their names hanging over their bed. It'll be so perfect.

I can't wait until you come home and see the ultrasound photo. I'd send it to you but I want to be here when you see it. I want to see your face light up when you see our two little babies growing inside of me.

I love you and I miss you and I can't wait for you to come home.

Love, the soon to be mother of your children,

Stephanie

Chapter 4
June 2016 – Jack

I walked into one of sterile offices the hospital had designated as a 'counselling space' when they couldn't find any other purpose for the few empty offices that sat outside the main hallway of the psych ward. I had always hated these offices and yet I was hit with a sudden pang of nostalgia as I realized that it had been over a year since I had stepped foot in one of these rooms. The last few months before my suspension, they had moved me out of these rooms, and had me doing home visits in the living complex which I always looked forward to, as these rooms were always so cold and bare. But revisiting this space made me remember when I had first started working here, this was where I counselled my very first set of clients.

I hadn't realized I had missed it this much until now. The room was small, square with just enough room for two comfortably plush chairs, a small coffee table and a small stand in the corner that held a pitcher of water and paper cups. The coffee table was cheap and had numerous scuffs from the amount of people who propped their shoes up as it was the only way you could stretch out in the tiny space. The table itself held a lone box of low quality tissues that tore your nose up more than it helped it, but besides that the room was empty.

Well not entirely empty. My client was sitting down in the chair across from me and was waiting for me patiently.

The first thing I noticed about her was how striking her appearance was. She had bright, curly, red hair that hung down past her shoulder and appeared to be well looked after. Not a single hair fell out of place. Her eyes were a light brown and freckles decorated the bridge of her nose and the top of her cheeks. Her skin was darker than most red heads and it was made even darker by the freckles that marked her arms. She had a slender frame but you could see the muscular definition in her arms and legs. She was sitting with her feet planted, knees together and hands folded delicately in her lap.

If a teacher was instructing her students how to sit with proper posture, they would use her as an example.

I got over my momentary fascination and extended my hand to her.

"Hello! Is it Krista?"

"No, actually it's Crista." She grabbed my hand gently and gave it a gentle squeeze.

I paused mid-handshake and looked at her. "I'm sorry?"

"It's Crista with a C. You called me Krista with a K?" I could see her hiding a smirk. I had seen this same smile with every disruptive classmate I'd had in school. The one who messes with substitute teachers and makes life hell for all the students sitting around them. For some reason or another, I always ended up befriending this kid, so I decided rather than being put off by her sarcasm as I imagine her previous counsellors had been, I would match it.

"How do you know what letter I was using when I called you Crista?"

"There's more emphasis if you're Krista with a K. More a Kuh sound. Crista with a C is gentle, you can hear the Cri in the name. You didn't say Cri, you said Kuh."

"Well you've got me there, Crista with a C." I smirked at her. "My name is Jack with a K."

"It's nice to meet you." She smiled at my playfulness and I could tell it was genuine.

"So tell me, you could tell the difference? Crista with a C?"

"Of course! Can't you tell when people are mispronouncing your name?"

"Jack isn't exactly a name that gets mispronounced often I'm afraid." I realized I was still holding her hand and I let it go quickly. Her fingertips lingered on my hand slightly as we both pulled away from each other and I caught another quick smile on her lips.

"You never get called Jacques? Or what about Jack with no K?" I had trouble containing my laughter as I shook my head no. "Well Jack with a K, I guess that's why you can't tell the difference when someone says your name with a C or a K. You have to experience it to understand, I suppose"

I shrugged at her. "I mean, there are worse things to be called, I suppose, but I totally get it. I would certainly never want to be called Krista with a K, that's for sure!"

She finally let out the laughter she had been holding back throughout the entire introduction and I felt a quick flutter of emotion as I remembered what it was like connecting with clients. I also felt a warm feeling as I listened to her laugh which was infectious and sweet.

It was the type of sound you welcomed and wanted to hear more of.

She then stuck her hand back out for another handshake. I looked at it puzzled.

"Well Jack with a K, it's nice to meet you." I smiled and shook her hand again.

"It's very nice to meet you, Crista with a C."

I released her hand much more gently this time and I took my seat across from her. I was reaching into my bag and pulling out a notepad and pen when I stopped mid-air and dropped them back into my bag on the ground beside me. Her eyes drifted to my discarded notepad and she raised her eyebrows in confusion at me.

"Aren't you going to take notes? What are you, one of those people with a perfect memory or something?" she asked.

"Do you want me to take notes?" I asked as I leaned back in my chair and crossed my legs. I interlocked my hands and rested them on top of my head. I could see the confusion in her gradually growing as she saw me lean further back into my chair in a very casual position. It was clear she was used to the properly postured and attentive stances her previous counsellors would take before each session.

"Well, aren't you supposed to figure out what's wrong with me?"

"Do you think there's something wrong with you?" I threw the question back on her without hesitation. She sat stunned for a few seconds of silence before replying.

"I don't know."

"Well if you don't know, why would I just force myself to find something wrong with you? Maybe you're perfectly fine. Are you familiar with apophenia?" She leaned a little further back from me and her head tilted to the side as she tried to figure me out. She finally shook her head no so I continued. "Well, apophenia is when you start looking for things to support your theory, regardless of the evidence in front of you. You start looking for connections that aren't there for things that may be unrelated.

"If a psychologist or a counsellor determines that you have a condition or a mental illness, then they start looking for every piece of supporting evidence while ignoring all of the other details that might disprove their theory. If they think you are bipolar, then they examine every single change in mood; if they think you're schizophrenic, then they start looking at every single inconsistency or instance of erratic behaviour. They stop listening and just focus on diagnosing. I don't do that. I let you tell me what you think is wrong." Her confused expression told me that either I had gone into too deep of an explanation or that she didn't believe me.

"Don't worry, this isn't a psychiatric technique. I'm not trying to secretly earn your trust by doing something different than everyone else. Instead of forcing myself to overanalyze any flaw you might have so I can throw a quick diagnosis and treatment plan, I choose to get to know you. I have you tell me about you, instead of reading the notes and reports of other people who wrote ABOUT you. You know what I mean?"

"But the other psychiatrists—" she paused as I cut her off.

"Ah, fuck the other psychiatrists," I said.

Her eyes widened with shock as she let out a bark of laughter. The sound of it filled me with a positive feeling I couldn't place and soon enough I couldn't help but join in on the laughter.

"Are you allowed to swear in counselling session?" she asked as she wiped the tears of laughter out from under her eyes.

"Probably not," I said and shrugged. "But if I didn't swear, then I wouldn't be me. And if I'm asking you to be sincere with me, isn't it only right that I'm sincere with you?"

She stopped laughing but her smile stayed on her face. "Can I be sincere with you, Jack with a K?"

"Only if I can be sincere with you, Crista with a C."

"I think I'm going to enjoy working with you."

"And I think I'm going to enjoy working with you."

Her eyes moved towards the window and her smile slowly dropped from her face. I let my eyes drift to where she was looking and saw the windows which were sealed shut with double pane glass. While the hospital tried to make itself feel as comforting as possible, it was always impossible to forget you were in here. And the psych ward was the worst of all with its thicker doors, double-paned glass and extra security staff. The look on her face told me that whatever feelings of happiness she had moments before were now gone.

"How long do I have to stay in here?" she asked without taking her eyes off the window.

"However long it takes, that's what they tell me anyways," I said and I saw her eyes start to fill with tears. She didn't bother to move her hand to wipe them from her face; she simply let them down her freckle-covered cheeks.

I jumped back in to try and reassure her. "But you know, with the amount of work we could get done by my daily visits, I'd say sooner rather than later." Her eyes snapped back from the window and met mine. Tears still streaming down.

"I see you every day?" Her voice was half shock, half joy.

"That is correct. Mainly due to the fact that you're my only client." I smiled at her and hoped she would return it. She didn't and I felt a strange twinge of rejection.

"Your only one?" I suddenly heard a slight distrust in her voice. "I thought you guys carried a huge case load. That's what all the other doctors and workers have told me. Why only the one? Did you do something wr—"

The door opened and we both turned towards the noise. Katelyn was standing in the doorway with an apologetic look on her face.

"So sorry to interrupt, but, Jack, there's an urgent call for you." She lingered in the doorway which told me she wasn't going to leave until I joined her. I sighed and turned back to Crista.

"That's okay, I think we were done for today anyways. It was only meant to be an introductory meeting. Well, Crista with a C, it was wonderful to meet you. I suppose I'll see you tomorrow then?"

She wiped at her eyes and nodded her head. "Yes, of course! Thank you, and it was nice to meet you, Jack with a K!"

We both stood and shook hands again. I almost felt guilty leaving her alone in her moment of vulnerability but knew that this meeting was only going to be a short one.

I picked up my bag and walked back over to Katelyn who was still lingering in the doorway, never taking her eyes off of me. When our eyes met, I didn't bother to fake a smile; I simply held a blank expression the entire time in an attempt to make it hard for her to read me just had she had done to me. However, in truth, I was holding a blank face to try and mask the nerves and anxiety I was feeling over the mysterious phone call that Katelyn had felt was important enough that she come tell me about it personally. We left the room and continued down the hallway together.

"Who is it?"

"It's Terry, the head admin assistant from the College of Social Workers."

"Fuck!" I tried to whisper under my breath. But as is often the case when I try to whisper, I say it much louder than intended.

"Maybe lock up the cursing for when you talk to Terry?" she said in the most condescending tone she could use. I cursed at myself, this time in my head, for allowing her to see my brief moment of frustration.

Terry was the administrative assistant for the head of the disciplinary board for the College of Social Workers. You didn't get a call from Terry unless you had a hearing date to determine if your license to provide counselling to clients was either going to be suspended or terminated. More often than not, it was the latter.

I thanked Katelyn and walked quickly to my office where the phone's hold light was still on. I set my bag down and took a deep breath before picking up the receiver. But right before I took the call that would determine my professional future, I heard Crista's laugh echoing through my head and I couldn't help but smile.

The client everyone was trying to pass off on each other for being impossible to work with had opened up to me on day one. As a person I may be a wreck, but as a social worker I still had it. I thought of her and smiled. *I'm going to save my job*, I thought. And with that I picked up the phone.

Chapter 5
June 2016 – Jack

"What was the phone call about?" Crista asked with what appeared to be a slight look of concern on her face.

"I'm sorry?" I asked.

"The phone call from yesterday. It's not every day your boss comes and personally tells you that you have a phone call waiting."

"Oh that!" I said. "It was nothing. Nothing to worry about." I smiled reassuringly at her but stopped when I saw her roll her eyes at me. It was slightly exaggerated and intended for me to see. I'd seen this look countless times before from Amy, and experience had taught me that I was going to have to tread lightly.

I thought about how to talk my way out of this particular line of questioning when I decided against talking my way out of it. Yesterday I had told her that if she was sincere with me, I would be sincere with her. So I sighed and answered.

"It was a call from the disciplinary committee for the professional college of social workers." Her eyes widened and locked onto mine, her look of annoyance immediately turning to concern. I once again tried my reassuring smile and for the second time in a matter of seconds

I saw that it had failed.

"What happened?"

"Nothing I'm legally allowed to talk about."

"Is this why I'm your only client?"

"Yes."

It took me a moment to realize that I wasn't making eye contact with her anymore and that my jaw was sore from grinding my teeth. I snapped out of my momentary lapse of concentration and looked up again to meet her eyes, wiping away the look of frustration I had held moments earlier and replacing it with a grin.

"Hey, hold up a second, who's social working who here?" She smiled at that, but I could still see the faint lines of concern on her face, so I tried to reassure her. "Honestly, it's fine. It's a formality

47

more than anything. It'll all blow over like all of these disciplinary meetings do and I'll still be able to stay on as your social worker."

I didn't know who had more trouble believing the lie, her or myself.

We sat in silence for a few seconds before I steered the conversation back to her.

"So, Crista with a C. What do you want to talk about today?"

She sighed quietly. I could tell she wanted to stay on the previous topic but if we were going to get any progress, we would have to keep the focus on her. She sat quietly for a minute before her eyes lit up and she grinned at me.

"What's your favourite music?"

Without hesitation, I answered her, "Heavy metal and hard rock mostly. Well, that's not true. Heavy metal and hard rock from the early 90s to the early 2000s. But I'm also not opposed to a couple of oldies, thanks to my dad. You know, The Beatles, Leonard Cohen, Frankie Vallie. Yourself?"

"Indie," she said apprehensively. I could tell by the way her voice trailed off at the end that she was nervous as to what my reaction would be.

"Oh wow, indie!" I said with false excitement. I then picked up my bag and started stuffing it with my paper and pen.

"What are you doing?" she asked in a slightly confused panic.

"Oh, I can't talk to someone whose favourite music is indie, so I'm sorry you'll have to find someone else. Maybe I can find you a hipster counsellor who shares your love of indie? And you never know, they might even share a craft beer with you at their favourite local organic vegan eatery!"

"Oh shut up!" she yelled as she burst out laughing. I tossed my bag on the floor and joined in on the laughter. "It's not that bad!" she pleaded. I laughed even harder and she began balling up tissues and tossing them at me.

"I'm sorry, you're right. They're amazing, indie bands are the best bands ever." I held my hands up. "You win."

"You probably haven't even heard the good ones!" she said as she tried holding back more laughter. Her hand was clutching her stomach and she appeared out of breath.

"Well, which ones should I listen to?" I asked as the laughter began to subside.

"Well, my favourite band is Arctic Monkeys," she said with confidence. I read her face and could tell that she was waiting for me to mock her; she was challenging me and of course I did what she wanted and took the bait.

I gave her an incredibly skeptical look and snorted loudly. "Well, surely you're making that band up?"

She began laughing again. "I am not! Google them, they're a real band!" She kept moving her eyes towards my bag and my pockets, hoping I would bring out my phone so she could prove to me that they were real. I caught what she was doing and shook my head.

"Sorry, they don't let us bring our phone to client meetings anymore. But I'm making a note right here, to listen to them when I get back to my office." She peered over at my notebook to make sure I was being sincere and beamed when she saw that I was indeed writing their name in my book.

I tossed my notebook back into my bag and smiled at her. "I'm sorry for laughing; I should be more open to other people's music." She waved my apology away and smiled at me as our laughter finally began to quiet down. We sat in silence for a few seconds before she spoke again.

"It feels good to laugh," she said with a somewhat sadder smile on her face.

I couldn't have agreed with her more. Our initial sessions together had been spent building rapport, something that I often found other counsellors spent far too little time doing. Often these counsellors would learn a fact or two about their clients and try to force in some playful discussion about it, which to the client it was very clear that it was forced and not at all sincere.

I always tried to build the rapport through casual conversation rather than by forcing a slew of uninspired and uninteresting questions at them. If you spoke to some of these counsellors about your favourite sport, they wouldn't even pretend to know a little about it. They would simply tell you how much they don't watch sports and you'd feel walled off by them. If you told them you loved movies, they'd tell you how they only read books. I had seen so many clients reaching out to their counsellors only to be shut down—the counsellors thought talking about the issues at hand was the only way to reach the client. I, however, took that offer every single time and used it to build strong rapport with my clients.

With Crista though, I had forgotten that I was even building rapport with a client. I hadn't even felt like I was in a counselling session; I felt like we were just two friends talking about everyday things. I was forgetting that we knew each other for less than 24 hours and that our total interaction time was less than an hour long. It was a nice experience, and one that made me feel validated about my counselling techniques. For the first time in a long time I wasn't telling myself that I was a terrible counsellor and that I was responsible for Gwen's death.

The thought brought me out of my happy stupor and made me realize that in the past 24 hours since I met Crista, this was the longest amount of time I had gone without thinking about Gwen. Crista's voice cut through my momentary distraction and caught me off guard.

"Aren't you going to ask me anything about her?"

"About whom?" For a split second I thought she was referring to Gwen, but the confused expression on her face told me otherwise.

She was stunned and her eyes stayed on mine, studying me to see if I was making a joke again or if I was being genuine. Once she realized I wasn't making a joke, she spoke.

"My sister? The reason I'm here?"

I shrugged casually at her and said, "I didn't know you had a sister." She squinted at me, still convinced I was making a joke and I could see that this was nothing to joke about. She studied my face and saw that I was being sincere, and that I had no idea what the situation with her sister was.

"Are you serious? That's the entire reason I'm here. It isn't in my file?"

She looked at the thick file folder I had poking out of my bag. I looked down at it and waved it away. "Oh no sorry, I haven't read it yet, no. And well, I'm going to be honest with you. I literally never read a client's file before meeting with them."

"You don't?" she asked incredulously.

"Why would I read about you when I can just talk to you? If I read your file, I'm coming in here with preconceived ideas and I'm going to start looking for signs that will fit my initial theory."

"Apophenia?" she asked tentatively.

"Apophenia," I confirmed. "Plus, if I did read it, then I'll know everything about you and you'll know nothing about me, and in any conversation, that isn't fair. It shifts the power dynamic, which means that we'll never be on level ground. You'll be trying to figure me out while I've already had time to figure you out. So for those reasons, I don't read the client file."

Her mouth still hung slightly open. "So you know nothing about me?"

"You like Arctic Monkeys."

"And you do this for all of your clients?"

"Correct."

She shook her head in disbelief. "That's actually really amazing." Her eyes slowly lit up and her lips slowly formed into a smile. "So you're expecting me to tell you my whole life's story then? Is that it?" she asked with a bit of playfulness but it was clear that she was masking her fear with the humour in her tone.

"Do you WANT to tell me your whole life's story?" I threw the question back at her. She hesitated for a moment and looked away to ponder before she finally nodded her head. "Then let's start." I said.

She nodded again and took a deep breath. I saw her eyes rest on the box of tissues that sat on the small coffee table between us. Experience had taught me that anytime a client searched for the box of tissues, it was because they were expecting to use them. So I leaned over and pushed it towards her end of the small coffee table. She pulled a tissue out and looked up at me to give me a quick smile as a thank you before her eyes dropped again. "Where do you want me to start?"

"It's your story, Crista. You know where it starts," I said as warmly as I could. She sniffed loudly and exhaled through pursed lips.

"Her name was Jane. She was my twin. And she's the reason I'm here."

Was, not is, I thought to myself.

"How so?" I asked

"I—" she stopped and tears began pouring out of her eyes. She wiped at them with the tissue but it seemed like the more she wiped away, the more frequent the tears became. She tossed the used tissue away and pulled four more out of the box.

"Take your time," I tried to reassure her. "Remember we don't have to talk about anything you don't want—"

"I burned our house down," she said, cutting me off. I held my face still and didn't show her the shock I was feeling in that moment. I wouldn't believe this girl incapable of harming a fly let alone burning an entire house down. I sat in silence, allowing her an opportunity to continue.

After a few tense seconds, she spoke again.

"I burned our house down, and then I sat outside so I could watch it burn. So I could watch HER burn. I was watching her window, and I could see it starting to fill with smoke when the police grabbed me. I tried to fight them off so I could see and make sure

51

that her room burned just as much as the rest of the house. I wanted to see her in the flames, I wanted to see her die. They took that away from me, and so I lost control. I screamed in that car for what seemed like hours until finally they brought me here."

"What had made you want to burn her house down?" I asked as calmly as I could.

"Because I had no proof of what she was or what she did. Without any evidence of any kind then I had no way of making anyone believe me. It would have just kept happening."

"What would've kept happening?"

"The murders," she whispered. "All of her murders."

I sat stunned for a few seconds but maintained my calm composure. I couldn't show her the shock I felt or I'd risk losing her trust in opening up to me. So I pressed on as calmly as I could.

"Have you tried talking to anyone about these, Crista?"

She shook her head no and buried her face in her hands so her voice came out muffled. "I couldn't. No one would have ever believed me. Plus"—she let out a loud shaky exhale—"she would have killed me if I ever tried."

"How do you feel now? Now that you're telling me."

"Scared. I'm scared of what you're going to think of me. I'm scared of having to tell anyone else who isn't you. And it's so stupid but I'm still scared of her. Like if I tell you, she'll hurt me, just like she always used to."

She wiped at her eyes and let out another heavy breath through pursed lips. She grabbed a few more tissues from the box and closed her eyes as she tried to steady her breathing.

"How did she hurt you?" I asked.

"It's a long story," she said between whimpers.

"We have nothing but time. But again, tell me only what you're comfortable and ready to tell me, okay?" I said as I lifted the tissues and placed them on her lap so she wouldn't have to keep reaching.

"Okay." She rubbed at her temples with a pained expression on her face. "I'm sorry. Crying always gives me a headache."

"It's okay," I said as warmly as I could. "If you need me to call for a nurse so they can give you something for your headache, I can." She waved the idea away and shook her head.

She sniffed and wiped at her nose again. "Thank you but that's okay. Okay, sorry." She let out one final breath before speaking.

"It all started during summer break when we were eight years old. Our mother had taken the day off from work and had promised us a day in the park, just like we used to do when we were little.

When we arrived at the park that day, we were so excited because—"

Chapter 6
July 2000 – Crista

We saw that there was a dog. I had always been a fan of dogs and for years have begged my mother to let us adopt one but she had never caved. We were allowed to play with other people's dogs but we weren't allowed to have one of our own. And so when we arrived to the park and saw the tiniest Shih Tzu we had ever seen, I nearly yelled with excitement. It was a cream colour with small patches of black fur. It was tinier than most Shih Tzu's, which is saying something since they're already a tiny dog, it couldn't have been more than a year old.

We hadn't been at the park for five minutes before this dog had begun following Jane and me around. It was clear that the dog had been playing in the sun all afternoon as I could feel the comforting warmth on fur when I stroked his back. I wanted to just bury my face in his soft, warm fur, and he was so friendly that he probably would have let me. We thought after we gave his back a few strokes that he'd return to his family but he followed us and immediately grew attached to us. He was running between our legs, licking our hands, laying at out on our feet and even exposing his belly. The owners of the dog watched from a distant and nodded to us that it was okay for us to play with him. We looked up at our mother and the smile on her face told us it was okay as well.

We played with him, each of us taking turns chasing and being chased by him. Whenever we had thought he had had enough, he would come prop himself up on our hips and nudge his head under our hands before running away again. I was getting wore out from the constant running and screaming, but I was also having so much fun with this new friend that I had already come to love.

Our mother was too busy setting up the picnic we had brought to notice how dirty and sweaty we were getting. Had she taken notice, she probably would have forced us to send the dog back to its owners and to clean ourselves off before coming to sit down on the clean, fresh blanket she washed just for this occasion.

Jane and I played with him for what seemed like hours until all three of us were out of breath and completely exhausted. The dog was panting loudly and it was obvious he was in need of a drink. The family who he belonged to had laid out a large bowl that they filled to the brim with water from one of the spare bottles they brought with them. I heard the father call out for him.

"Rufus! Want a drink?" The dog took off running on his awkwardly short legs which moved rapidly underneath him. He had to take twice the amount of steps that an average sized dog would take to cover the same distance, and it just about melted my heart.

I thought about how the family had called him Rufus and to me, it wasn't the right name for him. He needed a cute name, something that drew attention to his mixed colouring.

Something like Patches or Bandit.

While I thought about what I would have named him if he were my dog, our mother called us over for lunch. I hadn't noticed how hungry and thirsty I was until that second; playing with the dog was a lot more exhausting than I had originally realized. Jane and I went sprinting over and saw the horrified look on my mother's face as she saw us sit down on the blanket in our dirty grass-stained pants. She knew how much fun we had been having with Rufus beforehand so she chose to ignore how much of a mess we were.

After lunch, Mom moved our picnic blanket under one of the large oak trees that bordered the bicycle path that ran throughout the park and along the park's river. The tree was tall, thick with fresh green leaves and provided us with the perfect amount of shade. The fallen leaves combined with the tall uncut grass made for the softest ground that was perfect for napping. Jane and I had wanted to return to playing with the dog but once we had sat down for lunch, we realized that we were in desperate need of a rest. Our mother settled down between Jane and me, so the two of us could lie down on either side of her. She slung an arm around each of us and we nestled ourselves in the crook of her arm against her body. It was incredibly comforting and almost instantly, I fell asleep.

I was sleeping for what had felt like hours when I was suddenly startled awake by the sounds of a small chipmunk trying to make its way into our picnic basket. Its digging on the wicker basket was frantic and made a surprisingly loud scratching sound. I tapped the basket with my foot and the small creature ran away and back up the tree it had originally come down from. I moved my mother's arm off of me which caused her to stir a little before returning to sleep. I sat up on the blanket yawning and rubbing the sleep out of my eyes.

In the distance Rufus' owners were throwing a neon-green Frisbee at each other and were screaming excitedly as it curved away mid-air, forcing them to run and chase it. It didn't look like an organized game at all, rather it looked like a game of keep away which I actually thought looked rather fun. What surprised me though was that Rufus wasn't chasing the Frisbee or trying to catch it when it came close to the ground. I looked around our blanket to see if maybe he had come back to join us while his family played, but he wasn't there. And not only was he not there, but Jane wasn't there either. Both of them were gone.

I stood up, stepped away from the tree so I could do a full 360 and maybe see where Jane and Rufus had taken off to. I frowned as I realized I couldn't see either of them anywhere. I turned to my mother to shake her awake so I could tell her about Jane's absence, but that was when I heard a faint bark off in the distance.

I cupped my ear and turned to the side to see if maybe I could hear it again. After a few seconds I heard it again, only this time I heard it through a thick patch of trees in the distance. I recognized the patch of trees as our mother had once taken us through there so we could come out by the river. She told us that this was the only patch of the river that wasn't directly beside the bike trail, which meant that it was the only place the small river creatures were undisturbed. For a brief second my face flushed with a jealous rage; Jane had woken up and left to play with the dog that we had both fallen in love with, and not only that but she had taken him to the secret place our mother had once taken us to. She was taking things I loved and hogging them to herself.

The dog barked again so I ran towards the sound. I didn't know what I was going to do when I found them; play with the dog or argue Jane for leaving me alone so she could have the dog all to herself. I invited her to everything I did, it was only right she did the same.

I ran into the thick patch of trees and looked for any sign of Jane and Rufus along the narrow path that ran between the trees that were awkwardly close together. When our mother first brought us here, we had only been four years old and could run through the path with ease. Now, however, I found myself almost turning sideways just to get through some of the thick patches of trees. I felt a little claustrophobic following the path but I was scared that if I left the path for some of the more spacious opening of trees that I might get lost with nobody knowing where I was. The only thing that kept me pressing along the path was the joy I was expecting to see on Rufus' face when he saw me emerge from the trees where I would pick him up and hug him against my chest.

So I marched on and heard the dog's happy barks getting louder and louder. From the sounds of it, he was incredibly happy and playful, just as he had been when we were playing with him before our lunch break. This only angered me more as I thought about how Jane was depriving me of the joy I had felt earlier in the day, and how she was hogging it all for herself.

I walked further along the path where the trees had started to separate and felt relief as I knew I had almost reached the quiet patch of land our mother had once shown us. My relief was brief, however, as I realized that Rufus' barking had suddenly stopped and it was silent at the end of the path. I slowed my pace until I finally stopped altogether. I tilted my head to the side in an attempt to hear if maybe he was barking off in the distance. I worried that maybe Jane had taken him back into the trees along a different path and I would emerge to find neither of them there. I could still hear the sound of the water from the river but I couldn't hear any barking, not even anything in the distance. I nearly shouted out of frustration as I was convinced that they had left the place that I was so desperate to reach. Had I only noticed them leaving a few seconds earlier, I might have caught up with them and maybe I'd be playing with Rufus at this very moment.

I was ready to give up when I saw a flash of red in the distance. It was the same flash of red I saw every time I saw my own reflection in the distance. I grew overwhelmingly excited and I burst out of the trees, ready to greet Rufus exactly as I had imagined it.

As I came out of the trees, I saw Jane had her back to me and was motionless on the edge of the water.

Chapter 7
July 2000 – Crista

Jane was crouched on her knees and appeared to be bending over the river. I saw that her arms were submerged up to the elbow and it appeared as though she was fighting to hold something down in the water. I stopped walking and began looking frantically from side to side for Rufus. I couldn't hear him barking anymore and I was beginning to panic a little. I didn't know why I was feeling the panic rising in my chest but I did. Something about this entire scene didn't seem right to me.

I ran over to Jane so I could ask her where Rufus had gone to, I was so worried by this point that I had completely forgotten about my plans of yelling at her for leaving me alone. When I finally made it over to Jane, she had stood up from the river and turned to face me. Her entire front was soaking wet and her hair clung to her sweat-covered forehead. She was noticeably exhausted and panting loudly, but I also noticed that a large smile had spread across her lips.

"What are you doing?" I had asked her. She dropped the smile from her face and walked towards me until she was almost nose to nose with me. I flinched back as her hand shot towards my face, but she was too quick for me and she grabbed a tight hold of me, making it impossible for me to turn away from her. She moved her face a few inches from mine and held my eyes with hers in an unbreakable stare.

"Tell anyone what you saw and I'll kill you." And with that, she flung my face backwards, causing me to land hard on my back. She stepped over me without any other acknowledgement of my presence and disappeared back into the trees. I laid perfectly still on my back, trying to hold myself crying out in pain and undoubtedly out of fear. There was something in the way she had said it to me that told me it wasn't an idle threat. She wasn't joking. She really would have killed me if I told anyone what I saw. But the truth was I didn't even know what it was that I had seen. She stopped what she was doing before I even had a chance to process anything, so I stood back up and looked to where she had been crouching.

I walked as quickly as my fear would allow me to, which was not very fast. My legs were shaking uncontrollably and made it difficult to walk any faster, and with each step I felt my heart rate increase to the point that I felt faint. Finally I reached the section of the river where she had been crouching and I nearly toppled into the water as my head spun uncontrollably. My fear was telling me to run, find an adult and stay as far away from the water as I possibly could.

I ignored the internal screams of my fear, however, and I pressed on until I was standing right at the edge of the water. The river was moving quickly and it was clear that if I fell in, I might wash away, but the water at the very edge of the bank was shallow, blocked by fallen branches and a few large rocks. It made for a small pool of calm water that was barely big enough for a person to fit in. A dog, however, could fit in just fine.

Rufus' water-logged fur made him look bigger than he actually was and his eyes lay half open as if he was nearly asleep. The very tip of his tongue stuck out from his partially opened mouth. The dirt under his nails matched the desperate scratch marks that had been made on the surrounding branches and rocks that circled the small pool of water. His little chest which had been heaving earlier that afternoon was motionless.

I screamed as loudly as I could. I screamed louder than I thought myself capable of screaming as I reached into the water for him. He was heavy, water logged no doubt, and his fur smelled of the river. I picked him up and held him to my chest, wailing in pain as I squeezed him harder and harder with the hopes that maybe if I squeezed hard enough it would push the water out of his tiny lungs and he would still be alive. He hung lifelessly in my arms and his head fell heavily to the side. I tried propping it back up with one hand but I felt how limp it was. I buried my face in his fur, hoping to feel the warmth I had felt earlier in the day but his fur was now ice cold and gave me no comfort whatsoever.

I turned to run back to my mother where maybe she would know how to revive him when I saw Jane standing at the entrance of the pathway. I was startled and tripped over my own feet, sending Rufus through the air and out of my arms. I looked at where he had landed and struggled to scramble back to my feet so I could pick him up again. When I finally regained control of my limbs, I planted my hand down so I could push myself to my feet but suddenly a burning flash of pain shot up my arm.

Jane had stomped on my hand and when I cried out in pain, she jumped behind me and covered my mouth with her hand. My face was slick with tears and I was having some success in fighting her off before she finally got a strong hold on my face that I couldn't break. She squeezed the hand that was covering my mouth until my tears welled up from pain.

"Bring him to Mom and I'll make sure everyone knows that you killed him. Understand?"

She kept hold of me until I finally nodded. With this she let go of my face, and reached under my arms, pulling me to my feet.

"Now, let's go back. Together." She pulled me into the patch of trees, and gave me a violent tug every time I looked over my shoulder to see where Rufus' lifeless body lay. We had only gone a few steps into the trees when I felt my stomach release everything we had eaten for lunch that day. Jane paused long enough to let me get it all out of my system, and when it seemed like I couldn't throw up anymore, she grabbed me by the arm and pulled me along again.

When I came out of the trees we saw our mother still sleeping on the blanket; she had thrown both hands behind her head now that we were gone and had formed a nice pillow for herself. Jane brought me back to the blanket where she laid down beside our mother and closed her eyes as she pretended to sleep peacefully. I wanted to scream at her, I wanted to confront her in front of our mother and show her everything Jane had done. But instead I dove onto our mother and began crying inconsolably.

My mother awoke confused and in a panic and began frantically asking me what was wrong. When I wouldn't speak, she wrapped her arms around me and immediately began trying to calm me down. I felt a hand stroking my hair while the other rubbed my back—it was her way of comforting us since we were infants. Only this time I felt no comfort. I couldn't speak between the sobs and I felt like I was going to vomit again. I could hear the panic in my mother's voice as she continued to ask me what was wrong. I had never cried like this before.

She pushed me back and held my shoulders in her hands as she looked me up and down, trying to see if I had any injuries or cuts anywhere. Her eyes then locked on my hand which was bloody and torn up from where Jane had stomped on it. Blood was pouring down my knuckles and dripping at the end of my fingertips. Her hand flew to her mouth and she made a small squeal of alarm.

"Crista baby, what happened?" my mother asked as she wrapped my hands in the extra paper towel she had brought for our picnic. I opened my mouth to answer and saw that Jane was glaring at me. Her stare had me terrified and frozen in place and I found that my tongue was just as frozen as the rest of me.

I shook my head from side to side and continued to cry. My mother finished wrapping my hand and picked me up and flung me over her shoulder. She was frail with a small frame, and at eight years old I was certain I was too heavy for her to pick up the way she did when I was just a toddler. But she did so with ease.

"It's okay, baby, let's go get that checked out okay. Jane, will you please pack up the blanket and carry the basket sweetie?"

"Of course, Mom! Is Crista going to be okay?" she asked as she folded the blanket the way our mother had taught her.

"Of course she is. We're just going to go get it checked out, just in case! Okay, baby girl?"

She said the last part to me and I still couldn't respond. I just buried my face into her neck and felt the tears continue to pour out uncontrollably.

Off in the distance Rufus' family begun calling out for him. The children were running through the trees seeing if they could find him while the parents wore concerned faces that told me they were more worried than they were letting on. The cries of the family, which had started off as concern, were now turning to panic. I turned back to Jane and that's when I noticed.

She had been watching the family and she had been laughing.

Chapter 8
June 2016 – Jack

Crista let out a violent sob that was more of a cry of pain than of sadness. She buried her face in her hands and slumped over until she was completely bent at the waist. I could hear her muffled sobs through her hands and I reached across for her.

I had temporarily forgotten about our no touching policy and placed my hand as gently on her back as I could. I could feel her shoulders shaking with each sob and tried the same technique she had told me her mother always used only moments before. I rubbed her back in a circular motion with one hand while stroking her hair with the other. She continued to cry into her hands but I felt her shaking subside.

After a few minutes of me rubbing her back in silence, she appeared to be calming down. Finally she sat up straight and wiped at her eyes and nose with the handful of crumbled tissues she had crushed in her hands. I grabbed some fresh tissues, handed them to her and took the used ones from her hand.

"I'm sorry, that's so gross," she said as she stared at my hand which held the used and crumbled tissues.

"It's perfectly all right. Besides, what's a little bit of snot and tears between friends, am I right?" She couldn't help but laugh. She wiped away the last of her tears, leaving her eyes puffy and a bright shade of red that nearly matched her hair. I threw out the last of her used tissues and came back to my seat across from her.

"How's your head?" I asked.

"In a lot of pain," she said as rubbed at her temples with her fingertips.

"Then let's get you back to your room. We can continue tomorrow, okay?"

"Are you sure you don't want to do any more today?" I could hear the reservation in her voice. She was trying to please me by talking more but I knew she was exhausted. Physically and emotionally.

"I only want to do what you're comfortable doing, Crista."

She smiled at me and continued rubbing at her temples. "Maybe that's all for today. Is that okay?"

"Of course it is"

"Will you walk me?" She looked down at the ground as she asked the question—it was uncharacteristically shy of her and her vulnerability was spilling out for me to see. I felt like a parent being asked to check their child's closet for monsters, she was scared and hadn't wanted to ask me but she was scared and this would comfort her. So I nodded and said yes. Her eyes stayed on the ground but I could see the faint smile that had formed on her face.

"Come on. Let's get you to bed." I stood first and held my arm out to her which she took without hesitation. We shuffled awkwardly around the chairs and made our way out into the hallway. I helped her walk along the painted lines on the floor which directed her back to her room and ignored the looks of the nurses and doctors who passed me by. Usually the counsellors were supposed to call for an orderly to come and take the patient back to their room as we weren't supposed to leave the room with them. I felt Crista's nail start digging into my arm as the staff continued to stare and I realized that she thought they were looking at her. So I leaned closer to her and whispered.

"Don't worry about them, they're looking at me. Not you. Ignore them." The more the staff watched, the harder I felt her nails dig into my arm.

We arrived at her room and I gently pulled her hand from my arm and opened the door for her.

"This is where I leave you," I said. She smiled weakly and walked past me. I watched her climb into her bed and with that I closed the door behind me.

"You have to call one of us next time." I nearly jumped out of fright. A short, curly-haired nurse in her mid-50s, whose face looked like it was permanently in a frown, had shuffled along behind me and managed to surprise me. Her name tag read Bernice.

"Why, Bernice, I did call! I've left you message after message and you've never called me back! Can't you give us one more chance, isn't our love worth fighting for?" I tried my most charming smile, the one I had used on countless nurses in the past when I needed a favour around the hospital. Unfortunately my smile and playful sarcasm were not enough to win her over.

"Call next time." She turned and shuffled back along to the nurse's station. I caught the eye of a young blonde nurse and rolled my eyes at her. She giggled and when Bernice looked over at her, she went back to her notes.

I began the long walk back to my office and found myself unable to stop thinking about Crista's story, which could not have been easy to talk about. It was apparent that she had been traumatized by the events and from how she spoke about it, it seemed as though she was still afraid. If I was being honest, it made me want to open up her file and read whatever it was we had been able to collect on her so far—maybe there was more on Jane. But at the same time I had meant what I told her when I said I wanted her to tell me her story rather than read it elsewhere, so I waved those thoughts from my head.

If I wanted to understand her for who she was, I couldn't read about her. So I began planning out how I was going to write my session notes when I returned to the counselling room Crista and I had just left so I could grab the bag I had left behind.

My mind went back to her story. If Crista at eight years old looked anything like Crista now, then I don't blame her for not telling anyone about Jane. No one in their right mind would believe that this girl was capable of anything closer to murder.

"No one would have ever thought Gwen capable of murder either."

Amy's voice had invaded my thoughts, leaving me slightly shaken and forcing my hands to shake so badly that I dropped my bag. If I had time to prepare myself before hearing or thinking about Gwen, then I found I was able to keep myself composed without any sort of issue. But in those times when she managed to slip through the cracks of my psyche without my being prepared, then it almost always lead to my mental walls breaking down, which always lead to the anxiety attacks. My heartbeat began to race and my breathing became shallow. The pressure in my chest was gradually increasing and becoming tighter as I felt the adrenaline pumping into my veins.

"She's still causing these, eh?"

Amy's voice weighed in again and I shook my head violently from side to side in an attempt to rid myself of it. I was trying to breathe through my nose but my lungs were screaming at me that they weren't getting enough oxygen, so I began panting loudly through my mouth. My chest was under an intense amount of pressure and I felt my diaphragm sticking to my ribs. It was as if I couldn't find any air at all.

Can't breathe.

I dropped to my knees and began unbuttoning the top few buttons of my shirt frantically, nearing ripping them off. I reached for my bag and after a second or two of searching through it aimlessly, I turned it completely upside down, dumping out the contents.

"You better find them soon!"

"Shut up!" I whispered quietly to myself. Amy's voice wouldn't leave me alone and each time I heard it, I felt my chest tightening that much more.

I began rifling through the contents of my bag and reading the label of each individual pill bottle until finally I came upon an old pill bottle I kept for emergencies. Xanax. My hands shook violently as I tried to unlock the top of the pill bottle until I was finally so desperate that I used my teeth and popped the lid. I tried reaching into the bottle to grab a single pill but my fingertips were numb and I felt myself on the verge of passing out. Finally, I turned the bottle over into my hand, emptying out the entire bottle. I plunged my face into my hand and used my tongue to fish through the handful of pills. I would only take one. I dry swallowed the Xanax and sat back against the wall, surrounded by the chaotic mess that I had just created. I lifted my head up high and began forcing myself to take deep breathes through the nose before exhaling slowly.

Five seconds in. Five seconds out.

I clenched my fists as tightly as I could and held them there for a few seconds before releasing. I began clenching my arm muscles, holding it for a few more seconds and releasing it. My counsellor had suggested I try muscle tension therapy whenever I experienced my most severe of panic attacks. I found that it often worked but the result wasn't immediate enough for me. Having the Xanax to speed things along, something I wasn't supposed to do anymore after my first month of receiving counselling, comforted me more than the actual muscle tension exercises. But they at least gave me something to think about.

My heart rate slowed, my lungs expanded and the sweat on my forehead stopped trickling down. I stayed leaning against the wall beside the door until I felt the room stop spinning. I sighed loudly and began rifling through my papers for my anxiety medication.

I found the bottle and popped two into my mouth and grunted as I dry swallowed these pills as well; the Xanax had gone down when I still had some moisture in my mouth but these not so much. I threw the bottle back into my bag and cursed at myself when I saw that in the process of dumping out my bag I had dumped out Crista's file. I blindly picked up each piece of paper and straightened them all out before placing them back into the folder. That's when my eye caught a line of text on the page at the top of the pile.

Crista's intake form, which had been completed by one of the hospital's psychologists, was sitting on top of the pile of papers. These forms were used when assessing patients for any diagnosable mental illness that would need to be treated for in addition to the treatment plan the social workers were meant to develop. There were times, however, that the forms contained additional research that the psychiatrists felt would be beneficial for the social worker. Crista's intake form had the 'additional research' section filled out, and something in it had briefly caught my attention.

I figured that I had simply misread whatever was written down on her form so I chose to ignore it and I placed her file in my bag. As I stuffed the papers into my bag, I found that my hand wouldn't release the folder as I thought of the words I thought I had seen written down on her intake form. My curiosity won out in the end, causing me to pull it back out of my bag and opening it to the page on which I had just closed it.

I skimmed through the page until I found the line I had been searching for. I felt the sudden urge to vomit as icicles formed in my chest. All the oxygen disappeared from the room as I suddenly felt light headed. I closed the folder and placed the papers back into my bag.

After cleaning up the rest of the mess I had made when I upheaved my bag, I left the counselling room, walking by the nurse's station before returning to my office. There was only a single nurse posted there at the time, presumably the others were out doing rounds, and I stopped off to chat with her. I couldn't help but notice that she was the one who giggled at my interaction with Bernice. Up close I realized how incredibly attractive she was—had this been any other day, I might have stopped off for some casual conversation and flirtation. But right now I only had one thing on my mind, so I propped my elbows up on the counter and cleared my throat before speaking. She grinned flirtatiously at me, ready and waiting for whatever it was I had to ask her.

"Hey, random question. How secure are these rooms?" I asked.

She raised an eyebrow but kept the smirk on her face. "Um, excuse me?"

I realized that she was misinterpreting what I was asking and thought I might be inviting her to a private counselling session in one of the empty rooms. I tried to keep my face serious to show her this was not the case.

"Sorry! That's not what I meant! I mean, how safe are the patients in here from any intruders of any kind?"

"Intruders?" she asked, the flirtation out of her voice.

"Yeah, like someone accessing this ward that isn't supposed to be?"

"Oh I see. Well it's incredibly secure for them. The only visitors that they can have here are just other patients; we don't let visitors into this ward." I breathed a sigh of relief and she leaned in towards me. "Shouldn't you know that? Or are you new around here? If you're new I can show you around."

Her cheeks began to redden and I tried to bite back from getting impatient at her flirtations. I had a real purpose for asking her these questions and I wanted to make sure that I got all the information I needed. "Thank you. I'm not new, I just haven't been counselling in this part of the hospital for a while. Thank you."

"I mean you can lock the doors from the inside as well and all of the windows are bolted shut. So no one could come in unless they had one of these keys," and she showed me the swipe card that hung from a lanyard around her neck. She grabbed the lanyard close to her neck and swung the swipe card around playfully while maintaining strong eye contact with me.

She had given me the information I needed, so I tried to hide my concern through flirtation. If she left with the impression that I was flirting with her, then hopefully that's all she'd remember about this entire encounter. I leaned on the counter and leaned in close to her. The only person I had spoken to this closely in the past year was Amy, I felt like I was out of practice but she seemed to be responding well to it.

"I appreciate the help. I'll have to thank you for it later," I said as I slowly stood up straight from the counter and letting my eyes linger on her before I turned away. She smiled at me the entire time and her cheeks kept their bright red flush. I turned to leave and I dropped the fake smile I had plastered on my face only seconds before.

Her room was secure, I thought. Crista's room was secure and that's all that mattered. I kept repeating this to myself in an attempt to convince myself that everything would be all right.

I arrived back in my office and turned on my computer. My instincts were screaming at me to not go online and verify what it was that the psychologist had written in his notes. I thought about what I had told Crista earlier, about how I never dive any further into a client's background as it could affect my day to day counselling with them. But this seemed too important not to check.

I googled the news articles from Thamesville around the time of the accident and found countless news articles detailing the fire damage, and the state Crista was in when they found her. I read article after article and couldn't find what I was looking for, which brought me a sense of relief. *Maybe the psychologist was wrong in what they wrote*, I thought.

My relief was brief as I ended up finally locating the article that I had been dreading to find. I read the entire piece, top to bottom, then scrolled to the top and did so again. I didn't want to believe what I was reading, but the article came from an official and trusted news site, so I couldn't argue the validity of the article.

The article had the exact line of text that I read in the psychologist's intake form, and it was that line of text that was causing me to break out into a cold sweat.

'Police reports state that no victims were found in the fire. They are still investigating the whereabouts of Crista's sister and so far have been unable to locate her.'

I thought of how violently Crista shook when she spoke about her sister, and how she was in near hysterics the entire time she recounted the story of them in the park. I thought of how scared she was, and how her sister had threatened to kill her. I thought of this, and I found myself asking myself, how can I protect her?

How can I protect her from her sister Jane?

Her sister, who was a murderer.

Her sister, who was still alive.

II

From: Sullivan, Daniel
Sent: Thursday, June 2, 2016, 11:58 AM
To: Buchanan, Travis <tbuchanan@thamesvillepolice.ca>
CC: Van Der Hyde, Wesley <wvanderhyde@thamesvillepolice.ca>
Subject: Crista Sunderland – Arson Investigation Update

Sergeant,

The Forensic Fire Department sent Detective Van Der Hyde and myself their investigative report along with all of their findings. They determined that the fire was indeed an act of arson and that the suspect, Crista Sunderland, was responsible for setting the fire that burnt down the house.

From what they were able to determine, the fire started outside of the second bedroom on the second floor that they believe belonged to her sister. The damage to the house left them unable to collect meaningful evidence that would directly point to Crista; however, their report corroborates what she told us in her initial statement. We have been successful in obtaining some documents and letters from a desk in the basement of the home that was impacted the least by the fire. We currently have staff going through the paperwork to determine if anything is relevant to our investigation.

Detective Van Der Hyde has submitted a request to the missing persons unit to use a few of their officers to assist us in finding the whereabouts of Crista's sister as her remains were not found in the fire. The window of her bedroom was found open and the bushes that sat under her window appeared damaged. Several of the branches were broken and there was a large patch of damaged leaves and branches on the top of the bushes that would fit the shape of a person. Our forensic teams searched for any additional signs of where she would have gone after landing on the bushes but have not found any luck so far.

Detective Van Der Hyde and I myself had wanted to send in a K-9 Unit to search for the sister; however, with no possessions or articles of clothing, we had nothing to give them. As a result, we were unable to determine which direction she would have gone after she escaped the house.

We've had uniform officers speaking to the neighbours about the Sunderland sisters and so far no one has been able to give us anything substantial.

The street that they live in is one of the oldest communities in Thamesville and currently does not have any street lamps. Each house has a small antique street lamp on the front lawn that barely does more than illuminate a small patch of sidewalk in front of each house. Thus no neighbours saw anything until the house was fully engulfed in flames, at which point we believe the sister had already fled.

We have contacted the staff at Middlesex County Hospital and so far Crista has not spoken as to the incidents from that evening. The only statement we have from her is from when we initially picked her up and she told us that she had to burn down the house to kill her sister.

We are remaining in contact with the hospital staff in the hopes that they can provide an update when they hear anything from her. We suggested that we send someone from our department to go in and speak with her, but the hospital staff stated that Crista is still in a severe state of shock and unwilling to talk with anyone. They also stated that they would prefer their own staff to assist Crista and that once they are able to get her to speak about the fire then they will contact us.

In the meantime, we are focusing our attention on her sister and her current whereabouts.

We are looking into women's shelters in the surrounding area but due to current legislation, we are unable to request a list of names of the women staying in each shelter. We were told that they aren't legally obligated to release those names to any governing body including the police, nor will they confirm or deny if anyone is staying in their shelter even if we give the name.

Once we hear from the Missing Person's Unit, we will begin to develop a more detailed plan of how we will find this sister to ensure that she is indeed safe and to determine that she was indeed the victim.

We have already laid charges of arson to Crista Sunderland; however, we still need to determine if we will be adding attempted murder, or first degree murder to her charges. All we know now is that Crista Sunderland did indeed start the fire with the intention to kill her sister and that she should be approached with extreme caution.

More updates to follow – DS
Detective Daniel Sullivan
Major Crimes Unit
Thamesville Police Department
City of Thamesville
dsullivan@thamesvalleypolice.ca
Ext. 49767

Part 2

III

Re: Middlesex County Hospital Employee Update Event Notice – November 2015

Hello Everyone,

Middle Sex County Hospital is hosting an employee update event that is optional, but highly recommended, for all staff to attend. We will be holding four different sessions which employees are encouraged to sign up for on the signup sheet outside of the Human Resources office.

In light of recent events, we thought it important to host this employee update event to remind staff what supports are in place for staff in need of counselling and support. Whether you were directly or indirectly involved with the incident at the Residence last month, we feel it important to remind all staff that their wellbeing and mental health is important to us.

We will be hosting guest speaker Malcolm Russell—professional public speaker, mental health advocate and author of two award winning novels on mental health and the workplace. He brings to us over ten years' experience of public speaking where he discusses trauma in the workplace, how to identify signs of trauma and what you can do to support yourself and one another.

We will also be discussing the new security measures for staff—namely those working in the Residence—and what our safety protocols will be moving forward. Your safety is of the upmost importance to us and we want to ensure that all staff feel safe, secure and supported.

We hope to see everybody at these events and if anyone has any questions, please direct them towards Jamie in Human Resources. She can answer your questions.

Thank you

Middlesex County Hospital Director, Bill Meyers

Chapter 9
June 2016 – Jack

"Do you believe in ghosts?" she asked.

"That depends," I said as I tapped my chin with my pen.

"On what?"

"On whether the person I'm talking to believes in them or not!"

Gwen raised an eyebrow in confusion then burst into laughter. She brushed her bangs which nearly came down to her mouth off to the side and then ran her fingers through the rest of her jet black pixie like hair.

"Well, what if I told you I believe in them?" she asked after her laughter had subsided.

"Well then I believe in them also!"

"Do you actually though?" Her voice was dropping in volume and I could tell she was looking not for a discussion, but rather for validation. I nodded at her before responding.

"I do. I have ever since I was a kid."

"Why?" she asked, her voice told me that she was genuinely interested.

"Have you ever heard of sleep paralysis?" I asked. She shook her head no. "Well, sleep paralysis is when you wake up but your body is still asleep. You can't move and as a result you start to panic, there's this unbelievable pressure on your chest and your heart rate skyrockets. But what's worse than any of that is you're not completely awake, so parts of your dreams start to seep into reality. Now imagine that this happens when you're having a nightmare, and then you can understand why for a six-year-old kid who slept in a room with no night light would be absolutely terrified."

"So did you actually see a ghost or was it just the nightmare?"

"Just the nightmare." I began feeling a shortness of breath and my fingertips began to twitch, the memories of my sleep paralysis episodes always left me feeling particularly anxious.

"Every time I had an episode, I would run to my parent's room and dive under the blankets. At first they didn't mind but as I got older, they had developed less patience for it. Eventually, my dad was so frustrated that he went to the library and signed out every single ghost book he could find so he could make me read them. My parents didn't believe in ghosts at all, and had they known it was just a sleep disorder they never would have made me read about them as much as I did. But my dad thought that if I believed in them, then I should try to understand ghosts so that I wouldn't be as afraid of them."

"Did it work?" Gwen asked as she continued playing with her bangs.

"Kind of. I kind of became obsessed with them for a short time. I think I was trying to overcompensate for my fear of them. Eventually, I learned sleep paralysis had nothing to do with ghosts, but by that point I had read so many books about hauntings and ghost hunts that it just kind of stuck."

"So you've never experienced anything paranormal yourself?"

I frowned. "I guess I haven't. But that doesn't make me believe in them any less. How about you Gwen? What's made you start thinking about ghosts and hauntings?"

I could tell she had been waiting for me to ask. I had wanted to set up the topic as best I could to alleviate any fears she may have had about being judged. She continued playing with her hair and refused to make eye contact with me.

"I've been seeing a ghost lately. And I know I'm all fucked up in the head and I hear voices. I know that. But this isn't that." Her voice was rising in agitation the further she spoke. "I read that a lot of hospitals are haunted. I never thought anything about it since I'm staying at one of these little apartments on site—"

"But now you're experiencing something?" I asked. She removed her hand away from her hair long enough to nod. Her hand moved back to her hair and I grabbed the stress ball I had brought to our sessions at the hospital and slid it over to her. I had recently introduced this into our session as Gwen had the habit of playing and tugging at her hair when she felt anxious.

During times of crisis, this left large bald spots where she ripped chunks of hair out inadvertently. She looked at the ball and immediately her face fell like that of a child being scolded. She moved her hand away from her hair and she grabbed the ball.

"Tell me what you're experiencing, Gwen."

"It's a ghost. I know it is. But how do you convince anyone you're seeing a ghost when you also have been diagnosed with paranoid schizophrenia?"

"Tell me about the ghost," I directed her.

"You probably won't believe me," she said as she scoffed. I smiled as I held eye contact with her so she could see that my interest was genuine.

"I didn't say make me believe, all I want you to do is tell me about the ghost. Tell me what you've been experiencing. All I want is the story. We can see what to do with it after that?"

She smiled briefly before her focus returned to the stress ball that she had now begun to pick at with her finger nails.

"Why? So you can let me die again?"

My heart dropped and I was suddenly hit with a violent feeling of nausea which I had to forcibly swallow down. "I'm sorry, Gwen, say that again?"

"Are you going to do the same to her? Are you going to let Crista die?"

My mind flashed to an image of Crista sitting across from me before flashing to another image of Crista lying lifeless on the floor. I shook the images from my head and my attention returned back to Gwen who was now leaning forward in her chair. Her hands were cupped in her lap and thick red blood trickled through her fingers.

"Gwen, what are you talking about? What's happe—"

A shrill high pitched scream rang through my head and I flinched away from the sound.

My hands instinctively flew to my ears and I turned towards the source of the scream.

Gwen was standing behind me, covered in blood. I turned back to face the chair and found it empty at which point the scream became louder until I turned my attention back to it. Gwen was staring at her blood covered hands and screaming louder and louder. I jumped from my chair and ran to her in an attempt to comfort her.

No wait! My mind screamed to my body but it was too late.

I wrapped my arms around her in what was meant to be a warm embrace, when I felt a sharp burning punch to the gut. A hissing sound came out from between my teeth as I looked down at the long piece of glass sticking out of my stomach. The blood that had covered her was now all over me, and my hands were stained red. I shut my eyes as tightly as I could and I felt my body start to sink down into the floor until I lay paralyzed. I was six years old again and the sleep paralysis had once again taken me over.

I wanted to move but my limbs became monstrously heavy and something was pressing in on my chest. My eyes, which I had held firmly shut, now shot open as a loud thud came from the floor directly in front of me.

Gwen's bloody corpse was sprawled on the ground in front of me. We were nearly nose to nose, and her eyes were stuck open as blood poured from the open wound on the side of her neck.

"You'll do the same to her"

"No I won't."

"Saving her won't save me."

"I know that!" I growled.

"Do you? You'll kill her just like you killed me!"

I felt a pressure in my hands and when I blinked my eyes open again, Gwen was lying under me as I straddled her body. I had my hands wrapped around her throat as she spoke.

"You killed me! You'll kill her!"

I tried pulling my arms away but the more I tried, the harder my hands pressed into her neck. I screamed and wailed as I struggled to move off of her. I felt the muscles in her neck weakening and the tendons started snapping under my weight. The blood vessels in her eyes had begun to burst and her face took on a shade of red that nearly matched that of the blood that poured from her neck. Tears streamed down my face and as they rolled off my face they fell gently on her cheeks, causing her to wince with every droplet.

"You killed us," she repeated until tears filled my eyes completely, blurring my vision. I blinked rapidly to try to get them all out of my eyes, and when my vision cleared, I saw that it was no longer Gwen beneath me. Now, it was Amy. I reared back in horror but my hands were glued to her throat and they refused to let go.

"You killed us," Amy's voice said as it mimicked Gwen.

"You killed all of us," Crista said as she was now beneath me. The redness of her face matched her hair.

Finally my arms gave out and I collapsed forward. I fell until I was on the hardwood floor of Gwen's apartment. She was standing over Crista with a shard of glass in hand. I tried to scream for her to stop but no sound came out. Instead, I sat silently as I watched Gwen plunge the shard into Crista's soft white belly. For a brief second, nothing happened and I breathed a sigh of relief until a fountain of blood came shooting out of Crista and she began screaming in agony.

Gwen stood tall over her and pressed the blood stained jagged end of the glass on the side of her neck.

"You'll do it to her too. You do it to all of them."

"No, Gwen, wait!" I screamed after regaining my voice.

The glass slipped in effortlessly and blood poured out of the deep wound in Gwen's neck and ran down the right side of her body where it all collected at the tip of her right hand. Blood dripped from her finger tips onto Crista's pained face but she seemed to pay it no mind.

I struggled to stand as the gravity of the room grew heavy, pressing my body into the floor. My heart began pounding against my chest as if it were trying to escape; the sound of it drumming aggressively was all I could hear. My breathing became short and I began panicking as I felt my lungs constricting.

My heart boomed louder and louder and I could see Gwen's lips moving but I couldn't hear a sound. My eyes grew exhausted and I felt my eyelids shutting against their will. I struggled to keep my eyes open but the more I did the heavier they grew.

With each blink of the eye, I began to notice Crista's body was moving closer and closer to me. Finally, she was inches away from me, just out of reach. I concentrated all of my energy into my hand and began pawing for her hand. Crista whimpered in pain while holding my eyes with hers; and in them was a desperate plea for help.

"You couldn't save me. And you can't save her." Gwen drove the shard of glass straight down into Crista's chest, silencing her. She stood tall and triumphant over Crista before turning her attention to me. Her feet shuffled against the wooden floors and I heard her steps getting closer to me. A hard kick in the shoulder sent me onto my back, and standing over me was Gwen, whose neck had not yet stopped bleeding.

"Jack. I'm so sorry!" She lifted her arms high above her head, her weapon in hand. Her arms flew down towards me as she drove the glass through my heart.

I shot up and found myself panting heavily. My body was soaking wet with anxious sweat and I could see that it had left a crude outline of my body on my bed sheets.

My heart was still thumping rapidly out of my chest and the pressure felt unbearable so I threw off the blankets as I sprinted to the bedroom washroom. My body was still half asleep and my feet were clumsier than usual, causing me to stagger run into the doorframe of the washroom. I grunted loudly as my hip throbbed in pain from the impact, but I ignored the feeling as I made for the sink.

I began fumbling with the cold water faucet as the pressure in my chest was causing me to become more frantic. Finally, water started coming out of the tap and I turned the knob until cold water erupted from the spout. The few seconds it took the sink to fill with water felt like agony and I thought I was going to pass out before the water rose high enough. When the water level finally reached a satisfying height, I threw my face into the icy face bath where I focused on holding my breath and slowly my heartbeat.

As the seconds wore on with my face in the water, I could feel the pressure easing from my chest. I lifted my face out of the cold water and drained the sink. I opened the medicine cabinet and found the spare bottle of Xanax I had been keeping up there. I had emptied out the contents into a spare pill bottle before returning to my psychiatrist on a refill of my prescription so I could have two full bottles in case of emergencies. The lingering pain in my chest told me that today was one of those emergencies. I popped two pills into my mouth, turned the faucet back on and hungrily lapped up the water.

My throat clenched unexpectedly and it was a painful struggle to swallow but I forced the pills down anyways. I turned the water off and sat down on the cold tiled bathroom floor with my back pressing against the tub.

"It won't be the same," I muttered to myself, "it won't."

I didn't bother walking back over to my bed; my most recent panic attack had left me completely exhausted without any energy left to walk back over to bed. I threw my body over the side of the tub and rolled in awkwardly where I lay in the fetal position before shutting my eyes.

My mind had been so preoccupied with worrying about Crista after our session that I had forgotten to take a sleeping pill before bed, which usually did an amazing job of making me have dreamless sleeps. I was kicking myself for being so preoccupied and making such a dumb mistake.

The nightmares had been a constant in my life for the past year, and the pills were the only thing that helped me avoid them. They made for an incredibly groggy morning, but I'd rather have that instead of a nightmare filled evening that almost always set off a panic attack.

I closed my eyes for what seemed like a quick second before I heard the distant sound of my alarm in the next room.

'Hey Jude, don't make it bad. Take a sad song and make it better.'

My eyes snapped open and I realized I had fallen asleep in the tub. I sat up and groaned in pain as my cramped joints and muscles popped. My neck made a particularly loud snap as I moved it from side to side.

'Remember to let her into your heart. Then you can start to make it better.'

Wow, really, Jack? You miss me that much you even made this your ringtone? Amy's voice slipped into the back of my head.

Every morning I woke to the sound of Mama Cass' Make Your Own Kinda Music. In fact, I looked forward to it every single day. Ever since Amy and I had watched the season two opener of Lost, I had sworn I would never choose another alarm. So why was this song—correction, her song—my alarm this morning?

You can bet the next time I hear that song, I'll smash my phone once and for all. I thought as I argued with the voice in my head.

When I finally managed pull my attention away from the music coming from the next room, I stood upright and my back popped loudly and I groaned in relief. Despite the cramps and tightness I felt throughout my body, I still felt better than I had in the middle of the night. I stripped off my sweat soaked pajamas and tossed them outside the rim of the tub and turned the water on full blast, allowing the rush of cold water to hit me in the face.

I turned the cold water up as high as I could tolerate and sat with my head directly under the shower head. I held my head as still as I could and let the water run down my face.

"It won't be the same," I said to myself as I remembered the image of Gwen pushing the glass into the side of her neck. I felt dizzy as the image was fresh in my head, and the only thing keeping me upright in the shower was the song coming from the next room.

You'll begin to make it better, better, better...

Chapter 10
June 2016 – Jack

"Is everything all right, Jack?"

I had tried masking my exhaustion before coming into work this morning. To everyone else it would have just looked like another one of my signature hangovers. My eyes were bloodshot, my hands were shaky and the bags under my eyes were noticeably large. The extra-large coffee I had carried in didn't help either, since I normally only bought extra larges for the really bad hangovers.

I had tried avoiding Katelyn's office this morning, the same way I do anytime I'm trying to hide my hangover. Unfortunately, my usual trick of looking like a man on a mission as I walked by didn't work today as she saw me walking by and called me into her office.

She looked like she was in a pleasant mood today but that went away immediately when she looked up from her computer and made eye contact with me.

"Jack, did you hear me? I asked if you were all right."

I smiled weakly at her as I realized several seconds had gone by since she asked me and I hadn't yet squeaked out a response. I thought briefly about telling her what happened to me last night, every part of me wanted to tell her about my ongoing panic attacks. But the other part of me didn't want to put myself in any position that would leave me vulnerable in front of her or any of the management staff. Instead, I just kept quiet about my anxiety, and went on letting her think I was hung-over.

"Yes I'm fine. I just feel a bit under the weather today. Sorry. What can I do for you?"

She kept her eyes locked on mine and it was obvious that she was trying to read my face.

She shook her head disapprovingly before turning her attention back to her computer.

"When is it?" she asked.

I didn't need to ask what she was talking about; she was asking about my hearing with the College's Disciplinary Committee. I sighed loudly and clenched my teeth hard before answering.

"End of the summer."

"Are you ready for it?"

I shrugged. "How do you get ready for it? No lawyer, no union rep, no support. Just a group of angry old board members who haven't practiced social work in a couple of decades but still find it fit to tell us how to do our job."

She sighed loudly and the look of frustration on her face was apparent. She was never particularly good at hiding her emotions.

"That's a great attitude to have before you go in. You'll win them over in no time."

"Well, what do you want me to say? In two months' time I'll have to revisit an incident which has ruined my life. Then after revisiting that trauma, I'm going to lose my license and with that my job here. I don't know how to get ready for that and I don't know what I'm going to do after. I just—" *Shit.*

The loud drumming of my heartbeat returned and I could feel the air in the room getting thinner. I stopped talking and began inhaling deeply and slowly through the nose.

Don't have one now. Don't have one now!

I felt my heart rate decrease and with that the deep breathes became easier. I felt my shoulders relax and my focus returned to Katelyn whose look of frustration had turned to one of sympathy.

It was the first time she had looked at me like that since I had come back to work. She nudged the box of tissues on her desk closer to me. I raised an eyebrow at it until I realized that during my little rant I had begun tearing up. I sniffed loudly and took a tissue to blow my nose. I thought about wiping at my eyes but I thought rubbing at them anymore might make me lose the last bit of white you could see in them.

"I'm sorry," Katelyn said, "I didn't mean to upset you. I just needed to know the date." I nodded and turned to leave. She went back to typing away on her computer. I paused just as I got to her door. I looked over my shoulder at her.

"Needed?"

Katelyn stopped typing and turned her attention back to me. "Sorry?"

"You said you NEEDED to know the date?"

She realized where I was going with this and looked away from me. "Let me know if you need anything, Jack," and with that I was dismissed.

I went back to my office and shut my door. I tried placing my bag on the back of my door on its usual hook but kept my fingers kept fumbling with it until finally I threw the bag across the room in frustration.

She needed to know when my hearing was, because management had asked her to find out. Management had asked her to find out, because they were getting ready to fire me.

I walked over to my bag and picked my phone out of my bag. If it had been damaged in my temper tantrum, it was impossible to tell with all of the existing cracks in my screen.

My finger hovered over the contacts menu before I made the decision to call her.

The phone rang twice. Three times. Four times. Voicemail.

Hi you've reached the voicemail of Amy Ryan. I'm not available at the moment, but if you leave me a detailed voicemail with your name and number, I will return your call as soon as I can. Thank you.

The voicemail recorder beeped and I sat in silence for a few seconds before deciding to just hang up. I tossed my phone back into my bag and let my head drop into my hands.

My interaction with Katelyn brought me back to earlier in the week when I had spoken with the administrative assistant to the board president for the College of Social Workers. The conversation had left me so frustrated that I had forced myself not to think about it until now.

***

"Hello, this is Jack Fletcher returning your call."

"Hello, Mr. Fletcher. We're calling to let you know we've scheduled your hearing at 1pm for September 3rd."

"Can I get back to you about the ti—"

"The time is non-negotiable. If you aren't able to make it at that time, then the board will have to make the decision with the information they currently have."

"Jesus Christ."

"Excuse me, sir?"

I sighed loudly into the phone. "Nothing. I said that sounds great."

"We'll see you then."

"Do I need to bring any—" Click. The line went dead. Every part of me wanted to call back and tell that woman off. I knew I was a dead man walking so it couldn't have hurt my chances any more than they already were.

***

As I was busy remembering this conversation, a loud knocking on my door startled me and brought me out of my daydream. I sat up and realized I had drifted into a light sleep as I had been thinking about my phone conversation. I sprang to my feet to answer the door and realized that I had stood too fast and got a spinning head rush as a result. I tried to ignore it and stumbled over to open the door.

Katelyn was standing in the doorway. She had a look of concern on her face. "Jack, you're late for your appointment with Crista." I looked back at the clock at my desk and realized I was supposed to be there 15 minutes ago. I cursed loudly and grabbed my notebook and her file before rushing back to the door.

Katelyn was still standing there, waiting for me. "Are you sure you're fine?" I nodded and tried to squeeze past her. She hesitantly moved to the side and didn't take her eyes off of me.

I rushed to the counselling rooms and peered into each one until I saw her. They had placed us in one of the larger rooms designed with a play area for children. It was a lot more colourful and brightly lit, which was a nice change from the drab and dreary grey walls of the adult counselling rooms.

Crista had her head bent down and appeared to be reading one of the children's books. I went to open the door and realized I had left my key card in my office.

I cursed again before I saw someone come up beside me. It was the blonde nurse from yesterday who I had made laugh when I was scolded by Bernice. She smiled at me. "Need a hand?" She held her key card up.

I smiled and nodded at her. She pulled the card back. "It'll cost you." I was flustered from rushing over here unprepared and was thrown off by what sounded like her flirting. Normally, I would have been calm and confident in this situation, but my disorganized morning had left me unable to find the charm I would have used in this situation. Instead, I just found myself shouting in agreement to whatever she was saying so she would let me into the room.

"Of course, whatever you want!" I cursed myself for the awkward shout in her face and hoped that it sounded like one of enthusiasm and not one of frustration. I was eager to end this awkward encounter and hoped that my blurting out a response was enough to do just that. For some reason, however, she didn't see the awkwardness in my response and she smiled playfully at me.

She handed me her key card and I felt her fingers linger on mine. The name on the key card read 'Melissa'.

"Thank you, 'Melissa'," I put an emphasis on her name as I opened the door and handed her back her key card. She blushed as she turned to leave and she made sure she threw me one last quick glance over her shoulder. I ignored this and rushed into the room and opened my mouth to begin apologizing profusely to Crista. Before I had a chance to say anything, Crista spoke.

"I fucking hated this book."

Chapter 11
June 2016 – Jack

My apology stopped on the tip of my tongue and it took me a moment to respond. It was the first time I had ever heard Crista swear; it had sounded so unnatural coming from her as it was still spoken softly and sweetly. Not knowing how to acknowledge what she said, I turned my attention to the book on her lap and my eyes lit up.

"I didn't know we had that book! I read that thing a million times as a kid. Who hates this book?" I said playfully, thinking that this would spark another fun rapport building conversation between us.

"Because it was her favourite"

I sighed heavily as I realized that she wasn't looking for a playful conversation like we had on one of our first meetings. She was looking for a real discussion.

"Jane's favourite?"

Crista nodded as she continued to flip back and forth between the pages. "She always made our mom read it to us. I'd protest as much as I could but she won out every time. I think I could even recite it to you word for word even now, after so many years."

"Actually?"

She looked up and saw the slight look of skepticism on my face. Her expression changed from timid to annoyed, and she stared directly into my eyes which left me partially unsettled. It was the same face Amy made right before she was about to prove me wrong.

"In a time before time, there lived two Princesses who were both deeply loved by the people of their kingdoms.
Those Kingdoms were named, Sun and Moon.

The people from Sun were happy, warm and full of dreams. They weren't afraid of anything, and sometimes this got them into trouble."

She kept her eyes locked on mine and was even flipping the page at the appropriate breaks in between text. She knew what was on each individual page.

I shook my head in awe. "All right! You win, you were right. I was wrong."

She smiled and closed the book. Her eyes lingered on it and I saw that she wasn't quite ready to let go of it yet.

I saw that she was struggling to hold her emotions as she examined the front cover of the book while running her fingers over the illustrations. Her finger tips lingered on the Moon Princess and a quiet scrapping sound began coming from the book's cover and I noticed that she was digging her nails into the book's jacket. Her face was starting to turn a light shade of red and I could hear her breathing increase in volume. I reached across and gently pried the book from her hands.

Her eyes snapped upwards as if her mind had just come back from somewhere far away.

"Were you thinking about her?" I asked.

"Yes, sorry I didn't mean to damage the book," she said as she examined the damage her nails had made on the book's jacket. She looked concerned and immediately remorseful as if she was worried she had actually hurt the princess on the book's cover.

"It's okay, you still handled it nicer than the kids typically do. Now tell me, Crista, what were you thinking about?"

Her finger tips hung in the air where the book was and moved as if she were still trying to claw the image of the princess from the book's cover. When she spoke her voice was distant and had lost the charming quality it normally held.

"The very first time we read this book was the very first time I saw her—"

She paused and I sat in silence, waiting for her to go on. Tears had begun welling up in her eyes and her breathing was becoming heavy and laboured. Her eyes were still distant and I tilted my head to better examine them and for a brief second it looked as though the timid look she normally held in her eyes had been replaced by one of fury.

"Crista?" I asked tentatively. Her eyes came back into focus and the timidity returned to them. She smiled apologetically before moving on.

"Sorry I—"

"It's okay," I said. "Remember, you don't have to talk about anything you're not ready to discuss, okay?"

She nodded and then went on. "The first time we ever read this book was at a sleep over. And it was the very first time that I ever saw her—" She paused again. As if the words were causing her physical pain. She inhaled deeply before forcing the words out. "It was the first time I ever saw her kill someone."

She lunged forward for a tissue after the words rushed awkwardly out of her mouth. She grabbed a few from the box and leaned back into her chair without looking up at me. Whether she was looking away from fear or some sort of shame, I couldn't tell. After a few seconds of silence, she looked up at me, to see my face and determine if I was judging her. But I wasn't, and my face showed her that.

I had held a look of sympathy on my face as I nodded at her, encouraging her that it was okay and that she could continue. She smiled and exhaled loudly before returning her attention to the tissues she had crushed in her hands.

"I saw her do it. And I didn't stop it. I wanted to stop her! I just wanted her to stop, I—"

As her voice trailed off, the willpower she had been using to hold back her tears broke and her eyes began leaking profusely. Despite the tissues she was holding in her hands, she wiped away at her eyes using the back of her sleeves in an almost childlike fashion. She brought her knees up to her chest and hugged them tightly as she buried her face in her lap.

I thought that she was making quiet sobbing sounds into her lap until I leaned closer and heard that she was muttering something to herself. Something I couldn't quite make clear.

"Crista?" I asked apprehensively. Her whispers became louder and it became clear what she was repeating to herself under her breath.

"I saw her do it," she repeated continuously, her voice never rising in volume or agitation. She sounded like a recording that was skipping again and again.

"I saw her do it."

"I saw her do it."

"I saw her do it."

I reached across the table that sat between us and placed my hand on her shoulder to steady her rocking. Once again she snapped back to full alertness and realized she had wandered back to whatever distant place her mind had travelled to.

"I'm sorry," she whispered.

I shook my head at her. "You have nothing to apologize for, Crista. If you aren't ready to talk about this, we don't have to."

"No. I want to. I have to."

I nodded and removed my hand. She stared at it as it left and almost looked disappointed.

I picked up the book again and examined it before turning my attention back to her.

"Tell me about the book. About the first time you read it."

She reached for the book again and I handed it to her. She flipped open to the second page. It was the first page where the illustrator introduces the characters that were displayed on the cover; it was the first page with the Princesses. Her hand lingered over the dark-haired Moon Princess and she refused to take her eyes off of her.

"She was always her favourite character," she said as she traced the outline of the Moon Princess. "Every little girl who read this book always loved the Sun Princess, but she was the only one I knew who loved Moon Princess more. I remember always thinking that she looked a little scary; even now I think the artist made her a little bit too creepy for children. When I was a kid, I think what scared me was how unhappy she looked; she didn't look scared, she looked angry. Jane always wore the same look on her face and I remember thinking how unsettling it was that she resembled her so much." She chuckled as her fingers began tracing around the Princesses face. "She even had the same frown as Jane, it was—" She cleared her throat before continuing. "It was terrifying. Like my sister was stuck on the page."

"When did you first read it?" I asked, directing her back to her original line of thought.

Crista began turning pages at random as she spoke.

"It was a sleep over. It was our friend Taylor's birthday party. I remember being so excited about it because it would be the first time I'd be sharing a room with someone other than Jane. I remember thinking it would be the first restful sleep I'd have ever since I saw her murder the dog. I think not being able to talk about it with anyone had left me unable to process and move on from what had happened. So when I finally had the chance to sleep in a room without the fear of waking up to her standing over top of me, well I was excited. I thought since there were other people there that I'd be safe and everything would be okay. It should have all been okay."

She placed the book back down on the coffee table and pushed it towards me. She kept her legs curled up on the chair and hugged them tightly in an almost protective manner. She propped her chin on top of her knee and looked back down at the book.

"The invitation for the sleepover had come in the mail. I remember it was a Sailor Moon Birthday Card Invitation. I don't know how I still remember that but I do. I had found it mailbox on my way back from school and went running into the house to show my mom. I remember when she read the card to me, it was in the same voice our teachers had used when reading stories to the class. My mother looked down at me and said—"

Chapter 12
October 2002 – Crista

"You are invited to a birthday party and sleepover for Taylor McKinnon."

I squealed with excitement. I had never been to a sleepover before. Sure I had gone to birthday parties, what ten-year-old hadn't. But a sleepover? I couldn't believe it. I reached up to take the invitation back from my mother who held it just out of reach and when I realized what she was doing, I began to hop up and down. She laughed as she handed it back down to me.

"Your very first sleepover. Are you sure you girls will be able to handle it?" I stopped hopping and I felt my stomach drop. My heart sank and I looked at the invitation again. In all of my excitement, I hadn't bothered looking at who it was addressed to. I just assumed that since Taylor was my best friend that it was addressed solely to me.

'*To: Crista and Jane.*'

I wanted to cry out in frustration. Jane wasn't friends with Taylor at all. Taylor was my friend and only my friend, I can't even think of a time her and Jane spoke. But when you're a twin, everyone always makes you include the other. They didn't even separate us at school. They put us in the same classroom every year with our desks next to each other. Even on the bus people moved out of the way so we could sit together.

Most twins would love having that constant connection with their other half. But we weren't like most twins and I could never be at ease with her at my side. I didn't know which Jane I'd be dealing with that day. Was it the Jane who shared her crayons in class with me while plastering on a fake smile for all to see? Or was it the Jane who would close the door to our room and pin me to the ground, threatening to kill me if I spoke a single word about what she did?

I sulked as I took the invitation to our room, hoping that maybe the party would still be fun, even if I had to bring Jane along. Taylor was my best friend at school and I wasn't going to let Jane's inclusion ruin anything about my first sleep over. Especially not with my best friend.

Taylor McKinnon and I had met on the playground one afternoon when I was trying to escape Jane. Taylor had been an incredibly shy and quiet girl who had never really stood out.

Nobody had ever picked on Taylor, simply because they didn't know she existed. While they were engaging in playground politics and establishing themselves in the schoolyard hierarchy, she would wander the fields picking dandelions and chasing the white fuzzy florets that flew off when you blew them. She was always happy to play alone and everyone else seemed to be happy to leave her alone. No one on the school yard ever seemed to notice her. No one except for me.

On the day Taylor and I met, Jane had invited me with her to the patch of trees beside the school during our morning class. I remember the way her eyes lit up when she told me about all of the small animals she had found in the trees and all of the ways she wanted to play with them. I felt sick as she described to me what she had done with one of the small tree frogs she had found the other day and when my eyes shifted to look and see if anyone else had heard her, I felt her pinch my arm and twist.

"Don't you dare think about telling anyone or I'll do the same to you. Now are you coming with me or not?" she hissed at me as tears welled in my eyes from the burn of her pinch. I nodded at her and swallowed back my tears. She smiled approvingly and went back to her school work as if the conversation had never happened.

The image of her holding the dog underwater flashed through my mind and I cringed as I thought about her doing even worse things to the defenseless animals that habited the patch of forest beside the school. When the bell finally rang for recess, I told her I would meet her out by the trees. As she ran off to start whatever atrocity she was going to start, I hid and hoped she wouldn't find me. I saw her come back to the school yard where she began looking for me, the dirt on her knees told me that she had either found a small creature to torture or she was already done with it. The look of impatience and frustration on her face was causing me to panic and I was terrified at the thought of what she'd do to me if she found me. But it was nothing to the fear I felt at the thought of having to sit and watch her kill whatever small creature she had managed to capture that day.

Jane had a look of fury in her eyes that made me wonder what would be worse. Her finding me in her current state, or her finding me after having hours to stew about my avoiding her.

I chose to risk the latter and I ran to the other end of the school yard where I knew she'd never look for me. That's when I bumped into Taylor.

I asked her who she was hiding from and she just shrugged at me. She told me she wasn't hiding but that she just liked how quiet it was in this corner of the yard. I saw that she had a handful of the white fluffy dandelions. She held the crude bouquet out to me and asked me if I wanted to blow the white fluff off and chase them with her. There was no formal introduction and no 'do you want to be friends'. Instead all there was, was a simple invitation to join in her game. She became my best friend from that day forward.

For every negative thing Jane said about me, Taylor said something positive. For every bump and scrape Jane gave me, Taylor gave me snacks and toys. It seemed the closer I grew with Taylor, the more frequent Jane's outbursts became. So naturally, having her come to my first sleepover at Taylor's house was not something I was excited about.

The week leading up to the sleepover, Taylor and I would meet every single recess and talk about all of the games we wanted to play that weekend. We could barely contain our excitement and as the week wore on, we started planning all of our future sleepovers as well. We had enough ideas to last us for years. We could be having sleepovers well into adulthood and we still wouldn't get everything on our list done.

The night before the sleepover, I was lying in bed, and I was too excited to sleep. It was the first time in a long time that I was in bed and not worrying about Jane in any sort of way.

Jane had momentarily lost her power over me and I was happy, actually happy for once.

I had been making a mental list of everything we would have time to do tomorrow when I heard Jane's voice come down from the top bunk.

"I'm your sister, you know?" Her voice was cold but you could hear a whisper of anger in it.

"What?" I asked.

"I'm your sister. Not her." And with that I heard Jane's breathing pick up the way it does when she's in deep sleep. I stirred uncomfortably but dismissed her moments after she spoke, it was unsettling but the statement had been so out of place that it confused me more than upset me. Either way, I wasn't going to let her take this excitement away from me. I was going to have a sleepover with my best friend, and it would be the best day of my life.

***

The day of Taylor's party arrived and when we showed up, I wasn't surprised by what I saw, or should I say what I didn't see. There was no one at the house when we showed up; it was obvious that Taylor didn't have a lot of guests. She had invited myself, Jane and her cousin Allie, who had sometimes come over when Taylor and I were playing. Guessing from Allie's impatient expression, I guessed that she had been dragged here and would have been just as happy staying at home and playing with her actual friends.

Taylor's house was a modest split level home with a sizeable backyard that held a fenced off in-ground pool. Around the side of the house sat a small swing set and slide that was just a little too small for us and was more fitting for a toddler. The inside of the house was incredibly tidy with photos lining the walls of Taylor and her mother. Taylor's father wasn't in a single photograph and there was no trace that he even existed. I never asked Taylor where her father was or why he was essentially wiped from existence, much like she never asked me why I wanted to spend time with her and not Jane.

I remember being disappointed that it was October and that the pool was closed for the season. Taylor and I had begged her mom to keep it open for just a little while longer so we could still swim after school started, but she told us she didn't want to risk us getting a cold right at the beginning of the school year. The pool wasn't anything like I remembered it being only a month ago; it was no longer clean and well maintained. Instead, it was covered in a patched up black pool cover that had sunken in under the weight of rain water, leaves and crab apples. My attention quickly left the pool and returned to the games Taylor and I had organized and prepared for the past week. We dragged Jane and Allie along as we moved our games from the backyard, to the front, to Taylor's room and back to outside.

What started out as a party for four quickly became a party for two as Jane and Allie would leave or complain about the game we were playing. But Taylor and I didn't care. We were having so much fun, the other two could have left the party entirely and we wouldn't have noticed.

The games lasted all day until we were finally so wore out that the thought of staying up all night, like we had originally planned, was impossible.

Taylor's mom, who we had told our plan of staying up all night to, laughed to herself as she saw the two of us yawning constantly and struggling to keep our eyes open as the night wore on. She told us if we changed into our pajamas, we could continue playing in Taylor's room until we were ready for bed. We tried to argue that we weren't sleepy yet but she could tell from half-hearted protests that this wasn't true. So we dragged ourselves to her room and changed into our pajamas. Jane and Allie were waiting in Taylor's room and had already changed as it seemed they were ready to go to bed immediately. They groaned when we told them we wanted to stay awake a little while longer.

Minutes later, Taylor's mom came upstairs to ask if anyone needed anything and Taylor asked her if she could read us her favourite story.

"Do you girls all want the story before bed?" Jane and Allie shrugged. But Taylor and I nodded enthusiastically. If it was Taylor's favourite book, then I wanted to be able to share it with her. Taylor's mom laughed and ordered us to get under the blankets before she would read us anything.

We all climbed into our respective makeshift beds, which mostly consisted of sleeping bags lined with a few spare blankets. I sat up and let the blankets cover my lower half—I didn't want to lay all the way down and risk going to sleep. I looked over at Allie and Jane and saw that they didn't follow my lead; both were lying down completely and Allie had already started snoring. Jane's eyes were half shut, and I knew that once she closed them, she'd be dead to the world. Only Taylor and I were wide awake and ready to listen.

Taylor's mom taught Kindergarten at the nearby elementary school and over the years had developed the perfect reading voice. She pulled a chair from the hallway and placed the book in her lap with the pictures facing us so we could follow along. As soon as she read the first line, it became obvious to me why she was a kindergarten teacher.

Her voice was loud, clear and she had this ability to pause at the perfect parts. It was obvious she had read this story to Taylor numerous times as she recited the words without even looking down at the pages. My attention soon drifted from her soothing voice, and turned towards this story that I had never heard.

IV

The Legend of Sun and Moon

In a time before time, there lived two Princesses who were both deeply loved by the people of their kingdoms.

Those Kingdoms were named, Sun and Moon.

The people from Sun were happy, warm and full of dreams. They weren't afraid of anything, and sometimes this got them into trouble.

The people from Moon were sad, cold and full of nightmares. They were afraid of everything; it was the only way to never get in trouble.

Both kingdoms had beautiful princesses who the people worshipped and loved.

The Princess from Sun had golden hair that shone brighter than anything in the entire kingdom! She wore dresses of gold that were as bright and as beautiful as her hair.

The Princess from Moon had shadowy black hair that was so dark, it swallowed the light around her! She wore dresses of black that were as dark and as beautiful as her hair.

One day a Prince did what no one had ever done. He travelled to both Sun and Moon. The Prince wanted to find a Princess to marry, and so he found the two most loved Princesses in the world, and asked them both to run away to his kingdom with him.

The Sun Princess said, "No. My people will discover fear without me here to protect them. I cannot have my people know fear."

The Moon Princess said, "No. My people will discover hope without me here to protect. I cannot have my people know hope."

The Prince, angry at both Princesses for not wanting to marry him, revealed that he was no prince but rather he was a terrible wizard. His plan had been to trick the Princesses into loving him and when he failed, he wanted to punish them.

The wizard cast a spell that even he could not break and he trapped each Princess in the sky where they were to remain forever, never to return to their kingdoms.

The Princess from Sun shone brightly in the sky and soon the people of Moon were finding themselves feeling happier and they were no longer afraid. The people finally felt hope.

The Princess from Moon darkened the sky and soon the people of Sun were finding themselves afraid and were no longer as reckless. The people finally knew fear.

The Princesses had brought hope and fear into the world and soon the people from both kingdoms learned that there are times when you need hope, and times when you need fear.

The people learned to love both Princesses and would gather each day to watch one go to sleep, while the other awoke.

The Princesses, in return, learned to love both of their new kingdoms and promised to stay in the sky forever, so the people would always know they were there watching over them.

Chapter 13
October 2002 – Crista

I had immediately fallen in love with the story and wanted to hear it again. My mind began racing as I thought of countless games Taylor and I could play where we pretend to be the Princesses from Sun and Moon. I could barely contain my excitement when I looked over and noticed that Taylor was sound asleep. The disappointment on my face was apparent and Taylor's mother smiled at me sympathetically before she stood to leave the room.

She flicked off the light and the soft glow from Taylor's Sailor Moon night light filled the room with a gentle blue green light. Disappointed that I wouldn't hear the story again and that everyone was asleep, I decided to give up and go to bed. I had a momentary selfish thought about shaking Taylor awake and seeing if she wanted to hear any of my ideas about the games we could play tomorrow. But as the room filled with the sounds of soft snoring and heavy breathing I found myself getting drowsy.

I had shifted into a more comfortable position and in doing so I made eye contact with my sister. I was startled and yelped in surprise. I covered my mouth and looked at Taylor and Allie to make sure I hadn't woken them. They were both still sound asleep and I turned back to my sister.

"You're awake?"

"I liked that story." Her expression didn't change and she didn't take her eyes off of me. I felt unnerved by the unsettling eye contact she held with me but thought I'd try to hide it as best I could.

"Me too," I said to try and break the tension. "Maybe we can have Mom get that book for us?"

"The Princess from The Darkness Kingdom was my favourite." Her expression didn't change but it was clear she was looking for some sort of validation so I smiled at her uncomfortably.

"Yeah, she was pretty cool."

"Are you sure you liked her?"

I was taken aback by her odd defensive tone and I hesitated before answering. I had never known my sister to seek my approval on anything before. Normally, she simply told me what she thought which usually meant I would be forced to agree with her or otherwise face the consequences. But this was the first time she had actually sought validation and it made me incredibly uneasy, so I simply nodded at her.

With that, she closed her eyes and turned over in her sleeping bag. As I had expected, it only took her seconds to fall asleep and start breathing heavily. I had already stopped thinking about how much I enjoyed the story; all I could focus on was my sister's strange reaction to it.

I closed my eyes and tried to forget about it. I let my mind return to all of the games Taylor and I were going to play tomorrow by pretending we lived in those kingdoms. It didn't take long for my mind to begin to wander before I fell into a deep sleep, where I experienced the most vivid nightmare I'd ever had.

Chapter 14
October 2002 – Crista

I had woken up and climbed out of my sleeping bag. Everyone else was still sound asleep, and I could see that there was no light coming from under the bedroom door. Taylor's mom must have finally gone to bed as well.

I crept over to the door and made sure to walk as quietly as possible and hoping her house didn't have the same amount of creaky floorboards that mine did. I slowly opened the door and peered into the hallway; it was pitch black and held a peaceful silence.

I inched the door open just a little bit wider before walking on my tippy toes and squeezing through the narrow opening in the door as quietly as I could. I walked down the hallway and passed by Taylor's mother's bedroom. The door was shut and I stopped to listen and see if I could hear anything coming from the other side. After a few seconds of waiting, I realized that her room was silent and that my midnight stroll would continue uninterrupted.

I had to contain my excitement and I forced myself to tip toe back to Taylor's room instead of sprinting as I had originally wanted to do. I slipped into the room through the narrow opening I had left myself when I had first snuck out and walked to Taylor's bed where I nudged her awake. She stirred at first before swatting my hand away. I progressed from nudging to shaking her continuously until she began protesting.

"Leave me alone. Go back to bed," she grumbled. I didn't stop shaking her.

"Everyone's asleep! We can keep playing but now we don't have to include them! We can play whatever game we want!" I whispered with my mouth pressed against her ear in case the other two heard me. I looked back over my shoulder to make sure we hadn't woken the others and saw that they were still asleep.

She groaned as she sat up and spoke through a yawn. "It's so late though."

"That's what will make it fun! We can pretend we're in the Kingdom of Darkness! Come on, it'll be fun!"

She groaned again but this time she threw the blankets off and rubbed the sleep from her eyes. "Okay, for a little bit then I want to go back to sleep."

"Of course! Now let's go before we wake them up." Taylor followed me out into the hallway and we shuffled our socked feet along the ground as we slid downstairs. We winced every time we stepped too loudly or bumped into any of the furniture. The house was so quiet that every sound we made was amplified and nearly gave us away. That was when I proposed an idea to her.

"What if we played outside?"

"Outside?" Taylor asked. I nodded at her and we looked out through the glass doors leading out to the backyard. It was a cloudless night and the almost full moon was providing more than enough light to be able to see outside. Taylor bit her lip in hesitation.

"Come on," I said. "All the windows face the front of the house. They'll never hear us!" Taylor looked apprehensive but finally she nodded and followed me outside.

The moment we walked outside, our bodies were slammed with cold night air that woke up completely. Taylor's drowsiness disappeared instantly as did her original apprehension. She became as excited as I was, if not more, and we began talking about the story her mother had read us and how I had loved it. We then organized a game where we were pretending to be the people from The Kingdom of Moon and we would have to find the Sun Princess.

We tried to control our giggling as we sprinted and chased each other through the backyard. One of us would pretend to be the Princess while the other would chase them and try to catch them so we could bring them back down from the sky. Whenever we finally caught the other person, we would always fall to the ground, laughing uncontrollably as we gasped for breath.

When the cold air began seeping into our lungs and making them burn, we finally had to stop running and we sat down heavily on the grass. I could see in Taylor's face that she was finally wore out and ready to go back to bed so I cried out.

"I see her!"

I pointed to the far side of the fence that surrounded the pool and took off running. Taylor stood slowly, shaking off her exhaustion and took off after me. We ran and laughed, pausing for a brief second while we worked the pool fence's small gate lock. Once we were able to unlock it, I ran to the edge of the water that had collected on top of the pool cover and peered down into the black abyss.

"Do you see her?" Taylor asked excitedly.

"There!" I cried.

She giggled while she pretended to look. I pointed again. "Right there! Do you see?"

"Where?" she cried out, laughing again.

"Right...." I grabbed the back of her head and plunged her face into the water. "There!" She tried to jump back startled and swatted at my hand but I held on tightly. Immediately, she began panicking and flailed her limbs violently. Her arms were looking for purchase on the pool's edge, but the wet and slippery pool cover kept making her hands slide. Her legs kicked up and down as she tried to throw me off like a bull to a bull rider.

The faint sounds of her screaming were silenced by the splashing water and I could hear her screams becoming fainter and weaker. Her legs began to slow down as her kicks became laboured and powerless. Her arms stopped looking for the edge of the water and they lazily pawed at my hands that were resting comfortably on the back of her head. I plunged her face in deeper and held her until finally she stopped moving.

I refused to let her go even now. I wanted to make sure she was really gone.

When I was satisfied, I let her go and moved behind her, lifting her legs to move her into the pool. Her body had become heavy and uncooperative which prevented me from throwing her far, but I was still able to get her into the water. Her body made a tiny splash as it slowly floated towards the middle of the pool before it began sinking down to the bottom.

I stood up, brushing off the leaves and dirt that the pool's liner had thrown on me. As I examined myself to make sure I had removed all traces of the incident, I saw that a few strands of Taylor's wet hair had weaved themselves between my fingers. I collected these strands and placed them along the pool's above ground filter, hoping that if anyone found them, they may think her drowning was a result of her hair getting caught in the filter's mesh basket. I walked back to the house, making sure I left the gate to the pool wide open. Silently, I made my way back into the house and carefully climbed the staircase, ensuring that every step went unheard. I needed to make sure that I had wiped away all evidence of Taylor from me so I crept into the washroom on the top floor and switched on the lights. My hands still had some of the pool water's debris on them so I opened the faucets just slightly so the sound of splashing water wouldn't catch anyone's attention. I washed my hands thoroughly and dried them off completely before reaching for the light switch. Right as my hand reached the wall, I peered back in the mirror to study my face. I wanted to make sure that Taylor's thrashing hadn't left any visible marks.

I caught my reflection in the mirror and studied my face; it was unmarked and unblemished. In Taylor's violent struggle she hadn't managed to cause any sort of damage to me whatsoever. I tussled my hair and rubbed at my eyes to make them appear red and puffy, so when I returned to bed no one would suggest I had been doing anything but sleeping.

I smiled at my reflection, proud of my deception and turned to walk back into the hallway when I came to a sudden realization. I turned back to the mirror and began touching my face, examining it and I gasped. This wasn't my face in the mirror. It was Jane's.

I gasped and sat straight up in my sleeping bag. The nightlight was still illuminating the room and I scanned the room in a panic and saw that Jane was quietly breathing in the sleeping bag across the room from me. I was panting heavily and I could feel my heart racing in my chest, that's when I began to cry immediately. I had just had the most horrible nightmare of Jane killing my best friend. She had drowned her and even took pleasure in her death before she walked away as if nothing had happened.

I'll never forget the image of Jane smiling into the mirror as she looked at her reflection in a kind of morbid yet sweet satisfaction.

I continued crying until Allie and Jane woke up. The light under the door came on and Taylor's mom rushed in.

"Girls, is everything al—" she paused. "Where's Taylor?"

My heart dropped and the world became silent. I felt an uncontrollable cry building in my chest when I spun towards Taylor's bed and saw what I was dreading. When I had seen Jane sleeping in her sleeping bag, I had assumed that the entire thing had been a dream so I hadn't bothered turning around and looking for Taylor. The blankets on Taylor's bed had been thrown to the side, just like they had been in my dream.

In my nightmare.

The cry that had been building in my chest finally overwhelmed me and spilled out.

Taylor's mom, who was in her own state of panic, ignored me and turned for the hallway where she began calling out for her daughter. Her calls started off calm but the more they went

106

unanswered, the more hysterical they turned. Her footsteps became heavy as she began stomping throughout the house as she ran from room to room.

I heard Taylor's mother enter the family room with the glass windows that lead to the backyard and then a shriek of panic that made all three of us who were still in Taylor's room flinch.

"No. God. Please baby no!"

The three of us went running down to see what was happening, even though I had a sick feeling I already knew what it was. When we arrived at the family room, the glass doors were wide open and Taylor's mom had already taken off outside. We could see her running out to the pool where she pushed the fence gate open as hard as she could. It slammed against the fence and the echo from the impact was loud enough to wake the neighbourhood. But the sound of the metal on metal clash paled in comparison to the sound Taylor's mother made when she cried in agony.

My crying intensified with hers. Allie, who normally never showed much love for Taylor, had begun crying as well. It was upsetting for us as children to see an adult, who we normally relied on for emotional support, to have a full blown breakdown. They were supposed to comfort us when we were in pain; they were never supposed to be in pain themselves. We stood in the open doorway as the same cold air I vividly remember from my nightmare blew on us. None of us felt the cold, however, instead all we could focus on was Taylor's mom clutching Taylor's blue swollen lifeless body against her chest. Her cries had finally woken the neighbours and the lights from the neighbours' homes began turning on as people were rushing outside to see what the commotion was. We heard the wailing of ambulance sirens approaching the house from the distance and before we had any time to process what was happening, the front doors to Taylor's house burst open and in rushed two paramedics who went sprinting to the back of the house.

Once they caught sight of Taylor's lifeless body, they stopped. The look the two of them exchanged told us what we already knew.

Taylor's mom was screaming at them, "Save her! Save my baby!" The paramedics began moving quickly but it was apparent that they knew their attempts to revive her would be useless.

They attempted a few unsuccessful rounds of CPR before they had to make the inevitable call.

I'll never forget the sound Taylor's mom made that night. It was like nothing I've ever heard before and it was like nothing I've ever heard again. It was a scream of pure anguish. My heart dropped, I cried louder and Allie came over beside me. We held hands as we both wept uncontrollably. I was shaking uncontrollably when I suddenly remembered what I had seen in my dream.

I had seen Jane's face in the mirror, looking proud of what she had done. I turned back to look at her and saw that she was wearing the exact same expression that she had held in my nightmare. Her eyes never left the scene of Taylor's mom holding her daughter. I felt my face flush with fury—it was an anger I had never felt before. I wanted to lunge at her, to scream at her and have her admit to the world what she did. I felt the hand that wasn't holding Allison's ball up, and I was ready to pounce when Jane finally broke her attention away from Taylor's corpse.

She saw the look of pure hatred in my eyes and she shrugged. She pressed her finger to her lips and walked right up to me before whispering in my ear.

"I told you. I'M your sister. Not HER." She dug her nails into my arm as she did so and I felt my eyes well with tears that I would refuse to let her see. And with that she walked back to the open doorway where she peered outside again.

It was the first time my anger outweighed my fear. It was the first time I wanted to hurt my sister. I mean really hurt her. But it was also the first time I realized she would never let anyone get close to me.

I was hers, and I was trapped.

Chapter 15
June 2016 – Jack

"After that, Jane asked to hear the story of the Princesses every single night. She told my mother it was because it made her think of Taylor which made her happy. My mother thought this was a nice sentiment so she was always quick to dismiss my protests and asked me to be a little more sensitive to Jane.

"Jane would smile at me every single time she won this battle. Not only because she had once again gotten her way, but because she knew it also reminded me of Taylor and what she did to her. It was her subtle way of reminding me what would happen if I let anyone else close to me.

"It was her way of reminding me what she would do if I disobeyed her ever again."

The tissues she held in her hand had started to darken and turn red. She saw where my eyes were focused and pulled away when I reached for her hand. She turned away from me and opened her hand, letting out a small gasp and grabbing a handful of tissues to wipe the blood away from her palm. I could see traces of blood on the tips of her fingernails where she had dug them into her hand as she had been recounting the story.

"Here, let me call one of the nurses and they can patch you up."

"I'm sorry this is so embarrassing." She continued to do a poor job of wiping away the blood on her hand. The wad of tissues were now smeared with blood and the more she tried to clean it the more of a mess she made. I pulled a few more tissues out, folded them neatly and reached for her hand. She didn't pull away this time. As I wiped off her hand, she looked down at her lap, like a child who's just been scolded. I wiped it away gently and saw the four distinct marks left on her palms from her fingernails. I frowned and pressed the tissues down on top of them.

"You have no reason to be embarrassed. That took so much courage, what you just told me. I'm proud of you." She placed her uninjured hand on mine. She was still looking at her lap and wouldn't look up at me.

"Thank you," she whispered. "You don't think I'm a horrible person for never telling anyone about what happened to Taylor?"

"Of course not! God no, not at all, Crista. You were in an unbelievable situation that no one should ever be in, it would be easy for me to say I would've done differently but no one knows until they're in it. Plus you were a child, you were so scared. I would never think you're a horrible person for that. If anything, I'm proud of you for not letting it completely break you. You're still here, you still fought to survive. I'm so proud of you."

Her face flashed with a smile of appreciation before she broke down again. These tears were different though, these tears sounded like tears of relief.

"And I have to tell you, Crista, not many people would have been able to experience what you experienced and still be standing. I know I wouldn't." Gwen flashed through my mind for a quick moment, but I dismissed the thoughts and returned my attention back to Crista.

"You can still smile and you can still laugh. And for me, that's the biggest take away from all of our sessions so far. You show a lot of strength, Crista. I think you're a lot stronger than you think." She squeezed my hand tightly then let go so she could wipe away another tear.

"Thank you so much," she laughed awkwardly. "I'm not great at taking compliments. I was never used to hearing them." I joined in her awkward laughter.

"Well, I'm full of them so get used to them, Crista with a C."

"I will, if you get used to my awkward reactions, Jack with a K."

At this we both laughed again. Her eyes were red and puffy but finally had stopped producing tears. Her cheeks were red from the constant wiping and her nose was raw from the constant blowing. She looked worn out emotionally and physically, but she looked relieved as if a gigantic weight were now off her shoulders. It was clear that she was extremely vulnerable at the moment, as she had let me into a place she had never let anyone in before, and I felt unbelievable guilt.

She was only able to open to me about everything because she believed her sister to be dead. I wanted to tell her that the police hadn't found her remains amongst the fire and that they were still searching for her. I felt the words on the tip of my tongue and I was so close to speaking them aloud when I looked at the smile she was wearing and decided against it. I couldn't rob her of her momentary happiness, even if it was just temporary. I wanted her to enjoy this moment of relief. For the first time since I met her, she had appeared slightly unburdened. I would have to wait before I told her anything.

"You've accomplished a lot today. How about we end our session here and let you get some rest. I can only imagine how exhausted you are."

She nodded and winced slightly as she rubbed at her temples. The pained expression in her eyes told me everything I needed to know, that I had pushed her as far as she could be pushed and that was all we would be able to cover today.

"Come on," I said as I helped her to her feet. "Let's get a nurse to clean up your hand and then let's get you to bed."

"Walk me again?" she asked tentatively.

I smiled at her. "Of course," and with that we left the counselling room. We walked by Melissa to whom, I now remembered, I had agreed to some sort of arbitrary date before I had started this session. She turned away when she saw that I had caught her staring at me and it looked as though she had turned a bright shade of red. I smiled back politely in case she saw me before I turned away from her. Crista noticed the encounter and elbowed me in the ribs.

"I think she likes you." I rolled my eyes and laughed dismissively. "Oh, don't pretend you don't know!" she said as she began laughing. I felt like I was on the school yard again. Friends teasing friends about girls.

Only we aren't friends. She's my client. She is my client and nothing more. The last time I blurred this line, Gwen happened.

I walked her to her room and noticed the older grumpy nurse again. I signalled her over and before I had a chance to speak or show her Crista's hand, she spoke to me.

"I told you to call one of us to take her back," Bernice said after she had snuck up behind me. Her tone had an extra layer of sass in it today. I chose to ignore it and pretended to be as pleasant as I could be with her.

"Well, if I called one of the nurses instead of coming myself, then I wouldn't get to enjoy these little encounters of ours! Tell me, Bernice, are you married? Do you have a husband? Please say no, if you tell me yes, then I'll be forever heartbroken!" Her angry glare intensified. I knew that I wasn't being charming whatsoever, I had ventured into the realm of obnoxiousness.

I turned my attention back to Crista who was shaking and holding a finger to her mouth as she struggled not to laugh. My failure to charm the grumpy nurse had managed to amuse Crista at least, so I still considered that a victory.

"She's hurt her hand, would you be able to have someone take a look at it?" I asked.

With that, Bernice grabbed Crista's hand, inspected it and nodded. She pulled her away from me and chose not to engage in any further conversation. Crista looked over her shoulder and smiled at me before Bernice tugged her along. We both laughed and I waited until Crista was back securely in her room before I left.

Chapter 16
June 2016 – Jack

"Jack!"

"Hey, Ames. Sorry about calling you earlier I just—I didn't know who else to call but I'm fine now."

"Another anxiety attack?"

"No it wasn't that. It was just work stuff but it's okay now. I know you're busy, sorry I didn't mean to make you worry."

"Is it about your new client?" she asked. I wanted to ask her how she already knew I had a new client, but Amy was still friends with a good chunk of the people from the office. The people who had once been my friends as well.

"No. That's actually the one thing that's been going well. I forgot how much I missed it."

There was a slight pause on the line. "Well, you were always good at that."

"For the most part," I said under my breath. Unfortunately, I said it louder than I thought and Amy had heard me.

"Jack, not right now. I don't have time for a pity party right now. I know that's harsh but I really don't. I just needed to call to make sure you were doing okay and that you weren't going to hurt yourself again." *That had only happened once.* "Are you going to hurt yourself again, Jack?"

"No," I replied abruptly.

She sighed heavily and with that I knew the conversation was over.

"I have to go. I'm already running behind for a meeting. Take care of yourself, Jack." And with that she hung up. I felt rejected. I didn't know what I was expecting when I had first called her. I think my intention was just to pour out my emotions to the person who I used to be able to do that to. But I think secretly I had hoped she would acknowledge my vulnerability and maybe part of her would soften and she would remember why she fell in love with me. Of course I would never admit this out loud.

I had hoped for a conversation that lasted longer than thirty seconds. But I think over the past few months I had abused my phone privileges with her.

I turned on my computer screen and began typing away my case notes from the day's session with Crista. It was a mindless task, as all I had to do was recreate key points from the conversation we had just wrapped up. No speculation, no emotional input, I was simply to stick to the facts of the interaction. Summarizing the session only took me a few minutes and I found myself wanting to leave out key details. Details that I felt might hurt Crista's chances of being released once her file was review by the Head Psychiatrist on staff.

"Just like you left out details for Gwen," Amy's voice said in my head.

I ignored her voice and turned back to my case notes. When I finally finished, I saved the file and closed it. I scrolled the mouse over the start menu to log off when my hand froze. I could see the folder where I had saved all of Gwen's case notes on my desktop. My eyes went back to the start menu and I opened it. I even hovered the curser above the log-off button before my hand froze again.

"Don't do it. You know it isn't going to help anyone if you reread that," Amy's voice said again.

I was reliving countless conversations we had had in the weeks leading up to our separation. Amy had the unfortunate task of being my own personal Social Worker after I went on my leave of absence. She was assigned this role through sheer proximity and I chose to ignore the strain that it was putting on her. Amy spent whatever time she wasn't teaching and counselling clients, counselling me.

At the end of each day, she would come home exhausted and ready to relax.

Unfortunately for her when she came home, I would bombard her with my emotional baggage and a good chunk of the time I was drunk when I did it.

She was sympathetic at first. She ignored her exhaustion and would council me through my worst episodes. She was the one who set up the original appointment with the psychiatrist so I could finally start receiving medication for my anxiety and depression symptoms. She would pick my prescriptions up at the store and even counted them out for the week for me. Amy had known that the Xanax I was originally prescribed was only meant to serve as a temporary and short-term fix and that I wasn't supposed to continue taking them once my symptoms subsided. The problems arose when I was convinced I still needed them and she began withholding them from me.

When she took away my access to the Xanax, I began mixing my other medications with a heavy dose of alcohol, which the labels very much advised against. It was dangerous to consume with any amount of alcohol, which I then took as a personal challenge.

At first I would try to cover it up so when she came home, she wouldn't notice but my level of drunkenness soon escalated and she began confiscating all of my medication until I was sober. I would berate her for this. I'd shout awful things at her and tell her that the situation with Gwen was her fault. If only she'd helped me get a position with the university, instead of the Psych Ward with the hospital, none of this would have ever happened.

I became irrational, verbally abusive and outright dysfunctional. I would beg her to unlock the laptop so I could revisit my case notes I made for Gwen. I said I wanted to see where I had gone wrong but we both knew it was a lie. I wanted to reread the notes and punish myself for everything.

"Then what happened?" her voice asked, probing me to continue on with the memory.

Then there was the incident. It was the incident that finally pushed her over the edge and caused her to leave. It was when I inflicted 'self-harm', as the social work community would say.

To non-social workers this is referred to as a suicide attempt.

It was a day when Amy was teaching her late-evening class which typically ran until about ten o'clock. I had been waiting for her and trying my hardest not to drink everything in the house. I was proud of myself for holding out as long as I did, and thought that since I was actually sober for once, I should turn my attention to something productive. Unfortunately, my brain turned its attention to the thing Amy had been trying to hide from me for months.

The computer with Gwen's case notes.

In my sober state, I was able to think a lot clearer than I had the last few times I had tried unlocking the computer with the new password Amy had put on there. I had focus I hadn't had in weeks and it was enough to let me correctly guess the password.

Once I typed it in and hit enter, it brought me to the desktop where the folder labelled 'Gwen' was sitting there in plain sight. I didn't hesitate before I opened up the folder. I began opening files and case notes in random order, skimming through some, and overanalyzing others.

I read through all the files I could until I couldn't feel my fingertips anymore. My heart was racing and I couldn't breathe. I knew it was another anxiety attack but this one was worse than the others. Amy and my psychiatrist had taught me some breathing and grounding techniques but almost immediately I could feel the severity of this particular attack and I knew those old techniques wouldn't work. I felt an unbelievable urge to cry and my body shook with an uncontrollable surge of anxious energy. My chest was tight and an invisible hand wrapped itself around my heart and squeezed it until I felt myself on the verge of passing out.

I began weeping and begging the universe to stop these attacks. I couldn't handle them anymore and they hurt so badly. I didn't want to feel like this anymore. I cried and I cried until finally I thought that I knew a way to make the tears stop. I was going to find a way to make my anxiety stop forever.

I went into the garage and found some spare strands of thick electrical wire from an old extension cord I always thought I would get rid of. I didn't know how to form a noose——I had never had any skills with knot tying. So I made a poor excuse for a noose using the electrical wire and I strung myself up. My feet were propped on an old step stool I had stored in here that was just tall enough to get me into my noose. I was shifting my weight side to side, doing my best to tip the stool over, when the garage door opened.

The garage's interior was lit up by the headlights from Amy's car, which was waiting to pull in. The car sat idle for a moment before the car door swung open with Amy jumping out faster than I thought she could move. The car was still running with the keys in the ignition, any pedestrian could have come and stolen it without issue. But Amy didn't care about the car.

She sprinted towards me and grabbed a pair of wire cutters on the way. The muscles in her arms became pronounced as she squeezed the wire cutters as hard as she could. The electrical cord fell down at our feet and I collapsed with it. Amy tossed the wire cutters aside and held my face to hers. The pain in her eyes was unmistakable. I closed my eyes and moved towards her only to feel her pull away. Suddenly my face exploded with a sharp pain that left it on fire. I felt my cheek begin to throb and there was something running down it that I originally thought was a tear until I wiped at it and felt blood.

Amy was never one to slap, Amy was one to punch, and she had a powerful punch. She had cut my cheek with her ring and also left my eye socket bruised and swollen. I was too stunned to say anything to her, so she simply stood up and walked away. I thought she was walking back towards the house but then saw that she was getting back into her car. The engine roared as she put the car in reverse and peeled out of the driveway. It was the last time I ever saw her.

The next day a group of movers came and began removing her things. All of her clothes, her favourite pieces of furniture and even the files from her personal office. It wasn't too long afterwards that a 'for sale' sign was planted outside our home. I didn't dispute it or even try to convince her to come back. I simply packed up my things, found a cheap apartment and moved in there. I never asked her if the house sold or what my share of the sale would have been.

Those are things a normal person would do. Instead, I would call her drunk, crying to her, asking for her help, apologizing until I was near begging. This was usually followed up by a call the next day where I would apologize and she would berate me once again for my behaviour. It was a new routine in our relationship I wasn't particularly fond of.

"You've dealt with the whole thing just great, if you ask me," her voice taunted again.

I rubbed at my temples and cursed at myself for turning my internal voice of reason into her voice. Her voice always lingered in my head at the exact moment I didn't want it to.

My attention turned back to the folder sitting on my desktop, and I could feel my heart rate increasing with every second my eyes lingered on it. The temptation to open it was gradually getting stronger and I moved the curser over the folder.

"The last time you visited Gwen's case notes, you put the final nail in the coffin of our marriage. What possible good could come from reading it again?" I heard her ask.

"Jack." I clicked on the folder.

"Jack." I right clicked and hovered the mouse over the 'open' option.

"Jack!" I was startled away from my screen. I realized that the voice I had been hearing hadn't been Amy's voice at all. I looked up over my monitor and saw Katelyn standing in the doorway. She had her coat in one arm and her purse in the other. I smiled before turning back to my computer. I moved the curser back to the start menu and clicked on the log off button.

My computer screen returned to the login window and I turned the monitor off. I stood and stared at her blankly for a few seconds. The confused expression on my face said it all.

"You heading home for the day or are you sticking around for a little bit longer?"

I shook my head. "No, no, I'm done! Just had to log out of my computer. I'll walk out with you."

She nodded and left to wait for me by our main door. I grabbed my bag and my phone. I turned on the screen hoping to see a text or missed call from Amy. Maybe she'd be apologizing about the rushed conversation or she'd offer a time when she had more time to talk. Instead, I was met with a blank screen—no new messages—I sighed and tossed my phone back into my bag.

Maybe she'll call me soon? I thought.

She'll call me soon. She'll see I'm getting my life together and she'll call me soon.

V

East Thamesville Elementary School
1542 Lincoln Rd,
Thamesville ON
December 2, 2002
Mrs. Stephanie Sunderland
I'm writing you today to discuss a poem that your daughter Crista recently wrote in class.

I want to start off by telling you that she isn't in trouble, nor am I deeply concerned about the content of her poem. We both know that Crista is a highly imaginative young girl who has excelled in her writing at such a young age. Often the children in class look forward to hearing her journal entries when we invite the students to come up and read their most recent journal entries.

While the other children write about their weekend, their pets and their families, Crista writes highly imaginative and detailed stories. She often takes the names of the children in class and inserts them into her story so they feel a part of it. Everyone loves hearing her stories, myself included.

The past two weeks we've been reviewing poetry in our Spelling and Grammar unit to try to introduce students to the classic ABAB and AABB style poetry before we move on to more advanced techniques.

Last week I assigned the children an in-class assignment where they were to write a poem using this style about any subject matter, and when they were done they were to present to the class. I worried that Crista might write about her friend Taylor who she is still obviously mourning. We all are.

I wanted to wait and give her an opportunity to write what she wanted, in the hopes that if she did write about Taylor then maybe it would be therapeutic. Then of course, I'd decide if it were appropriate to read to the class, in case it upset anyone. So I sat at my desk and marked some of the homework from the night before when I looked up and saw that Crista was nodding off at her desk.

That wasn't abnormal for her as I know she has struggled with sleeping ever since Taylor's death. She told me once she suffered from nightmares and that you were making her see someone about them, so I didn't punish her for sleeping. Instead, I waited a few minutes and calmly walked over with the intention of gently shaking her awake and asking if she'd like to sleep in the nurse's office.

So you can imagine my surprise when I saw that Crista's paper was filled with a poem, and not only that but it was a brilliant poem. She used repetition, which is something that I definitely never taught the children. She didn't follow a rhyme scheme or anything that I reviewed with them the past week.

When I read what was on her page, I was delighted with how advanced this was for a child her age. I read the content and I have to admit I found it to be slightly dark; however, I also thought it might be due to the recent trauma she experienced. I shook her awake and she was alarmed, thinking she was in trouble. I kept my hand on her shoulder to assure her that it was okay and I wasn't mad. I then asked her about her poem and she looked terrified.

"This is my nightmare…." she mumbled as she pushed the paper away from herself. I told her it was okay and that I thought it was brilliant. But she refused to touch it. I excused her from reading in front of the class as it was clear that she was very visibly shaken by the words she had ghost written. I almost wondered if she was writing as she was falling asleep as I know children tend to do. Their hands move in accordance with the images they see and so they end up writing words that they never intended to write and have no idea what they meant. I thought this would be the same but she told me that this was very much the details of her nightmare.

I picked up the poem from her and told her I would keep it so she wouldn't have to. I then took it to our vice principal, not with the intentions of bringing up any concern, but to show him the quality of the poem. He insisted we talk to Crista again about the poem to see if she would be interested in entering the upcoming Ontario Writing Competition for Students. The winner of the competition would travel to Ottawa and receive recognition from the head of the Minister of Education, along with a small monetary prize that would be used towards future university tuition.

I approached Crista with this idea. She wouldn't have to use the poem she had written—although I was positive she would win with it—rather she could write any story she wanted. Any of the fun stories she used in class could at least place her in the top ten if they were slightly polished.

I thought she would be excited and eager to take the chance since she always loved coming up to read her stories. In fact, we would joke that she was always the main event since I would always pick her last since hers were the stories everyone wanted to hear most.

I was surprised, however, when she broke into hysterics and said that no she would not be writing in the competition and would never write a story ever again. I asked her why not and she told me that she never wanted to write anything like what she wrote ever again.

I told her it was okay and that she didn't have to write if she didn't want to, at which point she finally looked relieved. I asked her if I could keep her poem and she was reluctant to say yes but eventually nodded yes. She asked me if it was because I was going to tell her sister that she wrote it. I didn't know how to respond since this wasn't the question I had been expecting from her, but I told her that no the poem was just for the two of us and no one would see it. I thought it odd that she wouldn't want her sister of all people to read it but thought that was something you could address.

However, I am going to break my initial promise as I've attached the poem for you to read. The reason for my sending you this note and this letter is because I believe that Crista's skill at writing is too good to throw away. I hope that once you read her poem that you agree and encourage her to continue writing. I don't intend for you to speak to her about the Ontario Writing Competition for Students, I simply want you to encourage her to consider writing once again.

I hope I don't seem too forward in my note to you and I do hope that you strongly consider my request to speak to her. You have a brilliant daughter with an amazing gift and I believe that if nurtured, she could become a brilliant writer. I am at the school most days until about 5pm and school lets out a little bit after 3pm so you can feel free to drop by any time to speak with me. You can also call the main office and they will direct your call to me. I look forward to hearing from you, and I hope you can see the same brilliance in your daughter's writing that I can.

Sincerely,
Mrs. Elaine Ellis
East Thamesville Elementary School

VI

The Face in the Mirror

By: Crista Sunderland
I see my fire red hair but I do not see my face.

I see my light brown eyes catching the light's reflection but I do not see my face.

I see my freckles that splatter my cheeks but I do not see my face.

I see my porcelain white skin but I do not see my face.

I see my eyes following me as I move away from the mirror but I do not see my face.

I see my smile spread across the mouth as I tremble but I do not see my face.

I see my perfect row of white teeth as it laughs but I do not see my face.

I see my hand reach through the glass and grab me but I do not see my face.

I see my fire red hair turn to white and I see my face.

I see my light brown eyes darken to pitch black and I see my face.

I see my freckles fade from my cheeks and I see my face.

I see my pale skin turn ashen grey and I see my face.

I see my death in the mirror and I see my face.

I see my death.

I see my face.

I see my sister's face.

Part 3

Chapter 17
July 2016 – Jack

I awoke to the sound of my front door slamming loudly. I sat up as best I could before toppling over the side of the bed. I grabbed my forehead and shut my eyes tightly, wincing in pain. The room was spinning out of control and I couldn't focus on anything. I tried standing but my legs felt sluggish and heavy. Finally, the bedroom door swung open and I stumbled back down to the ground as I tried to turn and face my visitor. I was half lying, half sitting awkwardly on the ground when I looked up and saw who it was.

"Ah shit."

She stood in the door way and scanned the room in an obvious sign of disgust. My bedroom was such a chaotic disarray that the only thing missing from it was a table in the corner to cook some meth. Any flat surface was covered in either bottles, clothing or fast food scraps. Her eyes continued studying the room with a look of revulsion and finally her eyes settled on me, where the look she had held seconds before only intensified.

I sighed loudly.

"What are you doing here?" I grabbed a pair of sweatpants that was half hanging from my nightstand and I slipped them on clumsily. I looked down and noticed I had put them on backwards, I tried to play it off nonchalantly but she noticed immediately and began shaking her head.

"This is what you've become? All you ever did was complain that you never lived on your own, and now that you do, this is how you live?"

I sat up and rubbed my temples. Her voice had steadily rose in volume as she began her lecture and the sound of it was driving a spike through my brain. I was ready to offer a counter argument, a rebuttal of any kind, when I noticed that my mouth was unbelievably dry. My tongue stuck to the sides of my mouth and it felt incredibly swollen. I inadvertently let out a sigh in her direction and she waved her hand in front of her face as she turned away from me.

"Jesus Christ, Jack, did you drink a distillery? I think I just got a little bit drunk from your breath." She kept waving her hand in front of her face. "When's the last time you showered?"

I ignored her question and walked over to the small bathroom attached to the bedroom and turned on the faucet. I threw my head into the sink and began lapping up water hungrily and noisily. When I felt I couldn't drink anymore, I began holding mouthfuls of water to try and work it around and rehydrate the inside of my mouth.

I looked over my shoulder and saw that she was now standing in the doorway of my bathroom. She was brushing the bangs out of her eyes.

"You still haven't answered my question." I said with a slight irritation in my voice.

"And just what question is that?"

"What are you doing here?" The agitation in my voice was rising.

"Checking in mostly. Seeing how my death is affecting you. Not well from what I can see."

"Gwen, I——" I stopped speaking as I looked at the clock I kept in the bathroom. It read 7:02. I closed my eyes and began focusing on the time.

When I open my eyes, the clock will read 8:30.

I said this to myself over and over again. Repeating it almost like a mantra. When I firmly believed that the clock would read 8:30, I opened my eyes and felt a quick rush of panic as I saw that it simply read 7:03.

"The old lucid dream technique? Alter something small to see if you're dreaming? I forgot that you were the one who taught that to me! Why did you show me that again?"

She was smirking as she asked and I knew that she already knew the answer. I cupped my hands under the running water and began splashing my face, hoping that would wake me up and maybe end this hallucination. I wiped my face off and saw her in the same spot she was in before——she hadn't moved.

I sighed as I turned to face her.

"I showed you this so you could try to see if you were dreaming whenever you would see your 'ghost'."

"Not really a technique you find in your Social Work textbooks, is it? Showing a client how to differentiate between dreams and reality? Between humans and ghosts?"

"It wasn't a ghost! It was just your fucked up head!"

"Jack!" she said in a mocking tone that was whiny as if I had just offended her. "You've never sworn at me before! I'm offended!" A smirk spread across her face again and I felt my face flush with anger.

"What do you want?" I yelled. My throat was still raw and the growl that had come out of my throat had made it burn even worse.

"You're dead and I can't bring you back. So either tell me why you're here or leave me alone." I turned my attention back to the sink and continued lapping up water until my stomach started to feel bloated. I wiped my mouth and turned back to her. She was still there, and I saw that her short black hair with the long bangs had turned lighter in colour, it was almost red.

"You think you can save her? Look what you did to me. Hell, look what you did to Amy. You break people, Jack. You push them beyond the point that they should be pushed until finally they break. You're going to push her too, and just like everyone else around you, she'll break."

I grabbed the plastic cup which held my rarely-used toothbrush and I turned and whipped it at her. The cup smacked into the wall and left the tiniest mark on the paint. I scanned the bathroom and my bedroom for her, but she was gone.

I walked out of my room and heard a quiet conversation coming from the living room. I peeked out the door and saw Gwen sitting on the old torn fabric chair she told me she had picked up on the side of the road. The chair was the piece of furniture that had stood out the most in her apartment. It had a distinct olive green fabric that I was sure wasn't used anymore, and the arm rests exposed the heads of the sharp wood that had once sat underneath.

That chair that had sat in her apartment from day one was now sitting in my living room.

"What's that doing here?" I asked but Gwen ignored me. Instead, she spoke to the figure who was sitting across from her in a dark wood table chair. The figure held a pen and paper in their hand but wasn't making any notes.

"I saw him again."

"It's a 'him' now?" The figure asked. Gwen nodded and leaned forward as she began rocking back and forth.

"He talks to me while I sleep. I can't always tell what he's saying but sometimes I can. He whispers to me and I can't get him to stop. I——"

She stopped speaking and began to shake uncontrollably. Her hands, which shook the most, moved to her eyes in a clumsy attempt to wipe them of the tears that were forming. As she did this, her bangs fall in her eyes, only instead of brushing them aside as she always did, she simply left them there.

"He tells me things. Bad things. He"——she sobbed violently as she tried to continue——"he tells me to hurt people. And I don't want to! I don't like hurting people! I know I did when I wasn't on my meds, and I know everyone is scared of me and thinks I'm going to do it again but I won't. I don't want to!" Gwen's voice was rising uncontrollably and she was nearly yelling at this point.

"Who is it telling you to hurt?" the figure asked.

Gwen fumbled into the pocket of her hoodie and pulled out a crumbled pack of cigarettes. Her hands were shaking even worse than before and it made it nearly impossible for her to fish a cigarette out of her pack. When the figure offers to help her, she raises her hand and shakes her head from side to side. One crumbled white cigarette finally tumbles out of the cigarette pack and onto the floor where she awkwardly picked it up before struggling to place it in her mouth. Watching her try to handle the lighter was even more awkward and at this she allowed the figure to flick the lighter on for her. After a few deep inhales of smoke, her hands began to settle and she appeared more composed.

"It's telling me to hurt people I know." She paused and looked down at the ground. "It's telling me to hurt you."

"Do you want to hurt me?"

"No!" Gwen cried out. She inhaled deeply on her cigarette again and let the long finger of the ash hang off precariously.

"Gwen. I have to ask, and I need you to be honest with me. Do you have a plan to hurt any of these people? The people the voice is telling you to hurt?"

Gwen gripped both sides of her head and folded over onto herself. Her fingers began scratching at her head furiously and she began moaning.

"No! I just told you no! I don't want to hurt anyone! But I can't get him to stop! All I want is for him to stop! My meds won't even help because it's not a voice like the other ones. This one is real, and I know it's a ghost, but no one believes me!"

"Gwen, I believe you. But I need you to tell me what you need from me? What can we do to keep you safe from harming yourself or anyone around you?" the figure said.

Gwen's face was red and she was breathing heavily which created a slight raspy sound from her throat. She was getting noticeably agitated and the soothing voice of the figure wasn't helping ease her at all. I wanted to rush in there and comfort her, I wanted to stop the line of questioning but my feet wouldn't move. I was forced to watch.

"Gwen?" the voice asked again.

"Let me leave here."

"We're working on that. But we have to make sure you're ready to live on your own, risk free, before we let that happen. Now you're making good progress, Gwen, but we still have work to do."

Gwen buried her face in her hands and said something inaudible through muffled hands.

The figure asked her to please repeat it. Gwen slowly took her hands away from her face.

"I said—" Gwen looked up and made eye contact with the figure... "I said then kill me."

Gwen then stopped looking at the figure sitting across from her and looked at me. Her demeanour changed entirely, and she was no longer the scared and timid girl I had been watching only moments earlier. She had a smile on her face and her head was tilted to the side.

She pulled her collar down and lifted her neck towards me so I could see the blood pouring out of her wound. She stood and walked towards me with her collar still pulled down while she held a grin that plastered itself on her face. I tried to move towards her again but slipped in something wet under my feet. I looked down and found Gwen's blood pooled at my feet. I jumped back in horror and when I did, I noticed in my hand there was a glass shard that was digging into my hand, cutting the palm. Gwen's blood stained the end of the glass shard.

I tried to take another step back as I dropped the shard and felt my feet fly out from under me. I had slipped in the pools of Gwen's blood and was hanging in the air, falling in what felt like slow motion. I held my breath as I prepared for the jarring sensation of my back hitting the hardwood floors of my apartment.

I landed flat on my back, but the sensation wasn't hard or impactful. It was soft. Surprisingly soft. I sat up and found I was sitting in my bed. The lights were off and my room was as it was before Gwen had come in. I laid back down hard and exhaled heavily as I realized it was all a dream.

Just a dream, I kept muttering to myself.

I climbed out of bed and walked to the bathroom where I flicked on the lights and opened the medicine cabinet where I grabbed the last bottle of sleeping pills I had. I opened the childproof lid and groaned when I looked inside.

Empty.

My hands were starting to shake and the thought of going back to sleep and dreaming of Gwen was making my hands shake even worse. I turned to go to the fridge where I would try to find some sleep medicine. This particular sleep medicine was made by Smirnoff.

I went to turn off the light in the bathroom when I turned back towards the sink to look for the cup that held my toothbrush. It sat peacefully on the bathroom counter and I breathed a sigh of relief, it was all dream. But still I knew, today was going to be a shitty day.

Chapter 18
July 2016 – Jack

"Is this necessary, Katelyn?" I asked as I stared vacantly with blood shot eyes at the plethora of cliché motivational posters she hung around her office. It was the type of motivational BS you'd see plastered all over a high school kid's Facebook wall. The 'inspirational' quote set against a backdrop of nature. One of the posters in Katelyn's office read: "Keep your head up, keep your head strong", with an image of a forest that I'm sure the original photographer had no idea was being used in this motivational shit.

I scoffed as I noticed the one directly above her head that she had displayed most prominently so it would be the first thing you'd notice when you went into her office. It was an image of the Grand Canyon and it read: "Imperfection is Perfection". I'd never met anyone who hated me for my imperfections more than Katelyn.

This was this kind of meaningless messaging I kept out of my counselling sessions with my clients. I didn't tell them to keep strong and be hopeful that things would work out. I'd be real with them and empathize with their feelings rather than dismissing their emotions by telling them to stay strong.

She wasn't looking at me and was absent mindedly filling out the information boxes for the employee evaluation form that she was required to complete with me once a month. It was the agreement that the Union Rep had made with the Board when they were forced to keep me on for the time being. I was required to receive monthly employee evaluations from Katelyn and counselling from the psychiatrist assigned to the Hospital's Employee Assistance Program. Failure to adhere to these guidelines could result in discipline with the option for dismissal. "Katelyn," I tried pleading to her again. "I'm honestly fi—"

"How have your counselling sessions gone with your client?" she asked as she ignored my pleading. She kept her eyes on the evaluation form with her pen was in her hand. She wasn't going to let me out of this easily. I sighed in defeat.

"Crista."

"Sorry?" she asked.

"My client's name is Crista. Do we not give names to our clients anymore?"

"The department feels a certain detachment from our clients would help us serve them more objectively and more effectively. Growing close relationships with them can result in personal feelings overshadowing the necessary work they need to recover. I'm sure you of all people can understand that." Her voice was cold and robotic as she spewed off this very well practiced speech. I rolled my eyes and continued.

"Well, Crista. Oops I'm sorry!" All of the sarcasm poured out through my voice, I couldn't help it. "I mean, The Client is doing better and she's moving along quite nicely in her recovery. Still a bit of a way off before we can talk about independent living or release though." She sighed loudly and I knew I was really testing her patience; she simply kept her pen to the paper and I knew she was waiting for me to continue, only without the sarcasm. So I did.

"She's experiencing several symptoms of PTSD and high levels of anxiety."

"Physical or psychological?"

"Both," I said. "She stated that she experiences insomnia and when she does sleep she experiences very vivid nightmares. She shakes uncontrollably when speaking about the trauma she's experienced and that's only when she's able to speak about it. For the past month we've had daily sessions and only on a few has she really spoken about her abuser. It's physically and mentally taxing on her. Plus there was an incident when she spoke about her trauma and inadvertently harmed herself."

"Harmed herself how?"

"She dug her nails into the palm of her hand. The nurses told me it wasn't too deep and that they had seen much worse self-inflicted injuries but it concerns me. Her abuser has left her with some very intense mental health issues. Based on her descriptions of her experiences of her abuser, I can't help but wonder if there were mental health issues that ran in the family. Undiagnosed of course."

"What do you mean, in the family?"

"Her abuser," I said. "It was her sister."

Katelyn nodded and continued jotting down notes. "What's your plan of action for her then?"

I thought of Crista when she was laughing and happy. We had had several sessions where her sister didn't come up once and I saw what a positive person she could be when she wasn't focusing on her trauma. On those days I felt ready to submit a report to Katelyn confirming that Crista was ready to be released into supportive housing and out of the hospital.

Then I would remember the report which stated that no one had been found at the house, and the very real chance that Jane was still alive. I had grown very fond of Crista and the thought of her being released to an unsecure location where her sister could at any moment retaliate frightened me to my core. I was torn between my need to protect her and my need to do my job to the best of my ability.

I had spoken with Detective Sullivan—the police officer in charge of the investigation and who had initially brought Crista in—and he had informed me that they were aware that no one had been in the fire and that they were still looking for Jane. I hadn't wanted to ask him in what capacity they were looking for her; was she seen as a victim or a threat to society. How much of Crista's stories did they really know?

Crista herself stated that she hadn't gone to the police because she thought that they wouldn't believe her. But with Jane now completely missing and the thorough investigation into her disappearance, one can't help but wonder what skeletons would be brought out of their family's closet.

Until I could find more information on what the police knew about Jane, I didn't feel right releasing Crista. I knew that realistically the charges against her would either be dropped or she'd be declared not criminally responsible for her actions due to her mental health. Once that was declared, she'd be released into a treatment centre, which would undoubtedly have less security and easier access than the hospital. And a place with no security and easier access was exactly the type of place that Jane Sunderland could walk right into, and that was something I wasn't prepared to let happen.

"Jack?" Katelyn asked. I hadn't realized that I had gotten so lost in my thoughts. I turned back to her and shook the distracting thoughts from my head.

"My current plan of action for her is to assist her in developing an awareness for her triggers"—which we've already done—"finding methods that allow her to speak about her trauma openly"—also already done—"and of course establish healthy coping behaviours when her PTSD is triggered." That part we actually hadn't figured out, but we weren't far.

Katelyn nodded in approval, and there appeared to be the slightest look of admiration on her face. For a moment it seemed that she remembered what it was like when I was on my A-Game. She then put her pen down and looked me in the eyes.

"And you?"

I raised an eyebrow. "And me?"

"You've stopped attending your counselling sessions. So either you're a lot better, or you're a lot worse. Judging from the very apparent hangover you've brought into work today, I'd say it's the latter. Though at least you did shower and shave today; there were some days when it smelled like we were working in a distillery."

I laughed quietly and ran my hand over the smoothness of my cheek. "That's not the first time I've heard that today." I realized the silly mistake I had made and hoped she didn't ask me where I had heard it. What would I even say? The figure of Gwen who recurrently haunts my dreams said it to me?

"I wouldn't say I'm better or worse. But yes I've stopped attending."

"How come?" she asked abruptly. I took a deep breath and exhaled loudly, knowing that my answer was going to upset her.

"Because I don't think it's right that a psychiatrist who's being paid by the hospital is assessing my recovery to see if I'm ready to continue working AT said hospital. The hospital where I'm incredibly unpopular to the point that they've already written my letter of dismissal pending the college's decision. The psychiatrist you've hired has a subjective interest as an employee of the hospital."

"They're not our employee," Katelyn interjected.

"Third party contract," I said. "Same thing. They have their own interests in the matter, and if they want to maintain a good relationship with the hospital and renew their contract, then they have to keep the hospital happy. Telling the Board that I'm psychologically recovered and able to perform my job well isn't exactly the way to get a first class ticket to the Board's good books. Telling them I'm damaged and unable to do my job, now that's a sure fire way to keep the Board happy. So why would I go to a counsellor who is actively working to screw me over?"

"That's quite the victim complex you've got there."

"Oh don't plead ignorant, Katelyn, you know that's exactly what's going on here. I'd be just as happy to see a private

134

psychiatrist with no ties to the hospital, but you and the Board made damn sure that wasn't an option."

"That was the deal YOUR union rep agreed to—"

"That deal was bullshit!" I shouted without meaning to. Katelyn didn't flinch or even react to my raised voice. She was unnerved and had a hardened expression on her face that I had only seen when she was ready to discipline me.

"Look, Jack. I'm concerned about you. Your work with your client—"

"Crista."

"With your CLIENT," she reiterated, "looks impeccable. It sounds like you've built a good rapport and have been able to get a lot of information from her that the other counsellors weren't able to. You have a great relationship with her and that's something that isn't exactly easy from what other counsellors told me. So that's amazing to see."

"But?"

She leaned forward and made strong eye contact with me. She didn't speak for a minute and we sat in uncomfortable silence until she finally chose to speak again.

"Your work is strong, there's no surprise there. But you personally, that's a whole other story. When you came in reeking of booze every other day that was concerning, but at least it explained your appearance. Lately though, you stopped smelling like alcohol but you don't look any better. Your eyes are bloodshot, you're falling asleep at your desk, your hands are shaking more and more noticeably, and I see your door closed a lot more than it used to. You're displaying all the signs and symptoms of burn out, as well as some other more severe mental health issues."

"I'm fine," I tried to say but she waved away my answer immediately.

"You've been through hell and back. You haven't even had proper time to mourn, so it would make complete sense if you weren't ready to be back yet. Burning yourself out and pushing yourself beyond your limits isn't going to help anyone."

"Katelyn," I said and paused. I found myself wanting to choose my words carefully to avoid turning this discussion into an argument. "This is all I have right now. This is what's keeping me going. When I go home, all I want to do is talk to Amy but I can't. When I'm alone with my thoughts, all I want to do is not think about Gwen, but I can't. This"—I motioned with my arms to my

135

surroundings—"this is all I have right now. THIS is what's keeping me from burning out."

"Well, then you have to start seeing the psychiatrist again."

I threw my head back and groaned. "Fine!"

"Good," she said and then jotted down her final note. She then handed me the evaluation which had summed up our conversation. I signed it without reading and handed it back.

"I'll let them know you're moving forwards in your recovery right now but that you still require psychological counselling." She handed me the card of the psychiatrist I was to contact to arrange another session. I took the card and sat back down. She didn't say anything else; rather she just continued looking towards the door to her office. It was her way of telling me this meeting was over.

I got up and left, making the short walk back to my office. I waited until I was out of sight when I took the psychiatrists card and tossed it in the small shredder I kept behind my desk.

I tried putting the end of the conversation out of my mind and focused my attention on Crista. I had an appointment with her first thing after lunch and I needed to figure out what my next move would be with her.

I needed to find out how the investigation into her sister was going. I needed to find out how much of danger Crista was actually in. I needed to find out what I could do to protect her.

But most of all, I needed to find out just how dangerous Jane really was.

Chapter 19
July 2016 – Jack

It was another week of sessions with Crista before I was able to find out more information about Jane. We had spent the previous week discussing coping strategies when her anxiety would peak—ironic I know—and we spoke about different grounding techniques to use when she felt as if she was spiralling downward. We took breaks from the counselling from time to time to discuss movies, books and of course, her terrible taste in music. The more progress she made in her recovery, the harder I found it to have her open up about her sister.

I found that I began losing my train of thought during our counselling sessions because I would often focus on how to turn the conversation towards Jane. The more I thought about it, the more I lost concentration during our actual discussions. When I was finally ready to give up on my technique of subtly hinting towards this line of discussion, she offered me an opening. I had arrived for our session with a cup of green tea for her—her favourite drink—and a black coffee for me. I had run out to the coffee shop across the road to get them, as the in-house tea and coffee we had was deplorable. She was grateful and it helped ease us into conversation that day.

We had been discussing what her life was like living at the hospital. Namely how terrible and bland the food was, how the smell of sterile equipment made the entire place feel cold and how the staff treated her. At the mention of the staff, she perked up.

"Oh! Speaking of the staff! She has a crush on you, you know?" Crista said with a smirk on her face as she blew at the steam rising out of her cup of tea.

"Who?" I asked, pretending to be completely unaware of who she meant. I took a sip of my black coffee and cursed quietly as I burned my tongue.

"You know who!" she laughed. "I hear her and the other nurses talking about you at the nurse's station right outside my room. I thought I would be bored without a TV in my room but let me tell you, those ladies are better than any TV show you could ever watch!" She looked up from her tea and saw me smirking.

She shrugged. "I don't normally listen to other people's conversations but the choice was do that or write in my journal. I think I chose wisely." She then nodded to the window. "If I hadn't been listening in to their conversation, then I wouldn't have noticed that she's walked by our window about four times. She stares in every single time, I can't tell if she just wants to look at you or if she wants you to notice her and smile back. It's a mystery."

"What do you think I should do when she walks by again?" I asked with a bit of mischief in my voice. She scrunched up her face as she thought about it, then her eyes lit up.

"Blow her a kiss!" We both began laughing.

"Isn't that a bit mean though? Mocking her crush like that?" I asked.

Crista shrugged and turned back to the window. "Isn't she being a bit weird? Walking back and forth so often? If she's going to be weird about it, I think you should too!"

Crista began laughing again and began blowing fake kisses to the window of our room. I soon joined her again in laughter and then without warning Melissa walked by our window for the fifth time. She stopped as she locked eyes with us, a deer in caught in headlights. She blushed, realizing she had been caught and she rushed off past the window.

At this we began howling with laughter. It took us a few moments to get our composure back and when I went to take a sip of coffee, I started laughing again and that got Crista laughing all over again.

"I feel terrible! She's probably so embarrassed," I said as I wiped at the tears I had in my eyes. I took a couple of deep breath to calm down my laughter.

Crista did the same and looked at the window. "I can't wait to hear her telling the other nurses about it later. I'll let you know what she says."

"You don't have to do that Crista." I shook my head as I said it, trying to show her I wasn't interested in pursuing the one-sided crush.

She shrugged. "I know I don't have to. But I want to, it's the only entertainment I have here."

"I'm so glad that my love life is so entertaining for you!" I said with a mock smile. She was sipping her tea and had to stop herself as she laughed lightly.

"It is very entertaining. Thank you for giving me something to laugh about. Any other details of your love life you think will entertain me?" She held her eyes on me as I absent mindedly looked down at my left hand.

The faint tan line of where I had worn my wedding ring was nearly gone. Seeing it slowly disappear hit me with an unexpected shot of grief. I suddenly felt nauseous as my stomach tightened. I swallowed hard and looked back up at Crista as I put a fake smile on my face. But I was too late, she had caught my expression and she was staring intensely into my eyes. Studying me.

"I'm sorry," she said as she quickly tried to backtrack. She could immediately tell that she had accidentally upset me. I waved her apology away but she continued trying to apologize profusely.

"It's fine. Really. You don't have to apologize, Crista," I said as I tried waving off her apology.

"Who was she?" she asked. "The woman you loved?" I looked into Crista's eyes and saw a genuine look of sympathy. I hadn't been expecting to talk about this today and was taken aback by both her question but also her sympathy.

"Her name was Amy. She left a while go. I'm still getting used to it I suppose." She smiled warmly at me and I reached for a tissue. I expected tears to come but none did. I exhaled loudly and looked back up at Crista.

"Do you still talk to her?" she asked.

I shook my head. "She stopped speaking to me entirely about a month ago I think." I paused in thought. "Yeah, I'd say it's been about a month since she spoke to me."

"I'm sorry to hear that. I really am. How did you—"

"I drove her away," I said, cutting her off. "I made some questionable choices and drove her away. At first I thought it was temporary. But I think it might be for good."

Crista pushed the box of tissues towards me and I waved it away. "It's okay. It happens. Not every marriage is built to last, right?" I exhaled loudly then chuckled softly as I looked at her. I asked, "How do you do this to me every time?"

"Do what?" she said. The playfulness now gone from her voice.

"Get me to talk about me, when we're supposed to be here talking about you?"

Her eyes dropped to the contents of her mug. She swirled her tea around and I noticed that she was biting at her lip. It appeared as if she had something on the tip of her tongue that she wanted desperately to get out, but was afraid to.

"Is that what you'd like to talk about today, Crista? Relationships?"

She was in the middle of raising her mug to her lips again when she paused mid-air. The cup hung a few inches below her mouth as if frozen in time. She licked her lips then set the cup back down gently on the table.

She tightened her lips, looked down and began nodding up and down. Her eyes moved towards the tissues on the desk and, as had become our custom, I nudged them towards her. She grabbed them and thanked me quietly before she began playing with the rim of the mug.

"Crista, we don't have to talk about this if it makes you uncomfor—"

"His name was Troy Williams. And he was the only boy I ever loved."

She paused and downed the remainder of her tea. I held out my hand and offered to take it from her. She shook her head and placed it in her lap and began tracing her fingers over the coffee shop's logo that was printed on the side of the cup. I saw that tears had started coming down her cheeks but she was still managing a smile.

"He was a good guy. Like a genuinely good guy, you know. He wasn't a jock, he wasn't a brainiac and he definitely wasn't a loser. He was just Troy. And everyone loved Troy. Especially me. I'll always remember when I first met him."

Chapter 20
September 2007 – Crista

I had been running late for my period 3 Advanced History class which sat at the exact opposite corner of the school from my period 2 Advanced Biology class. I had become a master of weaving in and out of crowds, and normally I was able to make it to my History class with a minute to spare. Coach Podolski, the school's track coach, frequently told me that I ran better than some of his top athletes and if I kept it up that he'd reserve a spot for me on Varsity. It had only taken me a week to map out the best route to my next class, and by the end of the month I could have run that course in my sleep.

The day I had met Troy, there had been a fight in the hallway. Two senior boys had decided that the middle of the hallway was the best location for their fist fight over whatever stupid thing it was that boys fought over. It took all of a few seconds after their fight started for the hallway to explode into chaos. Students herded around the fight until they were packed in shoulder to shoulder, some even fought amongst themselves just for a better spot to view the action.

I had sprinted right up to the edge of the crowd and after a few failed attempts of trying to penetrate the wall of students, I gave up. I knew the next fastest route to my class would take me through the cafeteria so I turned and sprinted off as fast as I could.

The cafeteria sat empty with the exception of few seniors who had third period spare, and dedicated this period to countless hands of Euchre. My eyes focused on the card-playing seniors just a little too long and I had somehow failed to see the yellow 'floor slippery when wet' sign the janitor had just put out. I took one step on the wet floor and my smooth flat bottomed shoes slipped out from beneath me with a large squeak. I hung in the air for a full second before I came crashing down onto the hard tiled floor, feet straight up in the air. I was so suddenly taken off my feet that I hadn't had time to prepare myself for the impact, and as my back landed on the floor, my head snapped back. The back of my head made an audible smack and tears filled my eyes immediately.

My head began to throb and I was struggling to stand when I felt a powerful hand reach under my arm and another hand slip onto my waist. I looked up and saw him. I tried to speak but my ears were ringing and my speech was slurred. He let me go and my knees quickly gave out under me—luckily he was able to catch me immediately. He held my face and spoke to me, but I couldn't understand anything he said. Before I could try to get him to repeat himself, he whisked me off to the nurse's station.

He held me firmly on the arm and waist but not hard. It didn't hurt; instead, it had felt incredibly secure. Safe almost. He walked extremely slowly and took the majority of my weight on his hip. He was strong enough to simply lift me up and carry me on his own, but he appeared to be moving me as little as possible.

My vision went in and out, and I hadn't even noticed we made it to the nurse's station. Since both of his hands were occupied, he began kicking at the door to try and alert someone that we needed help. The nurse came running out immediately and upon seeing my pupils she rushed me into her office and onto the first aid bed as she moved to the phone.

I finally blacked out and woke up several hours later in the hospital to my mother screaming at the doctor and nursing staff. She was hysterical about the fact that I hadn't woken up yet and that they hadn't been able to see the extent of my concussion.

I tried to speak but my tongue still felt heavy in my mouth, almost as if it were being held down by a tongue depressor. I turned slightly and saw Jane sitting in the chair beside the bed.

She was working on her homework and somehow was tuning out my mother's screams without any effort. It took her a full minute before she realized I was staring at her, at which point she looked up at me and stared blankly into my eyes before she returned to her work.

I remember I began to writhe in panic as I worried that they were going to leave her alone with me. Even when I had the ability to fight back, I was completely useless against her. God knows what she would do to me now that I was completely incapacitated.

Luckily for me, my mother never left my side and stayed with me, until the doctor's released me home where I was to remain in bed rest.

I missed two whole weeks of school with a concussion, and even though the school advised my mother that maybe I take the whole semester off, she ignored them. While she was incredibly careful with my recovery, she was also incredibly strict about school. And falling behind an entire semester when I was near the top of my class wasn't an option for her.

My mother had kept me resting in bed for the two weeks with minimal TV, no phone and no computer. It sounds boring but truthfully it was one of the best two weeks of my life. Mom had Jane sleeping in a different room and told her that I was not to be disturbed. It was the longest I'd ever gone without having to see my sister.

It was one of the best times of my life.

On the Monday that I was to return to school, my mother stopped me on my way out the door. Jane was already outside, halfway to the bus stop and completely unaware that I was lagging behind. Although maybe unaware isn't the right word; disinterested is more like it.

My mother placed her hand on my shoulder and had a slightly mischievous smile on her face. "Crista, who was that boy?"

I didn't say anything, and I didn't need to. The confused look on my face told my mother everything she needed to know. She couldn't help but keep that mischievous smile on her face as she patted me on the arm and said, "Oh I see."

Still confused, I asked her what she was talking about. She laughed as she opened the door for me to catch the bus.

"I think you may have a secret admirer then," she said as she continued to giggle. I turned to face her before she could shut the door on me.

"Who? Mom, who's my secret admirer?"

She grinned and said, "The boy who took you to the nurse's office. What was his name?"

I gasped and my hand flew to my mouth to try to hide my excitement. I could feel my cheeks burning and turning a bright red. My mother noticed my blushing cheeks and couldn't help but laugh.

"Troy?"

"Is that his name?" she asked. "Well, whatever it was, he came by the house every day to make sure you were alright. I sent him away telling him you couldn't have any visitors but it didn't stop his daily check-ins. Make sure to thank him when you get to school, alright?"

I was stunned and unable to speak. I wanted to ask her a million more questions but my mother had pointed behind me at the approaching bus and closed the door on me. I could see the bus coming from down the street so I cursed and sprinted for my stop. I made it just in time and found Jane hadn't even noticed I was gone; she had her face buried in her book that she wouldn't take her eyes away from until we got to the front doors at school.

I couldn't focus during class at all that day and just kept trying to plan my route so I could run through the cafeteria at the exact same time he would be there. I planned and re-planned and then planned again how to best run into him. Would I look casual about it? Would I let him know I sought him out? Would I pretend I didn't know him? Would I thank him?

All of these questions came into my head, and when I saw that the clock was a minute away from the end of Period 2, I could feel my hands turn sweaty and my heart began to race. I felt sick to my stomach and all of my planning had gone out the window to the point that I started figuring out alternate routes that would help me avoid the cafeteria. The mere thought of going near the cafeteria made me feel light headed and anxious, so when the alarm rang, I picked up my back pack and bolted for the door so I could get to my next class earlier than usual. I had only taken two steps when I ran directly into him. I heard him make an audible 'oomf' sound as my shoulder drove into his chest.

I looked up into his face and I froze. My cheeks had turned a bright red and suddenly I felt as if my face matched my hair. I stammered as I tried to talk and then my heart dropped when I saw him rubbing at the spot on his chest I had crashed into.

"So you just always crash into things then? I gotta tell you, I'm a little bit sore after this crash so I might not be able to carry you back into the nurse's office this time!"

A loud obnoxious laugh escaped my mouth and my hands immediately flew to my mouth to try to cover the sound. I turned an even darker shade of red and my eyes went to the ground. I tried to apologize for my crashing into him and my embarrassing laugh but my mouth turned to sand paper and I couldn't find any words.

"Tell you what?" he said. "Why don't I carry that bag for you to your next class? I'd hate to have given you another concussion AND make you carry your heavy bag." He grabbed the bag from me and his hand lightly brushed my shoulder. I nearly cried out from the shock of his touch and wanted to protest but nothing came out other than more stammering.

"Where you headed, Red?" he asked as he smiled a smile that you only read about in teen romance novels, the type of smile that you don't actually think exists. If Prince Charming smiled at you, it would have been the same smile that Troy had on his face right now.

He propped my backpack onto his back and said, "You want to help me out here, Red? This bag isn't really all that light and I'd like to make sure you make it to class on time."

"BIOLOGY!" I yelled out. He scrunched up his face in a 'that was weird' kind of expression and then laughed as he turned and held out his arm for me to take.

"Well then. Let's get you to Biology. Man, that's on the opposite side of the school, why did you go through the cafeteria? Surely there's a faster route." I didn't attempt to explain that I already knew that, as I was afraid it would come out as more word vomit.

He walked me to class and I began panicking about what to talk to him about. It was only when we arrived to my class that I realized he had been talking at me the entire time. He didn't care that I wasn't responding, he just kept talking to me and laughing at my wordless responses. I wanted to thank him but still found I couldn't speak, until finally he handed me my bag.

"So, Red, what do you say? Same time tomorrow?" I gawked at him without speaking, he laughed and said, "Then it's a date. See you then!"

The next day he was waiting outside of my classroom, ready to take my bag. And then he was there the day after that, and the day after that, until finally it turned into a daily meeting. It was the best part of my day and I think secretly it was the best part of his.

It wasn't until a few days into our new routine that I was finally able to find the courage to speak and that's when I started arriving late to class every single day. Our conversations would get so engaging that we'd lose track of time, I'd end up getting unreasonably mad that I even had to go to class and that I couldn't stay and talk with him. Shortly after that, he wasn't just meeting me after History class, but rather he was meeting me after single one of my classes. It even got to the point that he was walking me to and from the bus.

We never spoke about our status or had 'the talk'; we simply started spending all day every day with each other and just ended up being in a relationship. It was unofficially made official on the day that he walked me to the bus, handed me my backpack and kissed me on the mouth.

It was a quick, dry-lipped peck. The type of kiss you'd give your grandparents when you're a child, almost an obligatory kiss you do without thinking about. And yet, it was the best kiss of my life.

After that, our kisses became longer, more loving and soon enough we would find ourselves sneaking off between classes so we could kiss as much as we wanted without worrying about my bus driver leaving without me.

The more time we spent together, the more we loved each other. While other couples at our school would have relationships filled with drama, bickering and immature fighting, we differed. We became closer, more intimate and soon we were spending every hour of the day outside of class together. I would go to sleep texting him, and wake up and text him again.

The day he told me he loved me, I bawled my eyes out. I couldn't contain my excitement, and I just started to cry uncontrollably.

"I'm gonna be honest with you, Red. Not the reaction I was hoping for, usually girls are happy to hear that, aren't they?" he asked me as he laughed and held me in his arms. At which point I grabbed his face and kissed him as hard and passionately as I could. I told him I loved him too, and I had never seen him look so happy.

We were in love.

We were happy.

All was right in the world.

Until one morning, when Jane and I had been riding the bus together to school. I had been daydreaming of what Troy and I would do that day in our breaks between classes. Would we find a hidden corner of the school and kiss our breaks away? Would we lay out by the bleachers, where he would wrap me up in his arms and hold me as I nodded off to sleep? Would we spend time just getting lost in conversation? My mind had completely drifted away from the real world and I wasn't anywhere on that bus. I was lost in my fantasies where I was truly happy when suddenly Jane's voice ripped me out of my dream world and forced me back to reality, catching me off guard.

"You're spending a lot of time with him," Jane said abruptly. Her face had been buried in her book and she hadn't acknowledged me the entire morning except to roll her eyes at me when I asked if her book was for fun or for class. So when she had spoken to me, it took me completely by surprise.

"Who?" I asked.

"Are you spending time with more than one boy?"

146

"No?"

"Well then why did you ask who?" she said, still not taking her eyes off of her book. Her eyes were still moving side to side and despite our conversation, I knew she was still reading and even absorbing the words she read. It frustrated me that she couldn't even be bothered to give me her full attention.

"I just meant—" I took a deep breath and tried to hide the anger that nearly slipped into my tone. "I just meant, I didn't know that you had noticed that I was spending so much time with him. What do you care any—"

"I don't," she cut me off and placed her book in her bag as our bus arrived at the school.

I wanted to ask her why she brought it up but I could already tell that her brain had moved on to another topic and I no longer held her interest.

I looked outside the window and saw Troy waiting for me; his backpack was slung over one shoulder and he was wearing his blue plaid shirt that he knew was my favourite. It hugged his frame in all of the right places and made him look like he had come out of a 90s' grunge band. I turned away from Jane and hurried off the bus where I ran to him and threw myself into his arms. I wrapped my arms tightly around his neck and pressed myself tightly against him before pulling away and planting a long kiss on his lips.

"I'm happy to see you too, Red!" he said as he smirked and kissed me again. He grabbed my backpack from me and threw it on his free shoulder. I hooked my hand on the inside of his arm and let him lead me away into the school. As we walked, I turned and looked over my shoulder and saw Jane, standing outside the bus. Staring at me.

Staring at us.

Chapter 21
December 2007 – Crista

That December had been uncharacteristically warm. I had been used to wearing thermal clothing under my regular clothes as well as heavy winter attire. Most years it was so cold by October that most kids couldn't even go trick or treating unless it was in full winter coats. This year, however, the weather was still in the positives and you could go outside in a light jacket. Or, in my case, my boyfriend's oversized and extra comfortable hoody that he had brought specifically for me.

We had driven out to the woods on the outskirts of the town's borders. It was still in Middlesex County, but you weren't technically in Thamesville anymore. It was a spot where on Fridays and Saturday nights, teens would drive out to drink and get high. It was also a spot where on a cloudless sky like tonight, you could see the sky light up with stars. It was far away enough from the city that the lights and smog from the city didn't block out the night sky.

Troy had taken me out here specifically for that very reason. He had come out here once with his dad when he was a child, he told me. His dad had bought Troy a telescope and had taken him out to a specific clearing in the middle of the woods where they looked at stars together for hours. It was one of Troy's happiest memories and he wanted to share it with me.

I was planning on sharing something with Troy tonight as well. Myself.

I had been nervous throughout the day as our date approached. I constantly felt my stomach fluttering and my mind wasn't able to focus on any task throughout the day. Even when Troy was talking to me at school, I had had difficulty listening to him. All I could think of was what I had planned for us that night.

As scared as I was, it felt right and I felt ready. I had always been afraid that Troy would expect sex from me and would hate me if I held out on him. But the truth was, he was incredibly gentle whenever we were intimate and he never pushed me beyond my comfort zone. He never even brought it up or pressured me in any sort of way; he was a perfect gentleman about the whole thing, which was typical Troy. It made me love him even more.

As we pulled into the unpaved parking lot at the main entrance of the woods with the low log fence, I felt my face turn a bright red. I was getting nervous and scared but at the same time, I was getting excited. He ran around to my side of the car and opened the door for me, leading me out by the hand. With his other hand he turned on his heavy duty camping flashlight and led me into the pitch black opening of the woods. During the day you would hardly notice the opening at the edge of the trees, but in the middle of the night it looked like the opening shot of a horror film. Some sort of monster or witch would be in there and once we crossed that entrance, we would never return home.

I was trembling slightly but I felt his hand give mine a little squeeze. He smiled at me and said, "Don't worry, Red. The only thing you have to worry about out here are rabbits and maybe an owl or two. Nothing scary in these woods. Now come on."

He pulled me along and I let him. He made quick decisive turns through the trees and if I hadn't known any better I would have thought that he didn't even need the flashlight, he was moving purely on muscle memory. I struggled to keep up, but fear of losing him in the pitch black woods helped keep my feet moving faster than they were used to.

Finally, we emerged from a thick group of trees and we were in a small but unmistakable clearing in the forest. It was a perfect little circle with level ground and surprisingly soft grass. The open nature of this spot made it dangerous for animals as it was so exposed, so it was left completely undisturbed.

He laid down in the middle of the clearing and held his arm out for me to join him. I laid down beside him and slid up against him, nestled in his arm and absorbing all of his body heat. It was perfect and I wanted to lay there with him forever. We laid for several minutes without speaking; we were simply absorbed by the vastness of the star lit sky above us. I wanted to ask him question after question about constellations and the various star formations, but I didn't. The silence was unbelievably pleasant and it brought a sort of peace to the entire situation.

"So, Red. What do you think?" he asked as he turned towards me, still holding me in his arms. I inched closer towards him and held his face in my hands.

"It's beautiful. It's so beautiful out here, thank you for bringing me and sharing this with me." I brought his face to mine and kissed him gently. We held our gentle kiss for a few seconds before I kissed him again, this time more intensely and more passionately. Our breathing was getting heavier and my hands had begun to move down from his face. I pushed him onto his back and threw my legs over him. His hands moved to my hips and he gripped me tightly. My hands worked at his belt, as his hands began pulling off my shirt.

We stripped each other naked, and what happened next I'll never forget. It was quick, and it painful, but it was wonderful. He was gentle and he was passionate, his eyes never left mine. The look he gave me in that moment was one of love. I knew right then and there that he really, truly loved me.

When we were done, he held me tight against him for what seemed like hours before covering me with his sweatshirt. He kissed me again and again all over my face and shoulders and repeatedly told me how much he loved me. We waited a while before we dressed again as the feeling of being pressed against each other, completely naked and vulnerable, was unbearably sweet. Finally, the cool night air decided for us that it was time to put our clothes back on, and when we were fully dressed, he held me against him again and I nearly cried from joy. I was so happy in his arms, but the temperature was dropping off and even being wrapped up in him couldn't stop me from shivering.

"You cold, Red?" I nodded at him and he jumped to his feet. "Why don't we go back to the car? I'll turn on the heat and warm you right up?"

I shook my head no. "I don't want to leave here. Now come back to me," I said as I reached for him. He stepped towards me and held my hands before he brought both to his mouth and kissed one, then the other.

"Well then let me go back and get us some blankets. I have a few in the trunk. I'll be back in five?"

The face I made told him I was nervous. He smiled and chuckled lightly at that.

"I left the car unlocked, so if you're worried about me leaving you and driving away, I can give you my keys." He placed them in my hands but I shook my head.

"It's not that, I just don't like being out here by myself. It's fine with you here, but it's a little creepy with you gone."

He bent down and kissed my forehead, then my nose then my mouth. He then reached for my hand and intertwined his fingers with mine.

"I'll run. And I promise I'll be back in less than five. But I won't have you out here freezing to death." He kissed my forehead and began walking to the trees that we had come out of.

"Troy!" I called out before he walked into the trees.

"Yeah, Red?" He looked over his shoulder.

"I love you."

He came running over, bent over and lifted my face to his. He kissed me as hard as he could. When he let our kiss go, he pressed his forehead to mine.

"I love you too, Red." With that he was off, and into the woods.

It was the last time I saw him alive.

Chapter 22
December 2007 – Crista

Five minutes went by.

Ten minutes.

Thirty minutes.

An hour.

I was panicking and near hysterical, I didn't know what to do. It would be hours before daylight, but even then I had no idea how to get back out. Troy had gone off the main trail about a minute into our walk and I had lost track of where we were by then. I felt tears of frustration welling in my eyes, I didn't know what to do and I didn't know how to fix this.

I had left my phone in his car, but even if I made it to his car and found it, I didn't think I'd have any reception out there. I reached into my pocket and felt the keys that he had left me, so I knew that he hadn't driven off. But somehow this made it worse, it meant that he hadn't driven away like I thought he had the first few minutes he didn't return. My having his keys would have made that impossible, so it was clear that he was still there in the woods. But where?

I had begun pacing back and forth in the small clearing that I had initially loved, but now felt imprisoned in. I was trying to commit to the idea that I should return to the car. Even if he wasn't there, I would be a hell of a lot safer than if I stayed out in the woods for much longer. I tried to force myself to walk through the same clearing I saw Troy walk through but my instinct of staying put was too strong.

In the distance I heard a twig snapped, cutting through the unsettling silence and startling me, causing me to scream in absolute terror. My heart was painfully pounding in my chest, causing an unbelievable pressure on my lungs that made it hard to breathe. Another twig snapped, only this time it was closer, coming directly behind me. My mind ended its debate of whether or not it was safe to return to the car, and I took off at a full sprint through the trees, ignoring the burning pains in my chest.

My face and arms were being whipped by low hanging branches, and my feet managed to find every possible loose rock that was hidden on the trail, causing my ankle to roll repeatedly. But I clenched my teeth and pushed through the pain, determined to make it back out of the woods to safety. I ran for what felt like hours and still I hadn't arrived to the edge of the woods we had come in. I had been disoriented when we had first arrived but I knew for a fact it had only taken us a few minutes to get to that spot in the woods. I had been running for about fifteen and still wasn't seeing anything familiar. I only had the light of the starlit sky to guide me, but that got lost in the thick patches of trees.

The darkened path threw the ground into complete shadow and hid the sprawling tree roots that were ankle height. Had I had any source of light, I would have seen the one that I wrapped my around my foot, tripping me and causing me to sprawl painfully on my stomach. I tried pushing myself back to my feet but the ground, which moments before had felt hard and dry, was now wet and slick. I squinted as I tried to make out what I was laying in and realized it was a patch of slippery mud. The rest of the ground up to this point had been hard and tough, so why the sudden change in consistency, I thought.

My legs burned, the muscles tight and unresponsive. Standing was proving to be quite difficult, but I was determined to follow this new trail that I had stumbled upon. My body was sore from the fall, forcing me to hold myself up on the surrounding trees as I made my way along this new mud path. The thick tree tops were making it increasingly difficult to see, and my legs had been ready to give out at any moment when I finally saw a clearing. I hobbled towards it, hoping and praying that this was an exit. I knew it couldn't be the exit I was originally hoping for, but I just wanted out of these woods desperately.

A thick bundle of low hanging branches blocked the end of the path, but I was so hungry for freedom and to be out of those woods that I drove my shoulder through the line of trees. Branches snapped against my weight as my arms and neck got covered in what felt like a million tiny scratches. None of them drew blood, but they all stung immensely.

I reached for Troy's keys as my plan was to sound the car alarm and see just how far I was from where we entered originally, but my hand froze in my pocket. I realized I wasn't at an exit; in fact, I wasn't anywhere near the exit. I was staring at the large pond that sat at the centre of these woods. It had normally frozen over by this time of year, but due to the mild temperature it hadn't done so yet; instead, it just sat with a pool of ice water that emitted a chill you could feel from a distance.

I began crying with frustration and sat down hard on the ground, wanting to just give up. I just wanted to go home, take a hot shower and go to sleep in my nice comfortable bed. Instead, I was trapped in the woods, Troy was missing and I couldn't find my way home. I screamed with fury and frustration, ruining the perfect silence that the lake had held only moments before. My screams turned to sobs and I collapsed to the ground in a pitiful defeat. I didn't have the strength to keep looking for a way out, and I didn't have the energy to keep looking for Troy. I was in a lucid nightmare that I couldn't wake up from. It was one of those nightmares where you keep telling yourself to wake up, you remember waking up thousands of times, but in this particular occasion you don't know how. So you plead with your body to wake up, but it doesn't respond, and the more time passes the more difficulty you have in remembering just how to wake up until you think you're forever trapped in the dream.

I was trapped in one of these nightmares when a hand placed itself on my shoulder, jolting me awake. I tried jumping to my feet, but the wet grass under foot failed to provide my feet with any traction, causing me to stumble back down to the ground. I was too relieved to think about the throbbing pain in my tailbone that had been caused by my awkward fall. "Troy! Where were y—" I stopped myself mid-sentence as the moonlight caught the figure's face spot on, and revealed that my saviour wasn't Troy. My heart got caught in a vice as time seemed to stop. I couldn't process the cold fear that had suddenly invaded my thoughts, causing me to lose all ability to speak and move.

"Are you okay?" Jane asked.

I pulled away from her touch and recoiled in fear. Her face remained blank; my rejection of her touch didn't seem to bother her. I looked past her, hoping that maybe she had run into Troy in the woods and that they had been looking for me together.

"Where's Troy?" I asked.

"Are you okay?" she asked again in a tone that was cold and void of emotion. I shook my head before I burst into tears again. "I told you, you were spending too much time with that boy," she said as she grabbed my hand, yanking me painfully to my feet. Without another word, she began leading me into the trees when I had a sudden realization.

"How did you know I was here? How did you find me?"

She stopped pulling me towards the trees and turned to look at me with the fear inducing blank stare she had mastered overtime. She remained silent, unwilling to answer my question; the only noise that came from her was a dismissive scoff. She turned back towards the path, trying to once again pull me along with her. I planted my feet as firmly as I could in the ground and twisted my body away from her to free my hand.

She reached for my hand again and I pulled away even further. I had turned into a child refusing to go to bed and she was the mother who was losing her patience.

She began walking towards me, reaching for me, but I kept stepping backwards so I was just out of reach of her. I was picking up speed as I kept stepping backwards until finally my foot landed in the wet, slick mud I had found earlier, causing my foot to slip under me. My fall was quick and I was left disoriented for a split second. But that was all it took.

Jane seized the opportunity the second it presented itself, launching herself on top of me and pinning me down with her knees. Her knees were weighing down on my chest, compressing my lungs of the air they were so desperately fighting for. When I thought I was going to pass out from the lack of oxygen, she eased the pressure on me, giving me a momentary feeling of relief.

My guard was down as I thought that her assault was only going to be brief, but I was mistaken.

Before I had a chance to move or stand, she was dragging me and flipping me onto my stomach so I was face to face with the frigidly cold, pitch black lake water. A weight suddenly drove into between my shoulder blades, pinning me down to the ground, unable to move. I howled in pain as her entire body's weight drove itself into my spine, I thought if she pressed any harder that her knee would surely burst through my chest. I tried thrashing and bucking my hips, the way a rodeo bull bucks under the rider.

She held on; however, she had some unbelievable strength that allowed her to keep herself planted in place until finally she grabbed me by the back of my hair. My neck snapped back as she yanked my head back violently before pressing her face against mine, cheek to cheek. She breathed heavily into my ear as I continued crying out in pain.

"I told you I was here to help you. Why do you feel the need to be fucking difficult?" She then drove my face into the water and held tightly as I began to kick my legs with new desperation. Air rushed back into my lungs as she pulled my face out, allowing me to gasp for air for a few brief seconds before dunking me again. This time she held me longer and I thought that I was actually going to die.

When my legs finally lost the strength to kick, and my vision began to blur, she let me go, climbing off of my back. I got onto my knees and elbows and began throwing up the pond water I had inhaled. My lungs and throat burned with an unbelievable intensity, and my muscles ached from the failed effort of kicking Jane off of me.

"What's the matter with you?" I yelled at her, straining my throat, causing the burning sensation to worsen.

"When I ask you to come with me, you come with me! Do you understand? You ever question me again and I swear to fucking God I won't let you out of the water next time. I'll drown you just like I did him!" She screamed at me before she looked up towards the pond. I stared at her in horror, before my heart plummeted into a bottomless pit. I had felt fear before, but nothing like this before. This was the fear that you feel, not when you know you're in danger, but when someone you love is. That unexplainable feeling of dread that you have when you know that something awful is happening, but you don't know what. It's the feeling a person gets when their phone rings, and without even looking at the number you know there is bad news on the other line.

I had that feeling.

I looked to where Jane's eyes had become fixated, trying to see just what she could possibly be staring at. Even though I knew exactly what it was going to be.

When I had been searching for him in the trees, my eyes had struggled adjusting to the dark, but now as I searched on the pond's pool of pitch black water, they refused to adjust at all. The trees were one thing, but the large open pond with the pitch black water was another; the water swallowed light and made it nearly impossible to see anything. My panic rose at an alarming rate as my eyes continued to struggle to adjust. As I looked frantically over the surface of the water that was visible to me, I realized that shapes were now starting to take form, making my search easier. That's when I saw him. Floating face down.

Troy was dead.

The sound I had heard Taylor's mom make when she had found her daughter face down in the water was a sound I had never wanted to hear again. I never thought that I would hear it again, but when I saw Troy, that very sound came out of me. It was a cry of pure unfiltered agony that no one should ever have to make. I screamed and cried and felt the strength leave my body as I collapsed on the ground.

Troy was dead.

I wanted to fix it. I wanted to dive in, swim to him and save him. I hadn't known how long he had been in there for; I prayed it was only a minute so that there would be a chance that I could save him. Had I been able to think rationally, I never would have clung onto such an unrealistic desire, but as it was I was in a state of shock. The possibility of losing the person I loved most in this world was just too much for me, causing me to think out of desperation rather than rationality.

I jumped to my feet and ran into the water before I felt Jane's powerful hands pick me up from the waist and lift me back out, throwing me to the wet grass around the water. I stood and lunged at her. She side stepped me easily, causing me to face plant on the ground in front of her, which allowed her to once again pin me down.

My body suddenly went into a form of violent autopilot, as a powerful fury washed over me, allowing me to gain a strength I never knew I had. I shrieked in anger as I threw my hips up from the ground, throwing her off of me. She landed awkwardly beside me on her back, which was an opportunity I was not going to waste. I immediately jumped on her, wrapping my legs around her sides. I curled my right hand into a fist and tried to punch her but she caught it immediately. Her grip was strong, allowing her the ability to crank my wrist painfully backwards, not breaking it but coming close. I cried out in pain, pulling my hand away. She used the momentary distraction to reach for my face with her nails ready to dig into me. I caught the movements of her hands just in time and craned my face away from her claws. Her hands frantically swiped at my face, attempting to catch any piece of skin that they could. I had planted my hands on her chest to push myself further back from her nails, when I suddenly realized that she was paying my hands no attention. I used the opportunity presented to me by her primal recklessness to move my hands to her throat without any sort of opposition. A surprised squeak came from her mouth before my hands clamped off any further sounds. I squeezed with whatever strength I had left in my arms and felt her clawing hands start to weaken before they slumped at her sides.

I squeezed harder than I thought I could and I looked down into her eyes. They were red, bulging and yet, they were expressionless. Her entire face was expressionless; there was no pain, no fear and no anger. It was the same blank sociopathic stare she wore that was incapable of reactions. She wasn't afraid, she wasn't in pain; she was simply waiting for me to kill her, as if she had always been expecting this. I was so taken aback that I felt my hands loosen, and in my brief moment of weakness, she grabbed my wrists and threw my hands away before she tossed me off of her altogether.

She sat up, brushed her clothes off and walked over to me. I was in shock, I was cold and I was exhausted. My arms were burning with the strain I had just put on them when I was clutching at her throat; they were so burnt out that I had no fight left in me. I knew that she had won. So I chose not to fight her off as she lifted me up from under the arms, forcing me to my feet. She half carried, half dragged me away towards the trees. I wasn't sure what she was going to do to me, but in my exhausted state I had stopped caring. I had come to accept the fact that she was about to kill me.

Only, she didn't. Rather she dragged me along until she found her way back to the original parking spot where Troy's car still sat.

Troy's car would be there still in the morning, waiting for its owner who would never return, and finally after three days of it sitting in the parking lot, someone would report it. They would find his body on the pond's edge later that day. He was dead and so was the part of me that loved him.

No one had passed by the evening that Troy had died, and so no one saw that my mother's car had been parked beside Troy's for the majority of the night. Jane threw me into the back seat of our mother's car that she had obviously taken without asking, before she peeled out of the parking lot, leaving Troy and his car abandoned in the woods.

The roads were pitch black and the reflection of the car's headlights blotted out the once visible starry sky. I propped myself up on my elbow and grunted from the effort. My entire body felt sore and I ached all over, but I fought through it so I could get a clear look at Jane. She kept her eyes focused on the road and didn't acknowledge me as I stirred in the back seat.

I stared at the side of her face, the side I could see, half with rage and half with terror. Her face was as expressionless as it had been when I had been choking her, her eyes as distant and cold as always. I felt unbelievable grief for Troy, but my mind wasn't on him at this particular moment. My mind was focused on the fact that I had the chance to kill my sister, I had the chance to rid the world of a monster who had killed the two people in this world I had loved most.

I had tried to convince myself that the reason I hadn't killed her was from the fact that the look on her face had terrified me enough to make me lose my bearings. But the more I thought about it, the more I knew I was lying to myself. I hadn't killed her, because if I had killed her, then I would have lost my best friend, my boyfriend and my sister. My sister who I still loved.

The fact that I still loved my sister horrified me and made me start weeping uncontrollably in the back seat. Jane kept her eyes on the road and didn't bother turning around to face me; she didn't even bother looking at me in the rear view mirror. She simply stared straight ahead and spoke.

"What's done is done. I forgive you." She rubbed at her neck as she spoke. Her voice was hoarse and a little grainy but it still had that emotionless dead pan tone that sent chills down my spine every time she spoke.

I kicked the back of her seat once, twice, five times. I kept kicking like a child throwing a tantrum, I couldn't put my overwhelming emotions into words so I chose to act out the way a toddler does when they can't get their way. When the world is being unfair to them.

My kicks were weak and didn't carry a lot of force or speed, but they were enough to frustrate Jane, who finally wrapped a hand around one of my ankles. Her hands were so powerful, I didn't know how she had grown so strong, when I was still so weak. We were twins and yet she greatly outmatched me.

"Kick me again and I will make you walk back." I felt her grip tighten and I cried out in pain as I felt her palm squeeze tightly on my Achilles tendon. I stopped moving immediately, and she let me go.

I curled up on the back seat and tried to hide my sobs in the long sleeves of Troy's sweater that I hadn't even realized I was still wearing until right now. I didn't want to give her the satisfaction of hearing me cry any longer and I was trying to block it from her. She took pleasure from my displeasure and I wanted to rob her of that. I wanted to make her as miserable as I was; I wanted to take away the things that brought her joy like she had done me. I gritted my teeth and forced my sobs down. I took deep breaths and forced myself to stop shaking. I never wanted to be weak in front of her anymore, because if I was ever going to stop her, I needed to have her lose her power over me. She noticed my silence and finally looked at me from the rear view mirror.

She cranked hard on the steering wheel and pulled the car over to the side of the road. I was thrown around the back seat with the sudden swerve off the road, and before I could sit back up, Jane had put the car in park and was leaning into the back seat.

"I forgave you, now you're going to forgive me. I can see you plotting whatever it is you're plotting back here. And if you so much as try to tell anyone what we did, then I promise you I will hurt you. Worse than I did today. Do you understand?"

I sat up as best I could till I was nose to nose with her and I tried putting as much hatred into my voice as possible. "Hurt me! I don't even care anymore! Kill me for all I fucking care!"

Spit flew from my mouth and landed on her face. I saw her wince as more and more landed on her and I wanted to smile. Suddenly, she grabbed me by the face and pushed my face away from hers. She turned back towards the steering wheel and pulled back out onto the road.

For a brief moment, I was convinced that I had won the exchange and that I was making her lose her hold on me. That was until she spoke again.

"Maybe you don't care if I hurt you."

She smiled, it was the first time I had ever seen her smile since she killed Taylor.

"But you might care if I hurt Mom. You so much as try me again, and I'll fucking kill her and make you watch."

I felt the colour drain from my face and I felt as if I had been stomped on the chest. I wanted to shout back at her, I wanted to tell her to leave my mother alone or tell her that she would never hurt the woman who took care of us. But I knew that would do no good, because I knew that she would truthfully and honestly kill her if she had the chance. If I stepped out of line, tried to retaliate, tried to escape even, she would kill our mother.

My mother's blood would be on my hands. And I couldn't live with that, I could live with the fear of Jane but I couldn't live with the guilt of being responsible for my mother's death.

So just like that, she had established her power over me even stronger than she had before. She had taken full control of my life and I was powerless to stop her. She had killed my best friend, my boyfriend and would kill my mother if it came to that. She wanted me all to herself.

From that day forward, I was a prisoner

I was the prisoner of a sociopath.

I was the prisoner of a murderer.

I was the prisoner of my sister.

VII

From the pages of The Thamesville Gazette

Teen Drowns at Coleman's Creek
By: Monica Paradinha – Thamesville Gazette
Saturday, December 15, 2007

By the end of this summer, South Western Ontario had a total of 38 drowning-related fatalities. It was one of the lowest drowning rates in recent memory, and almost every single drowning occurred at unguarded beaches.

With the summer season over, everyone was expecting the number of drownings to remain at 38; however, this past week, on a warm December evening, that number rose to 39.

Thamesville Police were called out to Coleman's Creek early Friday morning when a group of late season fisherman had arrived at the Creek. The group of fisherman had intended to make one last attempt at the Northern Pike that were still occupying the water due to the unnaturally warm winter. When they arrived at the Creek, they saw that an unoccupied vehicle was sitting alone and it had a pile of leaves on it that made it appear as though it had been unoccupied for a while.

"There was fast food containers inside that looked kind of recent, so we thought that whoever had abandoned this car couldn't have abandoned it all that long ago."

The fishermen continued towards the Creek and upon arriving, they found the owner of the car in a scene from a horror film.

"He had drifted to the creek's edge and his body was so blue and swollen. It took us a while to realize that it was a person," one of the fishermen stated.

They called Thamesville Police and the Ontario Provincial Police who both arrived immediately. The teen has been identified but his name will not be released as per request of the family.

Early toxicology reports stated that the teen did not have any drugs or alcohol in his system. The cause of death looks to be drowning as he did not have any other wounds or marks anywhere on his body.

"The air might be warmer than it should be for a December, but that water is anything but warm," Officer Brady, the lead investigator, stated to us. "A few seconds in that water and you're looking at your muscles cramping, the air being sucked out of your lungs and it may even disorient you."

There were no witnesses to the event and friends and family did not know what reason he would have gone out there for. Police have not confirmed whether or not this is to be treated as an accident or a suicide. More to follow.

Chapter 23
July 2016 – Jack

"I kept waiting for the police to come and talk to me. But I don't know if Troy ever told his family that he was dating me, so they never came to my door. I wanted to knock on their door and tell them what happened. I wanted to tell them about how Troy was the most loving boyfriend ever and how he took me out there to share an intimate moment with me. I wanted them to know what happened to their son."

Crista exhaled loudly as she wiped at her eyes. "You think after I finally got rid of her that I wouldn't still feel trapped by her. But I do. She still has me in this sort of psychological prison that I can't escape from."

Her jaw hardened as she clenched her teeth together, the sound of her teeth scrapping against one another filled the silence of the room.

"Let's move you out of that prison. Let's work together so you don't have to feel trapped by her anymore," I said in a soothing yet direct tone.

While I instinctively felt the need to protect her, I knew that she didn't need comfort right now. What she needed was for me to challenge her and force her to overcome the barriers that this topic normally threw up for her. I needed to push her in a way that I had been too scared to push her before now.

"You always push everyone too far Jack." I ignored Amy's voice and continued on.

"You've told me so much about her. About the trouble and the pain she's caused you. Tell me about the day you stood up to her. Tell me about the last day you saw her. Tell me about the fire."

"I—" she paused. "I can't yet."

"Crista, we're so close! I know it. The more you let her hold you back from expressing yourself, the more she's going to have control of your life still." I could see her thinking about it; the words were just on the tip of her tongue. I was so close to getting them out of her, so close to helping her leap that last hurdle of her recovery.

"Isn't that a little hypocritical?"

My words caught themselves in my throat and I sat puzzled. She had never challenged me before; even when it was particularly difficult conversation she still never questioned me or my questions. I tried thinking of what to say but I was too stunned.

"How do you mean?"

"The phone call. From the first time we met, you told me it was nothing to worry about but it's apparent in your face every single time I see you that it is something to worry about. You wear it on your face every time I'm upset. I hear it in your voice every time you ask me a difficult question. Whatever it was that happened has kept you guarded, and now you're telling me to let my guard down from my past trauma. To push through so I can finally come to terms with everything. How can you expect me to do that when you won't do the same?"

I didn't know how to respond. I sat stunned and tried evaluating all of our past interactions in my head. Any time I had thought I was keeping my face stoic and unreadable, she was looking right through it. She was able to read me just as well as I was able to read her.

Before I had a chance to respond, she continued on.

"I've told you so much about me. I've told you everything I could about Jane, which is something I've never said to anyone before. Because you told me from day one that you would be as open with me as I was expected to be with you. But you haven't. Instead, it's just been me spilling everything."

I felt a slight bit of hostility in her tone that I had never felt before. I had grown so completely comfortable with her and her candidness that I didn't think she was still capable of throwing up these barriers around her.

"I'm sorry you feel that way, Crista, but that's my role," I said as I reverted to my counselling training. Remain calm during a hostile interaction and remind the client of boundaries. On any other client this may have worked, but on her it was the wrong move.

She scoffed loudly and crossed her arms as she leaned away from me. You didn't need to be an expert in body language to know she had just closed herself off to me.

"Right," she said angrily. "I forgot. This is just a job to you, isn't it? My life's pain is just a job to you so you can get me out of the hospital faster."

"No, not at all. Sorry, I misspoke."

"No, no. It's fine. I just can't believe that you would come in here, pretending to be different. Pretending to be sincere and open and willing to make me think you were trustworthy."

"Crista, I—"

"Don't even think about it, Jack," Amy's voice said.

"It's fine. I think I'd like to go back to my room now. I can't believe I trusted you with everything."

"You pushed her too far, now don't push her further. Don't do what you're thinking of doing and push her any further!"

"Crista, we're so close! I just want you to—"

"I want to go back to my room now!"

"Jack! Don't you dare do it! She's a client! You don't owe her this! Don't blur the lines again!"

"A client attacked me."

The anger she was wearing on her face immediately slipped away and her arms uncrossed as her hand flew to her mouth.

"A client attacked me, because I got attached to her and chose not to see the signs of her illness. She attacked me, nearly killing me and then she killed herself as I watched."

"Jack…no…"

Crista's eyes turned a bright shade of red as they quickly filled up with tears. The hand covering her mouth was shaking and she sniffed loudly as she tried to control her emotions.

"Jack!" she shouted through her near hysterical voice. "I'm so sorry! I didn't know! I didn't think it was—" her voice cut off as she swallowed hard in an attempt to hold back her tears.

"It's okay," I said as convincingly as I could. I knew that this was a Hail Mary, using my story to get her to tell hers was a last ditch effort I hadn't wanted to try. I knew that I wasn't emotionally or mentally stable enough to try this, but she was so close to achieving her own recovery that I had to try.

"What happened? Are you able to tell me?" Crista asked hesitantly, the anger leaving her as suddenly as it came.

"You've said enough. Don't tell her anymore, Jack. You're not ready to revisit this! Plus don't forget that she's a CLIENT! We aren't supposed to disclose this much of ourselves to our client's ever! Jack! Listen to me!"

"Okay. I'll tell you."

"You fucking idiot."

Chapter 24
November 2015 – Jack

Gwen had been one of my biggest success stories as a Social Worker. She was what we in our profession referred to as a 'rotating door client'. Someone who comes in and out of service so frequently and who has had so many different counsellors that you never really put her file away. Everyone has a story of when they counselled her, and anyone who leaves the organization will ask, "Is She back in counselling again?"

Gwen was the type of client that new Social Workers always picture when they say, "I don't want to work in mental health." She was the type of client that even the mental health activists who were always so vocal about the rights of people with mental health would fear. Most often, those vocal activists wanted to appear as though they cared about the clients, without wanting to actually interact with them as they were more often than not afraid of them. Clients like Gwen were the reason they became afraid.

So naturally, everyone at the hospital would immediately try passing her off to someone else the second she walked through our doors. Some counsellors lasted only one session with her while others could go a few days. No one in our field ever admitted it, but we all had those clients that we all believed were 'lost causes'. Our profession wouldn't ever allow us to admit that as we were supposed to be the advocates for the people the rest of society deemed 'lost causes'. But the truth is, a good chunk of those working in the social services felt the exact same way, despite the fact that they would never admit it.

Everyone felt this way about Gwen. Everyone except for me.

When I was excelling in my career, I had begun noticing that Katelyn was pairing me with clients who demonstrated the ability to recover from their crisis. With my success rate of helping clients be released, they wanted to keep my numbers up. Pairing me with someone who wasn't going to respond well to counselling and who would be back in a week seemed pointless to them. Katelyn had later told me she thought it was more effective to simply place them on a counsellor's caseload who already had a number of unsuccessful releases as it wouldn't be as apparent the next time our files were reviewed by the hospital's board.

I took this as a personal challenge, and when Gwen was referred back to our services, I jumped at the chance to be her counsellor.

I had never seen Gwen before; all I had to go on were the millions of horror stories that all of the other staff told me about her. So naturally, I pictured this violent, threatening monster who would be ready to tear my head off the first moment she saw me.

What I saw instead was someone who looked like they were pulled out of a 1990s grunge music video. She had short jet black hair with long uncut bangs that hung down over her eyes, piercings in both of her eyebrows, lips and nose. She wore fingerless black gloves and an oversized bomber jacket over top of a Slipknot T-shirt. Her jeans were ripped and torn, although that looked unintentional, and on her feet were large, clunky, black combat boots.

I sat across from her and instead of smiling or introducing myself, I simply dove into the questions.

"Iowa or Volume 3?"

"What?" she had asked stunned, clearly not expecting my question. Most likely she had been expecting a 'welcome' or 'my name is' introduction, instead of me jumping into a conversation over which Slipknot album she preferred.

"Iowa or Volume 3. Which do you prefer?"

"Ew! Oh my god, neither. Self-titled album, every day of the week!"

"Wow! I thought when you wore their shirt, you were actually a fan, but judging from the fact that their original album is your favourite then I see maybe I was wrong."

"Oh, fuck you, buddy! You think you like them better than me?"

"My ticket stubs from six of their shows suggests that yes, I kind of do."

"Oh wow, six shows? I guess I just kind of like them since I only went to thirteen of their shows. Which was easy for me since I followed them on tour, I didn't just wait for them to show up in my town."

"Well, I had to wait for them to show up in my town because that's where Corey Taylor was doing his book signing."

"You trying to impress me by showing off that you Wikipedia'd him and saw that he wrote some books?"

"Three in fact! I know that because I own all three and had them all autographed. So, you know."

"You're shitting me. You actually met the guy? AND got him to sign all three of his books?"

"I did indeed. I didn't say anything to him though, I was too awkward and star struck, but I can bring in each of the books and show you that yes I did indeed actually meet him."

"Well, fuck."

"Well, fuck is right."

She burst out laughing and brushed her bangs out of her eyes. From that moment forward Gwen and I began our working relationship.

Not every day was as successful as our first ones. I had prepared myself for the worst of her episodes, which believe me there were lots. Twice I had to call for the orderlies to come and take her back to her room because she became violent and hostile. But each time our sessions ended terribly, I would surprise her by being in the counselling office the very next day.

"Still haven't given up on me yet?" she would ask. I would simply smile at her and move on without acknowledging the episode. It got her to like me, which got her to trust me. So when I introduced the very unpopular topic of medication to try and regulate the schizophrenia she was suffering from, she told me she would try.

It was a struggle at first as she would complain about how the medication made her drowsy all day and how she felt too sick to get out of bed most days because of it. Sometimes this would lead to her blaming me for her feeling sick, and she would once again yell at me until the orderlies had to be called in.

Yet, she stuck with the medication. And after a few short months, it was apparent that she had made significant improvements. She was becoming much better adjusted during our meetings and the unpredictable nature of her outbursts ceased. Her mood improved as did her mental health. She would tell me that this was the best she had felt in years, and she gained a realistic perspective on her recovery.

In the past she would tell staff she wanted to be released as soon as possible and that she hated it at the hospital. Now, however, she was acknowledging that she required the additional support to recover and that she would take her time for her recovery. It was unbelievable progress and I couldn't believe what we had achieved in just a few short months.

Finally, she graduated to our residential care program.

It was the stage of our program people got to when they were nearly recovered.

It was the stage of our program that she had never believed she would reach.

It was the stage of our program that had finally sent her over the edge, and killed her.

***

She was recovering so well, and the people living on her floor all seemed to love her. They told me that she organized community meals with them all, she helped plan social nights and that she frequently supported everyone when the staff weren't available. She had come to be adored by everyone living there and at first I thought it was going to be a good environment for her.

She had spent her entire life being hated and pushed away by everyone. And now, she was loved and welcomed by staff and her peers alike. She was surrounded by a positivity that had eluded her throughout her entire life, and while I thought it was going to be a positive experience, it ended up becoming overwhelming.

She began silently experiencing nervous breakdowns as she felt overwhelmed by her new circumstances. When she supported the other residents with their breakdowns, she would take a lot of it onto herself. It would cause her unbelievable stress and she became exhausted physically and mentally.

I didn't know it at the time, but she was feeling so exhausted that she began forgetting to take her medication. She still took them when she remembered, but without the consistency of the scheduled doses, the medication became less effective. She unconsciously began deteriorating mentally and her schizophrenia began announcing itself at inopportune times. She didn't know this of course, and mistook her schizophrenia with something else.

She began to believe that her apartment was haunted, and that these spirits were sinister. No amount of reassurance changed her mind, and in the end, these feelings of being haunted are what drove her over the edge.

For weeks she had been telling me about her experiences with the haunting of her apartment. And I should have realized what she was going through at the time; she had shown signs that her schizophrenia was re-appearing. However, I overlooked it because I was so proud of where we had come. I didn't want to acknowledge

170

that she was slipping backwards. So I pressed her in her recovery, hoping that maybe some forward movement would help her move past her brief relapse.

When she began talking to me about the ghosts she was seeing, I thought I would humour her. I had always loved the occult and all things paranormal but I didn't particularly believe that they actually existed. So when she asked me if I believed in them, I had a gut feeling that I should say no, I shouldn't be humouring her hallucinations. But I didn't. Instead, I acknowledged her feelings and made her feel validated. I did so because I wanted to push her even though I could see she wasn't ready to be pushed.

I had come so close to helping her recover that I didn't want to slip backwards. I didn't want to fall into the same category as all of her previous counsellors. So I turned a blind eye and pretended like everything was alright.

Then the day of our final session arrived. It was the session that was supposed to determine whether she was fit to be released or not. If I recommended she be released, then she would be released; if I recommended she should stay, then she would stay.

It was clear to me from the moment I arrived that she was going to receive a 'not ready for release' decision on her review form.

I was ready for her to be disappointed by the decision. But I had no idea what actually awaited me.

Chapter 25
November 2015 – Jack

"I saw him again."

"It's a him now?" I asked. Gwen nodded and leaned forward as she began rocking back and forth.

"He talks to me while I sleep. I can't always tell what he's saying but sometimes I can. He whispers to me and I can't get him to stop. I—"

She stopped speaking and began shaking uncontrollably.

"He tells me things. Bad things. He…" She sobbed violently as she tries to continue "he tells me to hurt people. And I don't want to! I don't like hurting people! I know I did when I went off my meds, and I know everyone is scared of me and thinks I'm going to do it again but I won't. I don't want to!" Gwen's voice was rising uncontrollably and she was nearly yelling at this point.

"Who is it telling you to hurt?" I asked.

"People I know." She paused and looked down at the ground. "You."

"Do you want to hurt me?"

"No!" Gwen cried out. She inhaled deeply on her cigarette again and let the long finger of the ash hang off precariously.

"Gwen. I have to ask, and I need you to be honest with me. Do you have a plan to hurt any of these people? The people the voice is telling you to hurt?"

Gwen gripped both sides of her head and folded over onto herself. Her fingers began scratching at her head furiously and she began moaning.

"No! I just told you no! I don't want to hurt anyone! But I can't get him to stop! All I want is for him to stop! My meds won't even help because it's not a voice like the other ones. This one is real, and I know it's a ghost, but no one believes me!"

"Gwen, I believe you. But I need you to tell me what you need from me? What can we do to keep you safe from harming yourself or anyone around you?" I asked.

Gwen's face was red and she was breathing heavily. She was getting noticeably worked up.

"Gwen?" I asked again.

"Let me leave here."

"We're working on that. But we have to make sure you're ready to live on your own, risk free, before we let that happen. Now you're making good progress, Gwen, but we still have work to do."

Gwen buried her face in her hands and said something inaudibly through muffled hands. I asked her to please repeat it. Gwen slowly took her hands away from her face.

"I said——" Gwen looked up and made eye contact with the figure, "I said then kill me."

My heart sank and I realized I had been defeated. I had pushed her when I should have been supporting her, and in that mistake, I let her slip so far backwards that she was now at risk for harming herself.

"Gwen. I'd like to place a call to have some staff from the hospital come over. Would you feel better spending the night out of this apartment? Away from the voice?"

She nodded as she blew out another mouthful of smoke. I smiled at her and reached for my phone. My fingers were hovering over the call button when my phone sprang into life.

Amy was calling me and the ringtone she had programmed into my phone for when she called came blaring out of the small speaker.

'Hey, Jude, don't make it bad. Take a sad song and make it better.'

"Shit! Sorry, give me a second," I called up to Gwen while I fumbled with my phone to ignore the call.

'Remember to let her into your heart, then you can start to make it better.'

"Ah! Ignore call! Sorry, Gwen I—" the words froze in my throat as I saw her smash the glass that had been sitting in front of her. Her hands found the largest, sharpest shard and she pointed it towards her throat. I dropped the phone as I ran towards her.

'You were made to go out and get her.'

I grabbed her hand and tried wrestling the glass away from her, but her determination had given her a strength I hadn't been expecting. I was pulling her hands away from her, and trying to wrap

173

my hands around the edge of the shard. She was screaming in frustration until finally she stopped pulling the glass towards herself.

When she had stopped struggling against me, I thought I had won and I breathed a sigh of relief until I was punched in the abdomen. The impact from the punch lingered and I soon found it difficult to breathe. Gwen was standing nose to nose with me, breathing heavily into my face.

"I'm sorry," she said in the same shaky tone she had spoken in only moments before.

Tears began falling down her cheeks as she backed away from me.

'The minute you let her under your skin, then you begin to make it better.'

I looked down at the growing pain in my abdomen and found that the front of my shirt was stained red. I remember being upset because this was my favourite shirt that Amy had given me for my birthday.

I tried moving towards Gwen again but my legs gave out and I collapsed heavily on the ground. Gwen moved towards me, with the glass pointed down towards me. *This is it*, I thought, *this is the moment I die.*

'For well you know that it's a fool who plays it cool, by making his world a little colder.'

The glass in her hand turned away from me and I let out a sigh of relief. That was until she pointed the shard towards the side of her neck, and drove it in without any effort. Blood poured from her neck and she collapsed beside me.

'Nah nah nah nah nah nah! Nah nah nah nah! Hey, Jude!'

The world was turning black as she lay beside me. I reached for her fingertips which only seemed to sit inches away from me. But I couldn't reach her, and soon the world fell into a darkness.

'Nah nah nah nah nah nah! Nah nah nah nah! Hey, Jude!'

My eyes closed, and that was the last time I ever saw Gwen.

Chapter 26
July 2016 – Jack

"When they investigated her death, they found out that she had been experiencing these hallucinations, and that I had known about them. That was when they suspended my license and took away all of my clients. And that pretty much brings us up to today. So that's it. That's my story."

I had been completely unaware of the tears that were rolling down my cheeks until I was done talking. My hands were balled into tight fists and when I opened my hands, I felt them pop and crack loudly. My stomach felt as if it were on the verge of releasing everything it held, and my chest was heavily constricted.

My mind returned to the image of Gwen turning the shard towards herself and I felt my face begin to flush while my heart rate increased dramatically. I felt the inevitable coming on, when suddenly Crista's voice sliced through the oncoming anxiety attack.

"Is that what drove Amy away?" Crista asked.

"I'm sorry?" I asked, taken aback by her question. It was not the first thing I was expecting her to ask me about when I had finally finished my story.

"Earlier, you had said that Amy had stopped speaking to you recently, that you had driven her away. Was it everything with Gwen that had caused you to drive her away?"

"Yes. I didn't handle it as well as I should have and it got to be too much for her. So she left." I stopped myself there, without giving her any of the intimate details about my drinking and failed suicide attempt. I had just told her incredibly personal and intimate details about one part of my life, I didn't feel the need to disclose any more.

"Oh," she said in a tone that slightly rang with empathy, but partially rang with pity. I didn't offer her any further details which I knew she wanted. I was too busy still being in awe at how calm I had been after finally discussing Gwen with someone who wasn't my psychiatrist or Amy.

Telling the story had caused me a great deal of anxious feelings, but Crista's reaction to the story helped me move past my anxiety attack that I was positive I was about to experience. I couldn't believe how easily she had helped me out. She had helped me easier than anyone ever had before and she had done so unintentionally. I wanted to thank her profusely but I thought against it.

"Well, I tell you what, Crista with a C, why don't we end off there today? You don't have to talk about the fire today. We both put a lot of ourselves out there today, and I don't know about you but I'm feeling exhausted."

She smiled at me. "I am too. Thank you for sharing that with me, Jack with a K. I didn't mean to explode on you the way that I did. And had I known what had happened I never would have pried."

I waved her apology away. "It's perfectly alright. Now let's call Nurse Ratchet to come get you before she bites my head off again."

I placed the proper call this time and saw that the nurse who had arrived to take Crista away was Melissa. She was blushing and wouldn't make eye contact with me—it was clear she was still embarrassed after having been caught staring at me.

I felt guilty at having laughed at her earlier in the day when Crista and I had caught her peering in at us, so I thought I'd be extremely nice to her.

"I am so happy it's you picking her up and not my other favourite nurse!" I was helping Crista to her feet and helping bring her over to Melissa, so the snicker that had come out of her was only audible for me. "I'm thinking of becoming a nurse myself, you know? Just so I can spend time with her."

Melissa laughed and I was surprised at how pleasant and genuine her laugh sounded. The sound of it had made me want to try to get her to laugh again; however, the elbow that was subtly digging into my ribs wouldn't let me come up with any more clever dialogue.

"I'm glad I was able to make your day! I'll have to make sure to send her by next time, seeing as how she's your OTHER favourite nurse."

Melissa took Crista by the arm and smiled over her shoulder at me as she walked her away. I saw Crista's body give a small shake as she stifled a laugh and I waved bye.

When both of them were out of the room, I collapsed back into my chair. It was an exhausting session, but I felt that we had grown significantly closer. And I was just one session away from learning about the day that had sent her here.

After I spent a few minutes collecting myself, I returned to my office where I typed out the lengthy case notes that summarized everything she had told me about her old boyfriend Troy.

I was obviously going to exclude the fact that I had disclosed my own personal history to her. Especially since that was still an ongoing investigation that I wasn't supposed to discuss with anyone.

I had also left out how Crista had helped me move past my anxiety attack. I was continuously growing more fond of her as our sessions wore on, and it was clear to me after our session today that she was so close to being able to move on from the torment her sister put her through. She was still incredibly emotional any time we spoke of Jane, but she was becoming more confident and articulate in her story telling. She no longer stuttered and spoke through a shaky voice as she recounted these incidents. I was proud of her progress but needed to be careful as I had almost lost her today. I couldn't risk what happened with Gwen to happen with Crista, and have something send her spiralling downwards. But I wanted to do more than simply help her come to terms with her past trauma. I wanted to make sure she would never be bothered by it again.

So I picked up my phone and dialled the police.

"Ontario Provincial Police – Thamesville Headquarters," the voice on the phone answered.

"Hi, I'm calling from Middlesex County Hospital, my name is Jack Fletcher. I am calling for Detective Sullivan."

"One moment."

The phone rang a five or six times and I was getting ready to hang up when finally an out of breath voice came through on the other line.

"Detective Sullivan's desk."

"Hi, Detective. It's Jack Fletcher from Middlesex County Hospital. We spoke before about my client Crista Sunderland and the search for her sister."

"Oh yes," he said. "What can I do for you, Mr. Fletcher?"

"Well, I don't know how much you're allowed to tell me and I'm guessing it's nothing but I figured I'd try anyways. Crista's sister Jane—"

"Ah yes, the missing sister."

"So she's still missing?"

"I'm afraid so. We've conducted an incredibly thorough search but we still haven't been able to come up with anything."

"Damn it," I whispered away from the speaker. It was quiet, but not quiet enough as the detective had heard me.

177

"Is there a problem, Mr. Fletcher?"

"Well, I'm concerned but I don't know what I can and can't tell you as there isn't technically an immediate threat."

"As far as I'm concerned, I've already told you some information that's off the record. So anything you need me to keep off record then I'm happy to do so. As long as it isn't essential to the investigation."

"Right of course. Well, it's just that Crista has opened up a lot to me and I couldn't really believe that she could commit arson, let alone do it with the intention of killing someone. That was until I spoke with her about her circumstances. Detective, I believe that her sister Jane may have been incredibly abusive towards her, and that she may have committed acts of violence towards others as well. I'm concerned that Jane could be incredibly dangerous and that the longer she isn't found, the more likely she is to find my client and harm her. I don't know what this does for your investigation, maybe it doesn't change anything. But I just thought it was important for me to disclose to him what Crista has said about her sister."

There was silence on the other end of the phone and I was worried that somehow one of our phones had cut out.

"Detective?"

"Still here. I'm just trying to process this. You think she started the fire to kill her sister because her sister was a violent offender? Violent how?"

"Well," I said hesitantly. I hadn't wanted to break Crista's trust but at the same time I couldn't keep her here and protect her from Jane forever. "Well, from what Crista has told me, she was physically abusive to her throughout her entire life up until the present. And also, there's a chance that she may have committed some murders."

"Murder? Do you have anything to substantiate this?" There was a clear skepticism to the Detective's voice.

"I have names of some of the supposed victims."

"And these names, have you searched for any of them? Have you confirmed that they were indeed real?"

"No, unfortunately not yet. I didn't think to. What I can do is send you over their names, if that's alright?"

Detective Sullivan sighed heavily on the other end of the phone and I knew that he wasn't interested in doing the extra work. It was a weak lead at best and all of it was given to me from a patient currently residing in the mental health ward of a hospital. I realize I should have looked into this myself before asking to maybe give myself just a bit more credibility, but it was too late for that. I just had to hope he would actually conduct the search.

"Sure," he finally answered with a very clear impatience in his voice.

"Okay, the names are Taylor Mckinnon and Troy Williams."

"And you believe these were unsolved homicides?"

"No! That's just it. I believe that these were ruled as accidental drownings. Neither will appear in any murder investigation I don't think."

"You don't think?"

"Look, I know it's flimsy and I'm sorry. But everything she's told me has been consistent without any sort of gaps or holes in memory. It's all been too coherent for me to believe it was all a hallucination. I'm sorry if there's nothing, but I think that this may be important to your investigation."

Another loud heavy sigh. "Alright Mr. Fletcher. I'll take a look into it."

"Thank you, Detective. I'll call if—" click. The phone hung up and I was left looking—and feeling—like a hysterical pedestrian on a street corner yelling nonsense. When we had first spoke, I had told him I would disclose any information pertinent to his investigation and we had left on good terms. But I worried that now he was feeling as though he had made a mistake and was regretting the open line of communication we had established.

On the drive home I wanted nothing more than to call Detective Sullivan again and recount the entire story that Crista had told me up to this point. But I didn't see what good that would do other than distract him from doing the work he was actually supposed to be doing. Which was finding Jane.

Crista was so close to her recovery that I didn't want a newfound fear of her still living sister to set her back. Especially since I knew that tomorrow we would finally be discussing the fire that she had refused to discuss for so long.

It was a day that I knew would either make or break Crista. And I knew that I couldn't risk breaking another client.

Chapter 27
July 2016 – Jack

We had both been silent when we walked into the counselling room that morning. There was an unspoken tension in the room as we both prepared ourselves for the conversation we knew was coming.

Finally, I spoke first and broke the silence.

"Okay, Crista. Whenever you're ready."

She inhaled deeply and let out long slow breath through pursed lips.

"I'm ready."

"Okay. Tell me about the day of the fire."

"Okay."

Chapter 28
May 2016 – Crista

I was trapped in a perennial prison, and Jane was my guard. For years I had been protected and kept safe from my mother who had been willfully blind to the crimes her daughter continued to commit. I had always thought that I had been the one protecting my mother of the knowledge that her daughter was a murderer, but it turns out she had been the one protecting me.

My mother's death was devastating to me as Jane had kept me so entirely isolated from anyone I tried to care about. As a result, my mother became the only companion that Jane would allow me, and so naturally I grew unbelievably close to her.

The day my mother's cancer-ridden body finally gave out on her, I had been sitting at her bedside, clutching her near lifeless hand. It was a hand that had scooped me up effortlessly when Jane murdered the dog and I had been inconsolable. It was a hand that caressed my face when I bawled nightly over Troy's death, that was ruled an accident. It was a strong hand that was capable of taking care of me in every which way. And now, it was a hand that was too weak to grip my hand back, and if I did squeeze it there was a chance that I could bruise or even break it.

It was a hand that sat lightly in mine, as the last flicker of life left her.

On the day of her death, Jane wouldn't come to the house. She had simply ignored our requests to come spend our mother's last hours with her. I had tried encouraging her to hold on for just a little bit longer in case Jane did come by, but after a few hours painfully crawled by it became apparent that she wasn't coming.

I chose to spend the last hour of my mother's life no longer waiting for my sister but rather enjoying the company of the woman I loved more than anything in the world. We sat in silence, as I gently stroked her hand. Her breathing was slowing down and her blinking was becoming laboured. I knew it was only a matter of time, so I began to apologize about Jane's absence when my mother spoke and caught me unaware.

"Mom, look I'm sorry about Jane. I told her to come, I really did! I can't believe that she isn't here for—"

"Stop."

It was the first time she had spoken in a week as she had been too exhausted to carry on any sort of conversation. It pained her to talk and she was barely audible, but her voice was clear in the silence of the room nonetheless.

"Your sister isn't coming."

"No, we don't know that, Mom."

"Yes I do." She began coughing violently, the phlegm was thick in her chest and it made the cough uncomfortable to listen to. I grabbed the hand towel she had on her night table and dabbed at the spittle that flew onto her chin, but she brushed me away. It was a feeble attempt, but I knew what she was doing so I complied and left her face alone.

"Crista. Promise me."

"Of course, Mom, anything."

"Get rid of her. You need to make your sister go away."

My heart leapt into my throat and I felt my limbs fall numb. I nearly fell out of my chair as I struggled to grip what she was saying. I replayed her words over again in my head.

"Mom, what are you talking about?"

"Your sister needs to die. You need to finally kill her and forget about her. Your sister, I mean your real sister, died that day in the park and—"

"You know about the park?" I yelled at my mother as I stood up from my chair. My mother closed her eyes and winced. I realized that my shouting must have been like a hammer being driven through her skull so I apologized and sat back down.

"Of course I knew. A mother always knows."

"Why didn't you say anything? Why didn't you do anything? Mom, all those people that were hurt."

"I had to protect my child. So I did, for years. Murder after murder, but that was a mistake. Crista, please. She's dangerous, get rid of her. Get rid of her for good!"

"Mom, I—" my mother's coughing fit returned, only this one was longer and her body began curling up into a ball the more she coughed. I backed away from her bed and stumbled over the foot stool she kept on the side of the bed which she had used to give her the boost she needed to get into bed in her final month.

My mother's sudden revelation had left me feeling sick to my stomach, so I left the room and ran to the bathroom down the hall when I crashed into a familiar face.

"Sorry, I—"

"I don't care," Jane said as she pushed me aside.

My mother's coughs were still audible from the next room, and I wanted to run back and take care of her since I had just essentially abandoned her. I turned to walk into the room when Jane's arm came out and blocked my path.

"You had your moment with her. Let me have mine." I tried pushing Jane's arm aside but she turned and gripped me by the throat, pressing me against the wall.

I whimpered in pain as her hands cut off the oxygen and blood flow to my brain. She moved her face close to mine and examined it. She must have seen the submission in my face, so she let go off me and pushed me back down the hall. I stumbled backwards and tripped over my own feet as I landed clumsily on my back. I tried to sit up when the door to my mother's room slammed shut.

I cursed myself for being so weak and letting her get away with yet another assault. But the thought of challenging her again terrified me, since I knew that if I pushed my luck, she wouldn't stop. She would finish the job, much like she could have done so many times before.

I could still hear the sickening wet coughs coming from my mother on the other side of the door, before they fell silent. It was sudden, too sudden for that level of coughing to simply stop. I pressed my ear to the door and heard nothing at all, and in that moment I knew that my mother had passed away.

I didn't get to see my mother in the exact moment she had passed away—part of me was grateful but most of me was furious. Jane had ruined my final interaction with my mother, but she had also spared me having to actually witness her die.

***

It only took a day for my mixed emotions to turn to grief. And I began missing my mother so much that it had turned painful. For the first few weeks, Jane had left me alone; she hadn't come into my room nor did she bother abusing me. I was given an unsettling amount of time to grieve and be Jane-free.

Weeks after mourning and repeating my mother's words in my head, I was ready to confront Jane. I was ready to tell her about how our mother knew everything, and that I was going to put a stop to it. I thought I had the courage, and a newfound resolve that would let me get rid of any sort of power she held over me. That was until the day my door flew open and Jane whipped a bundle of wet clothes on my bed.

"Wash those."

"What?"

"Now." She turned to leave and I jumped up from my bed. I sprinted towards her and stopped myself when I was an inch away, and the scratches on her arms came into view.

"Jane. What are those?" I turned back towards the clothes soaking into my bed. "Jane! What did you do?"

"Now that Mom's gone, I need you to do this for me instead. Now. Go. Wash. Those. Clothes." With the final word she grabbed my face and pushed me back towards my room.

"I had to protect my child. So I did, for years."

I nearly threw up as I thought of my mother's words. The full gravity of them hit me, and I realized that she knew more than I did. These murders hadn't just happened once or twice, they had happened countless times and they were still happening!

Jane stood in the hallway, staring at me with her hollow eyes as she waited for me to pick up her clothes so I could go wash them. I was too shaken to protest any further or fight back, so I did as I was commanded and grabbed her clothes.

I stepped into our laundry room that our mother had kept meticulously organized for years. It had a variety of cleaning agents, laundry detergents and neatly-stacked baskets. I threw Jane's blood and water-logged clothes into the washer and reached for a bottle of detergent when my eyes fell on a large can of paint thinner my mother kept on the shelf. My mother always took care of everything around the house herself as she always told us that no contractor could do anything she couldn't. She re-shingled our roof, she fixed faulty wiring, and she painted the entire thing inside and out. This must have been from one of those projects.

The can of paint thinner caught my eye for the small flammable symbol it held on the front of the label.

'Extremely flammable', it read.

I began sifting through the various bottles on the shelf, to see if any more cans were lying around, which there were several. I picked up each can to test how full they were. It turned out that all of them were nearly full. There may not have been enough flammable liquid in them to cause a huge fire. However, there was enough flammable liquid in there to burn down a house.

Our house.

"You need to make your sister go away."

The door banged open and I turned back towards the detergent.

"Run another cycle on the washer after you take this load out. But add bleach. It'll kill anything that sticks around," Jane snapped at me. I nodded in agreement and she scoffed in disgust at my submissiveness.

I wouldn't be submissive for long. She would find that out shortly. Very shortly.

***

That evening I waited until she was silent in her room. Whether she was asleep or awake, I didn't know, but I crept downstairs and began loading an empty laundry basket with the cans of paint thinner. I packed the sides of the basket with towels in case any of them slid around and banged into one another.

Once my basket of kindling was ready, I took it back upstairs and kneeled outside of her room, the lights were off and there were no sounds coming from inside. I opened the first can and poured it over a thick shower towel. The towel absorbed every drop and the smell burned my nostrils, but I pressed on. I repeated the same process with the remaining cans of paint thinner and towels until I was left with an armful of extremely potent but flammable cloth. I began cramming the towels in the crevices of her door, and wrapped a small chemical-soaked hand towel around the door knob to her room.

I grabbed a book of matches from my pocket, striking one and using it to light the rest. The flame grew higher than I expected and nearly burned off my eyebrows. I held the flames away from my face and in my momentary distraction the door swung open.

Jane looked down at the bundle of towels on the ground and at the few that were still wedged in the door frame. She sniffed loudly and made a repulsed face before she saw the flame in my hand.

"So this is how you do it?"

"No. I—" I stammered. I took one step back and she stepped onto a towel, making a loud squish underfoot.

"You what? You wanted to kill me? You wanted to burn me to the fucking ground! Well then do it! Come on! For once don't be so fucking weak!"

"I—" I took another step back and Jane took a step off of the towel, moving closer towards me.

"Jesus Christ! You're so fucking weak, it's pathetic! I let you live, thinking maybe you would change, but no! You're as weak as our mother was!"

"You shut your mouth!" I growled. My feet were no longer moving backwards. "You don't ever mention her."

"Oh! Is that it? Is that the sweet spot? Well, come on then! Our mother was always weak, our mother was so weak that she never tried to find our dad, did you know that! She let him fuck her and then was too much of a coward to ever seek him out and tell him that he knocked her up! I couldn't believe it when I found out! So it's not surprising that you're just as pathetic. Like mother, like daughter, I suppose."

"That's not true. You shut your mouth!"

"You're defending her? She knew what I did and she did nothing! She washed my clothes, she gave me alibis, she did everything I asked her to! She was every bit as guilty as I was. And do you know what I did to finally repay her?"

"Shut up!"

"It was sad really, she didn't even fight back. She just laid down and let me repay her by holding that pillow over her face when she wouldn't stop coughing. She just let me hold her down like the weak little whore that she was!"

I lunged at her, driving my forehead into her chest and driving her backwards. She laughed as she fell back and I looked down to see that the matches in my hand had fallen and burned out. I turned my attention back to Jane, ignoring my plan to burn her down; instead, I jumped on her chest. I pinned her arms under my knees and I began wailing mercilessly on her face. She laughed harder with each blow, until finally one of the punches snapped her head back, causing the back of her head to slam on the ground. The sickening thud her head made left her semi-conscious and unable to laugh any further.

I stood and stormed over to our mother's room.

Our mother had always been fond of candles, and in her last few months she had insisted at always having some in her room. I opened the door, and sitting on the side table beside her bed sat a worn down barbeque lighter. I picked it up and tested how strong the flame was. It wasn't large by any means but it would do the trick.

I walked back to where I had left Jane and saw that she hadn't moved. I bent down and turned the flame onto the first chemical-soaked towel. It lit up immediately and after a few seconds, the rest of the towels became engulfed in flames. I walked away from the flames and saw Jane's motionless body lying on the ground, the flames creeping slowly towards her feet. I thought she was completely unconscious, that was until she spoke just loud enough for me to hear over the crackling of the flames.

"I'll find you, Crista. I'll kill you."

The words had come out in a raspy voice as she lay motionless on her back. She laughed afterwards before she began coughing violently, either from the smoke or the blood that had seeped back into her throat from her blood filled mouth.

"No, you won't," I whispered as I left the house. The hallway was filling quickly with a thick black smoke, and the flames were now spreading down the hall. I ran down the stairs and out the front doors where I would sit and watch them envelope the rest of the house.

I needed to see it burn. I needed to make sure she burned. I needed to make sure I fulfilled my promise to my mother.

I needed to make sure I killed my sister.

Chapter 29
July 2016 – Jack

"But I'm free from her now," Crista said as she choked back tears. "I'm free from her. Finally." She sniffed loudly and cleared her throat loudly. Her eyes were focused on the table between us; the look in her eyes told me that she wasn't in this room. She was back in the house where her mother had died, and where she thought her sister had as well.

I pushed the tissues toward her but she shook her head and pushed them aside. She wiped her face and then ran her fingers through her hair, pushing it out of her face. She looked up at me and for a brief moment it looked as though she was prepared to lunge towards me——the look was almost feral as if she was burning with anger and wanted to release it on the first available target.

"Crista," I said, trying to subdue the anger that was emanating from her. "That could not have been easy to talk about. Thank you for trusting me with that." My voice was shaky and unconvincing.

Her story had not only left me feeling unsettled, but also incredibly anxious. Crista was very clearly struggling with PTSD from her years of witnessing horrific event after horrific event, but the only thing helping her in her recovery was the belief that Jane was dead. I couldn't bring myself to talk about what would happen if Jane were still alive as I truthfully believed Crista was in the process of recovering. I knew I was going to have to investigate the fire and Jane's disappearance further. If I were to feel comfortable releasing Crista back into independent living, I would have to make sure I wasn't signing her death warrant.

Crista's eyes remained locked on me, and her anger held for a few moments longer before finally breaking. She smiled the same smile I had grown quite fondly of, and she looked back down at her bandaged hands.

"Thank you for listening."

"Crista, I—"

"Can we go back to my room please? I'm feeling dizzy all of a sudden."

She was swaying slightly and I immediately rushed over and grabbed her just above the elbow. Holding her steady while making sure I didn't grip her too hard, her arms had lean muscles but they were skinny. I helped her to her feet and we began the walk back to her room.

As I held her up, carrying her weight in my hands, I suddenly felt a rush of protective emotions. Maybe it was the fact that she was my only client that I felt overly attached to her, or maybe it was the fact that she chose not to confide in any other counsellor except for me. Regardless of the reason, I felt the need to protect her and to make sure she lived the rest of her life no longer in fear.

We passed the nurses' station and were only a few feet from her door when she suddenly dropped. Her body became limp and she collapsed dramatically and I nearly allowed her to hit the floor before I caught her in my arms. Her legs were caught behind her, creating an awkward arch in her spine that looked incredibly uncomfortable. I held her tightly in my arms, afraid to let her go down to the ground. I began screaming loudly for help, and it took me a moment to realize that someone was screaming at me to lay her down. I swivelled her around so her legs sat in front of her and I laid her down gently. The nurses came running over and placed a pillow under her head as she convulsed violently and frothy saliva came pouring out of the corners of her mouth.

Voices were shouting at each other so loudly and so rapidly that I struggled to understand a single one of them. I looked from face to face to see who was talking to me, and who was talking to each other, in the chaos I only saw one face looking at me.

It was the older nurse who had grown to dislike me. In the confusion and the yelling I saw that she had remained calm and had taken over primary care while the attending doctor rushed into the room. The nurse had never spoken a word to me; rather she had simply glared at me in an accusatory stare. It was the same look the paramedics have given me when they entered Gwen's apartment on the night when—

"When what? When you let her die?" Amy's voice rang in my head.

I felt my heart rate start to increase rapidly. My chest clenched as a phantom hand wrapped itself around my heart and squeezed it with an iron grip. The noises of the staff shouting over each other and the beeping of the machines began to drown out until the world was silent. I suddenly realized that it was becoming harder to breathe and my wind pipe had constricted to the size of a dime. I clawed at the front buttons of my shirt, ripping the top two off in the process.

Tears filled my eyes as I struggled for air and to keep the pain in my chest down.

I began looking around me frantically for a garbage can, a recycling bin, a bucket or just anything that I could be sick in. A large stainless steel garbage container sat beside the nurse's station and I stumbled over to it, tripping over my own feet and knocking it over in the process. The crash of the metal trash can alarmed everyone in the room along with all the staff who were stationed outside by the nurses' station. I tried sitting up but before I could. I violently threw up on the floor.

The sound of my vomit splashing against the floor reignited the sick feeling in my stomach and caused me to throw up once again. I heard voices all around me, and within seconds a sea of hands engulfed me. The hands, which were blindly clawing at me and pulling at me, were constricting me. They were occupying the same space which was giving me the very small amount of oxygen that I needed to survive. I swatted at them and tried escaping but that only seemed to make them grip me harder. I was getting more and more agitated and my voice was getting higher and higher. With both hands I pushed as hard as I could to whatever was in front of me.

Sound returned to my ears and I heard a crash as the orderly who had approached me fell flat on his back. My senses were returning to me, and I saw a crowd of panicked faces. Patients and staff alike, all staring at me in horror. Among the faces was Katelyn; she was pushing through the crowd to reach me and when she did, she grabbed me by the arm and began leading me away, apologizing to everyone as she lead me.

I was a boy being led by his mother, and I was completely ashamed about it. I turned back around to look into Crista's room and saw the staff with looks of relief on their face. I felt relief as I could see that her convulsing had stopped and everyone looked calm. My relief had made my panic subside, which unfortunately made me painfully aware of my current situation. I looked at the chaos of the scene and cursed.

"Fuck," I said, putting an extra emphasis on the K. Katelyn tugged at me a little bit harder and glared at me as we were still surrounded by patients and staff.

She brought me back to my office and sat me down.

"Water," I said through a hoarse voice. She nodded and rushed back to her office. In the brief moment she was gone, I fumbled through my drawer and found my cell phone. Without thinking my fingers moved over the same numbers I had memorized ages ago. I didn't even need to look at my phone to find the numbers anymore.

Hi, you've reached the voicemail of Amy Ryan. I'm not available at the moment—I hung up and dialled the number again.

"Come on. Pick up. Please Amy I—"

Hi, you've reached the voicemail of—"Goddamn it!" I threw my phone aside.

Katelyn came rushing back in with an opened water bottle; she had removed the lid for me and was pushing the bottle into my hands. The mother-and-child relationship we had created moments earlier was now being further established. She handed me the water and stood over top of me, insisting I drink. When I took a small sip, she tipped the water bottle back up and wouldn't remove her hand until I had guzzled half of the bottle. I pushed her hand away, spilling water on my already ruined shirt. I looked down at the spilled water and saw that I had also managed to cover it in my own vomit. I removed it and tossed it in the garbage bin beside my desk, leaving me in just my sweat soaked undershirt. I felt a pang of nausea return and bent over with my head between my knees.

"Well, shit."

Chapter 30
July 2016 – Jack

I could hear the scrapping of the spare chair I kept in my office as Katelyn dragged it across my office floor. The sound drove an ice pick through my brain and I winced as the sound came closer.

"Hey." Her voice was soft but commanding. She wanted me to look up at her, but my head stayed between my legs. "Hey!" she shouted this time and snapped her fingers beside my ear.

I sighed heavily and sat up. The look on her face was one I hadn't seen before today. It was a look of pity; she didn't empathize or sympathize with my situation, rather she felt sorry for me. It made me think of every horrible dream I'd had where I had experienced a great embarrassment of some kind that left me praying it was all a dream. Normally my prayers were answered when I would wake up and realize that none of that actually happened. Only this was real, and as much as I wanted to wake up from it, I wouldn't be able to. I was stuck in this dream, and stuck with the consequences of having just experienced the worst panic attack I had ever faced, in front of everyone I worked with.

"Look," I said, getting ready for my long winded excuse. "I'm sorry, I haven't been feeling we—"

"How long have you been having the panic attacks?" Katelyn asked, cutting me off midsentence.

"I didn't have—"

"How long?" she reiterated. Her voice was stern and slightly harsh but at the same time it made you want to be honest with her. As if she would be able to read through whatever lie you told her. I was now starting to see how she had managed to move up in this field; she had strong confident counselling techniques that could get anyone to open up.

I sighed in defeat. I cleared my throat, my mouth felt incredibly dry despite the half water bottle I just drank. I reached for the bottle and downed whatever was left before I spoke.

"They started about a month after—" my voice trailed off. "After Gwen"

"How frequently are you getting them?"

I shrugged. "Not often. Just every so often." I reached for my pill bottle that I kept in my bag and brought it out for her to see. She picked up the bottle and studied the label along with the contents. I felt a sudden pang of insecurity and uneasiness and wanted to grab the pill bottle back from her. As if the bottle was my secret, I didn't want her reading it or prying through the contents. I didn't want her to see how the pill count was lower than it should be for when it was prescribed or that I only have one more refill left before I'd be cut off. My only option to renew my prescription would be to go to the useless counsellor they had set me up with months ago.

She saw my hand twitching uncontrollably as I tried to hold myself from reaching for the bottle and she handed it back to me without a word. Her face stayed hard and her eyes locked with mine.

"Your doctor prescribed this?"

"Yes," I answered curtly.

"Do they help?" she asked.

"Somewhat. Some days the attacks are worse than others. And on those days, the entire bottle wouldn't help." I paused. "Look, Katelyn, I appreciate the concern but honestly I'm fine. Yes it was a bad attack, yes it's never been that bad before. But I'll go back to the counsellor and see if she can up the dosage so that doesn't happen again."

"What triggers them?" Katelyn asked without acknowledging a single word of what I had said. She saw through my fake plea and chose to move on.

"I don't know!" I threw my hands up in the air and turned away from her. I felt her eyes stay on me, burning through me. Seconds went by at an agonizingly slow rate until I felt uncomfortable with the silence and felt forced to break it. "Crista had a seizure. The way she was writhing on the ground, it looked like... well, it looked a lot like—" my voice trailed off.

"Her," Katelyn finished for me.

I nodded and reached for my pill bottle until I realized that if I downed them in the manner I normally did in front of Katelyn, she wouldn't be able to ignore that. So I simply took it and placed it on my desk beside my cell phone. Still no calls.

"Is that what's triggering them? Anything that makes you think of that day?"

I nodded reluctantly. "Yes. If I'm reminded of anything to do with her and I'm not mentally prepared for it, then it sets it off."

Katelyn hesitated before asking, "Her, being?"

"Gwen." I said in a half question half statement. "Who else would I be speaking about?"

"Well." Katelyn paused. "Amy of course."

I bit my lower lip and closed my eyes to try and mask the frustration I felt towards Amy, the woman who was ignoring my calls in one of my worst crisis ever. I knew that I was on incredibly thin ice, and taking out my frustrations with Amy on Katelyn would surely be the final nail in my coffin. I shook my head and took a quick glance back at my phone. No missed calls, no texts, no voicemails, no response.

"No. Amy is not the cause of my anxiety attacks. She actually was helping me for a while with them, but lately she's taken to screening my calls. Leaving me to kind of fend for myself," I scoffed again. "Helpful. Am I right?"

I looked back to Katelyn and saw the look of pure confusion on her face. The colour had drained from her face and it almost appeared as though tears had welled up in her eyes. I thought that this is what I must have looked like moments ago during my panic attack. This what the staff must have seen when I collapsed. I reached my hands towards hers in an effort to comfort her and she pulled away.

"What do you mean she's been screening your calls lately? Jack, have you been talking to Amy?"

My heart started beating faster in my chest and I felt my entire body start to prickle as I began sweating again. My face felt numb and my throat began clenching in a strange effort to hold down my feelings of nausea. Katelyn's demeanour and her questions were leaving me unsettled. Something about this conversation was making me feel incredibly ill.

"Well I was, until about a few weeks ago. She finally stopped returning my calls," I said, at which point Katelyn's hand covered her mouth as she let out a tiny gasp. "What?" I asked, my heart rate steadily increasing.

"Jack. Tell me about the day Gwen died."

My heart began beating irregularly and became a hot ball of pain in my chest. My breathing became shallow and I felt my back sticking to my chair as my body began sweating uncontrollably.

"Katelyn. I can't, I just had a panic attack when I thought about it! I can't!"

"Jack!" she yelled at me. "Jack, tell me about the day Gwen died!"

Tears filled my eyes and at this point I disregarded the control I had exhibited moments before. I took the pill bottle, scooped out three anxiety pills and popped them into my mouth, dry swallowing them.

"Please. I'm not ready."

"Tell me, Jack."

I reached for my garbage can which contained my already ruined shirt and I brought it up to my lap, in case I felt the sudden urge to vomit. Sweat was dripping off my forehead into the bin and landing on my shirt. My chest was feeling tighter and my head felt as if it I was sitting underwater, making all sounds from the surface muffled and unclear.

"Jack," Katelyn said in a more sympathetic tone. "I need to hear you tell me what happened that day."

"You know what happened!" Tears were now flowing down my face, but I didn't bother wiping them away, I simply let them fall off my face.

"I need to hear you say it," she said again in a commanding tone. I felt helpless and powerless to escape the situation. I exhaled loudly and struggled to find the strength to speak.

"It was supposed to be the last counselling session before I recommended her release from hospital care. I thought she was ready, so I arrived to finish our last session and then I planned on delivering the good news to her. Only that didn't happen. Nothing happened like I expected. Everything went wrong that day. Gwen attacked me, and then she killed herself! She attacked me, Katelyn, please don't make me remember it anymore."

"Jack," Katelyn said, with a quivering voice I had never heard come out of her before.

"That's not what happened."

That was when I blacked out.

Chapter 31
September 2016 – Jack

The stumble home from the pub that was only two blocks away from my apartment shouldn't have taken me as long as it did. But I had stopped twice to sit down when the world wouldn't stop spinning. I was taking deep breaths in an attempt to hold down the urge to vomit. The air was cool that night, which felt great against my clammy skin that had been unwashed for a few days. Being on paid medical leave twice in one year had left me completely unmotivated to shower or take care of myself.

My hearing with the disciplinary committee was scheduled for the next day and the support I once had from Katelyn before my second suspension was gone. She hadn't responded to my e-mails when I attempted to ask her for one final chance so I could keep my license. I hadn't been sure what my plan was or what I was even going to say to the committee. I had gone over everything I had prepared for the meeting and could feel my anxiety building to an unbearable level so I decided to visit the pub down the road for a quick break to clear my head.

The first pint of the ice cold lager had tasted so good and it had cleared my head of any bit of stress and anxious feelings. So I decided to have one more drink to settle my nerves completely before I went back to work. I was feeling great after two so I decided to have another. And another. And another. I had finally been forced to leave when I had attempted to stand to go to the washroom and tripped over the leg of a chair and knocked over every drink that had been placed on the table next to it. Everyone looked at me in pity as I stumbled outside while the bartender held me by the back of my shirt. He wasn't even throwing me out, he was steering me so I wouldn't crash into anything else.

When I stepped outside, I saw that the sky was clear that night, despite the fact that the street was lit up with street lamps. I could still see the star-filled sky which brought on a memory I hadn't thought of in ages.

I thought of the very first time I spent an evening with Amy under a star-filled sky which looked identical to this one. The air had been warm and it was the perfect temperature for a barefoot stroll through the grass. I remember the blue dress she wore that was patterned with black flowers. It was a sun dress that hung loosely at her hips and showed more of her shoulder than she'd ever shown before.

The head of the Social Work department was throwing a wine and cheese party at his old Victorian home which sat about a five-minute walk from the university. The houses surrounding the University were originally meant to serve as student houses when the university first opened, but they aged well and grew in value to the point that the only ones able to afford them were the wealthiest of professors. The head of our department was married to a corporate attorney and between the two of them they were able to restore this old home and put in every modern amenity. It was overly lavish for a home that stood five minutes away from a university. It belonged in a gated community in New England. It didn't belong here.

Everyone from our program had shown up to try and rub shoulders with the professors and TAs who were attending in the hopes to get either a reference or a job offer. My interview with Homes for the Homeless was coming up next week and I had more references than I needed. So I decided to spend the night with the person I knew all the other students would be avoiding.

The Ice Queen.

The bench swing sat at the very back of the backyard in the pitch black; we had stumbled upon it by accident when we had agreed to take a short walk together. It was an isolated spot which was far enough from the house that we could barely hear the music and conversation going on inside. We were in our own world and so we chose to stay and sit down.

"Do people really call me the Ice Queen?" Amy asked as her and I sat on the bench swing.

I choked on the wine I had been sipping and spit some of it back in the glass as I thought of what to say. "Um. I mean, who's to say, really. Do they call you the ice queen? Do they not call you the Ice Queen? Who pays attention to these things?" I stammered out as I avoided her gaze.

The bench swing sat in the pitch black and it was difficult to see one another, but I could feel her eyes on me. They were burning with a cold fire that only the Ice Queen was capable of delivering.

"Jack, do people call me the Ice Queen?"

Her tone intimidated me, which I somehow found strangely attractive. I felt compelled to answer.

"Yes, they absolutely do."

"Have you ever called me the Ice Queen?"

"What? No! Of course not!"

"How many times did you call me the Ice Queen?"

"Almost daily during semester one…" I dropped my head as I was caught red handed; she was no longer my instructor and yet she still held an authority over me that I couldn't deny. I knew that if I even tried to lie that she would catch me in it immediately.

"But in my defense!"

"I was a bitch," she said as she laughed.

God, I love that laugh. I had only heard it a few times the past year but I had immediately fallen in love with the sound. It was quiet and she would always purse her lips with this sort of mischievous grin, as if she was trying to hide the smile that wanted to find its way to her lips. It was in those moments that her eyes became warm, and I would want nothing more than to grab her and kiss her.

"I mean, like you weren't the nicest a human being has ever been but I get it." I laughed as I felt her knee bump into mine. I wasn't sure if this was intentional or accidental so I let my leg linger there and see if she would move hers.

She didn't.

"I know I'm not always the nicest but, God, I hate so many of those students. You know what I hate more than anything? Every year we ask the students why they applied for the program and what they want to do in this field. And every year over half of them say 'I want to help people'."

"Oh my God, I know!" I sat up excitedly as I recalled how annoyed I had been on the first day of school when I thought the exact thing. "And you could immediately tell that anyone that gave that answer was going to be useless! They didn't answer questions in class, they didn't contribute to group projects and they didn't care where their co-ops were!"

Amy was laughing again and I realized how animated I had become as I ranted about my classmates. I felt embarrassed and was happy that she couldn't see me since I was sure that my face was as red as the wine I had in my hand.

"Tell me how you really feel, Jack?" she said, mocking me.

"I mean, I guess some of them are okay," I laughed nervously as I tried to backpedal.

"If you say so."

We sat in silence as we swung on the bench swing. We had gone for a walk outside when the noise of the students shouting over each other for the professor's approval was getting to be too much. People were drinking too much to calm their nerves and it was starting to get a bit much for us both.

Amy had lightly brushed her fingertips against my elbow and gave the slightest nod of her head to the backyard in a silent invitation to join her. I felt my stomach turn from nerves and from the wine. There was a rush of blood to my face and I wanted nothing more than to go outside with her, while at the same time dreading it because of how nervous I felt.

We had kissed at the end of the year in her office, but hadn't talked to each other since. It was only a week ago, and every day I thought about finding a way to contact her but I only had her office extension and e-mail. I didn't think she'd appreciate having me e-mail her, 'Hey, loved that kiss, let's go for it again' being sent to her University of Toronto faculty e-mail.

I had no idea what I would say to her or how I'd even broach the subject with her when we stepped outside. While my brain raced over the different ways I could start a sentence, she began to speak to me and I responded without thinking. I was surprised how easily the conversation came between us. I couldn't even remember how we had started the conversation, it just seemed as though we dove into the middle of an already-existing conversation and then we never stopped speaking.

Eventually, we had walked more than we had intended and had made our way to the bench swing. I turned around to walk back towards the house but saw that she had sat down. She didn't invite me and I didn't ask to sit; I simply sat beside her, leaving a slight space between us.

As we talked, I continued inching closer towards her to see how comfortable she would be with closing this space.

Maybe the kiss had been accidental, or maybe it had just been a spur of the moment or maybe it didn't mean anything to her. I didn't want to make any assumption and kiss her again so I tried to test the waters with her.

I took a sip from my wine that was nearly depleted. I put my arm at my side and allowed my pinky finger to linger on her leg. It felt smooth and silky, and that's when I realized I wasn't touching her leg at all. I was touching the spot on the bench where her dress was sitting. If I didn't feel like an idiot before, I certainly did now.

I felt like a child pawing at his mother's dress. I brought my hand back to my side abruptly and realized that she saw the movement.

"That was embarrassing," Amy said as she broke the awkward silence.

She began laughing and I saw that her eyes were resting on my hand. She had seen my very lame attempt at contact and I felt my heart sink into the pit of my stomach. I wanted to run away back to the house and pretend that didn't happen. I wanted to avoid eye contact with her so she wouldn't see just how embarrassed and frazzled I had become.

"I took a midnight stroll with you, we're sitting under the stars drinking wine, I continuously brushed up against you and I've made eye contact with you about twenty times. I figured that your first move would've been to try and kiss me again, not poke me with your pinky like a high schooler."

"What? Oh no, see, I thought that, I mean what I thought was—" I cleared my throat as I stammered awkwardly.

"Oh, for God's sakes," she grabbed the front of my shirt and pulled me towards her.

Instantly, the awkwardness fell away and I grabbed her as I kissed her passionately. She pushed me away from her and I was wondering if I came on too aggressive with my kissing, but was relieved when she took the wine glasses from our hands and set them in the grass.

She then wrapped her hand around the back of my neck and pulled me back into her. She leaned back until I was lying on top of her on the bench and my hand searched for the skin beneath her dress. I felt the smooth skin of her thigh as my hand ran up her leg. My blood turned warm.

"Look at the size of this backyard!" someone shouted in the distance. We heard more voices join in and we realized that a large group had made their way to the backyard.

Amy pushed me off as we both sat up straight and fixed ourselves before anyone could show up. She grabbed our wine glasses and we walked as quickly and as quietly as we could through the shadows to try and join the group in secret.

We joined the group before the head of the department turned on his backyard lights and illuminated all of us. Relief flushed over both Amy and I as we saw that the house lights perfectly lit up the bench swing and that we had been so close to being caught in a very precarious position. She flashed me a mischievous smile as she turned away, pretending to not notice me.

After another hour, the party was dying down and a group of students were all planning their trip out to the on campus pub that was open until 3am. They had asked me if I was joining them. I looked over at Amy who I could see was still slightly flushed from our kiss in the backyard. I told them no, since I would be driving back home tomorrow morning to Middlesex County to see my parents and they all took my excuse without question. I then lingered around the front lawn while Amy stayed in the house for a few more minutes to make our silent escape much less conspicuous.

I had already called a cab, and when Amy stepped outside, we ran into the car together so no one would see us. Before I had a chance to tell the driver my address, Amy was telling him hers. I had wrapped my arm around her waist in the car and she was pressing up against me as she ran her hand along my chest. When we finally arrived at her house, it had felt like hours had gone by with the anticipation building to near unbearable levels.

We rushed inside and hadn't even kicked off our shoes yet when our mouths met once again, our hands aggressively peeling away the layers of clothing. We didn't even bother moving into the bedroom. We had sex right against the door to her apartment, and after catching our breath, we moved to the living room and did it again before finally moving to her bedroom where we capped off our evening with a third and final performance.

I didn't know then, but Amy and I were never going to spend a night apart after that. Every single evening after that, we either slept at her place or mine. Even when I'd make the two-hour drive home to Middlesex County, she would come with me and spend the night. When she'd have to come back to do some school work, we'd drive back to Toronto together and spend the night at her place.

Every night was perfect and better than the last. But I had never been able to get the image out of my mind of kissing her under the stars where no one else was around. We had been in our own world and I had never wanted to leave it. I had never wanted to leave her.

I had wanted to tell her about how perfect this night was and how I would do anything to recreate it. I had wanted to tell her how that was the happiest night of my life and how I would relive it forever if I could.

I felt my phone in my pocket and I attempted to dial her number numerous times but kept cursing as my fingers continuously hit the wrong numbers. Finally, I got the sequence of numbers correct and hit call. I had a beautiful speech written in my head that I knew would no doubt convince her to take me back. By this point I had made it back into my apartment and was stumbling in my living room as I waited for her to pick up.

Unfortunately, the words that came out of me were nothing like the words I had written in my head. What I had said was a slurred sobbing mess of words that were nearly incoherent. She had hung up on me when I had called her the first time. I had yelled out how much I missed her and loved her and needed her back in an incoherent jumble of words.

The second time I called, it had rung a few times before going to voicemail. The third time I called, it went straight to voicemail.

"Ames!" my throat wasn't working and gave each word a strange thickness. "Cull me bahck! I love you. Fuuuuck, I love you. D-d-do you remmbr stars? Hmm? The kissh undur the stars?" There was a loud crash in the voicemail next as I tumbled forward and fell headfirst into the ground beside my bed. I pushed myself back up to all fours and saw my phone laying a few feet from me.

I pawed for my phone and saw that I had somehow hit end call. I went back to the call button and called her for the fourth time. The call immediately went back into voicemail again, this time my message was a lot shorter.

"Bisch!" and then my phone died. I tossed it at the wall and then threw up all over my hands as I was crouched on all fours. When I tried pushing myself to my feet, my hands slipped in the vomit and I landed heavily on my stomach. The smell of the vomit hit my nostrils and I threw up again, not even bothering to sit up to do it this time. I simply turned my head and threw up as it pooled beside my face.

Tears began rushing down my face as I sobbed loudly. I hadn't cried like this since I was a toddler and was trying to get my mother's attention. I sobbed and felt sorry for myself.

Finally I pawed at my bed and pulled myself up to knees where I rolled my vomit-covered body onto the bed sheets that were in a desperate need of a wash. I passed out immediately and had only intended to sleep for six hours in order to attend the meeting with the disciplinary committee.

I slept for 13 hours and never made it to the meeting.

VIII

Ontario Professional College of Social Workers
Disciplinary Committee
Toronto, ON
September 4, 2016
Jack Fletcher,
As a failure to attend your hearing with The Ontario Professional College of Social Workers, the Disciplinary Committee made a decision based on existing evidence and witness statements.

This evidence found you to be in professional misconduct of the ethical standard set out by The Ontario Professional College of Social Workers in Sections 1.4 (A) and Sections 3.2. Violations of these standards results in immediate termination of your membership to The College.

You will not be eligible to re-apply for your membership at this time and will not be eligible to be employed by an organization which requires this professional affiliation.

This decision cannot be appealed at this time.

Any further questions you may have can be directed towards our general line.

Ontario Professional College of Social Workers

IX

Middlesex County Hospital
Adult Mental Health Department
Middlesex County
September 5, 2016
Jack Fletcher,
As result of your removal from the Ontario Professional College of Social Workers, Middlesex County Hospital is terminating your employment as this affiliation is a condition of your employment in your role.

You are prohibited from entering hospital grounds at this time as well as contacting any previous clients or staff. Your personal items will be sent to you. Any information you have saved on your computer will be reviewed and assessed for confidentiality before it is returned to you.

If you have any further questions at this time, you can contact our Human Resources Department.

Katelyn Thomas

Adult Mental Health Program Director Middlesex County Hospital

Part 4

X

From the Personal Diary of Crista Sunderland

I had the dream again. That same terrible dream that for some reason I can't get rid of. I'll go to sleep thinking of literally anything that makes me happy. Kittens, the beach, my favourite food even. And yet it doesn't matter, because every single night when I'm sleeping, I go back to the dream of the mirror. The dream where you stand, watching me, mimicking my movements while basking in my misery.

It was always the same dream every single night, but last night something changed. It was something that threw me off from the already unsettling images that I still haven't grown used to. It was the first time in the dream that I wasn't alone. This time, he was there.

I think of him every single day, hoping that one way or another he'll come back into my life and help me in the way he used to. Anytime they assign me to a new counsellor, I think of how much I hate them and how much I miss him. Despite how much I missed him, and how much I desperately wanted to talk to him again, he never once visited me in my dreams. Until last night.

I was standing in front of the mirror, the same mirror I'm always standing in front of. I was staring at your face as I always do, you mimicking my every movement in perfect synchronicity. I steadied myself for the part of the dream I hated most, when my face begins the process of slowly peeling and dying away. I held my breath as I always do at this part, when suddenly he appeared in the mirror beside me. He was standing perfectly still, his hands by his sides, eyes fixed on his own reflection. I tried speaking to him but no sound would come out of my mouth.

The more I tried to speak, the heavier my tongue weighed in my mouth. Finally my entire body became paralyzed from head to toe. That was when he began to move, his feet shuffled sideways, inching him closer towards me until we were side by side and I could feel his hand brush against the back of mine. I wanted to reach for his hand, intertwine my fingers with his but I was still stuck in place.

I could still feel the skin from the back of his hand on mine, and I could feel him beside me as strongly as I could see him. That feeling didn't leave me even when our reflections started to move. My body was still, as was his, and yet our reflections were turning to face each other. His reflection moved his hands onto my hips and I moved my hands to his chest. Our doppelgangers moved in closer and closer to each other until finally their lips were inches away from one another's. Our mouths partially opened and right before he planted his lips on me, my reflection slid her hands up from his chest and grabbed his throat. His eyes opened wide and he moved his hands from my hips to my hands as he tried to pry them away from his neck. But the more he struggled, the harder my grip became until finally he was on his knees. Red faced, eyes bloodshot and thick veins protruded on his face.

I wept and tried to beg the reflections to stop, but my paralysis held me in place, forcing me to watch myself kill Jack. I shook with frustration, trying to will my body to move even an inch so I could stop what was happening. But I couldn't, and I had to witness myself strangle him until he was lying motionless on the bathroom floor.

He died. I watched him die. And I'm the one who killed him.

I felt the vice on my body release, freeing my body to move as I wanted it to. I turned to face Jack as quickly as I could. I wanted to hold him, to apologize and to tell him how much I needed him and how I would never do what our reflections had just done. But he was gone. He was gone, and you were there.

When I looked back towards the mirror, there was no reflection. There was only darkness.

So I turned back to face you. You were beside me, and you came towards me. You came towards me and you grabbed me by the neck. Your strength was overpowering and I couldn't fight you off. I felt weak, my neck muscles tightening as they tried to resist your grip. Until even they were too weak for you, there was a loud crack and my body went numb. The world slowly turned dark. And then I died.

You killed me.

That's when I woke up. I woke up with the fresh memory of you killing me. The image of myself strangling a person I had grown to care deeply about, still burned in my brain. I killed him in my dream, but you killed him in reality. You took him from me and he may as well be dead to me. I can't see him and I can't speak with him. Once again, all I'm stuck with is you.

Just you.

I hate you.

Chapter 32
November 2016 – Jack

"It's absolutely unbelievable."

"I know I feel so horrible seeing him there. What a nightmare! Isn't there any other hospital they could transfer him to?"

"No, I asked Katelyn about that and apparently he can still be admitted here. He just can't receive any counselling from anyone that he knows. Which is pretty much everyone in the department."

"Poor guy. He really never recovered from that whole Gwen incident, did he?"

"Would you?"

"No, I guess not. Still though, can you imagine being brought back here as a patient? It's tough enough on a regular patient, but a former staff member."

"Do neither of you two have any work at the moment? I'd be more than happy to assign some if you two have an excess of free time!" Katelyn's voice boomed in from a distance.

The two staffers muttered quick apologies as they turned to scramble away, the sound of their feet shuffling away told me that they were gone. I turned over in my bed and saw Katelyn at the end of the hall, looking into my room. We locked eyes and she held my gaze for a few seconds before turning away and rushing back down the hall to her office.

Chapter 33
December 2016 – Jack

"Mr. Fletcher?" The orderly called into my room.

I was laying on my side, facing away from the door. I hadn't reacted to his shout and I wanted to feign sleep in the hopes that they would let me skip my first mandatory counselling session. I knew better than to hope for this, but thought that they might take pity on me as a former staff member.

"Mr. Fletcher, I know you're awake. You know that if you won't come to the counselling offices, then the counsellor comes to your room. Now which would you prefer?" he said in a tone one might use on a child refusing to go to the principal's office. I sighed loudly before turning over to face him.

"Who's my counsellor?"

"I'm not sure. All I know is that I was asked to bring you to counselling room 7, and that I'm to bring you back to your room when the session is done." He stood waiting at the door, it was obvious that he wasn't leaving until I came with him.

I sluggishly threw my blankets off of me, while standing from the bed at a snail's pace. The orderly looked incredibly impatient, and were he allowed to do so, I'm sure he would have physically grabbed me and yanked me to my feet.

I picked up the hoodie I had been allowed to bring into the hospital, minus the string that was attached to the hood in case I used that to harm myself, and followed him out of the room.

My mind began going over all of the other counsellors I had known when I was working here, trying to eliminate all of those who wouldn't be able to council me. I didn't think they'd stick me with one of the new counsellors, since chances were I'm the one that did their orientation. They couldn't put me with one of the more experienced counsellors since I would have known them for years. So who?

I stepped into the room, and when I saw a familiar face across the room from me, I felt no relief. Rather, I felt furious.

"Dr. Hamilton? Seriously!" I exclaimed a little too loudly.

Dr. Hamilton was the psychiatrist that was hired by the hospital to provide counselling to employees for the employee support program. While she ran her independent practice outside of the hospital, she was still technically affiliated with us, since she was the sole psychiatrist they would refer hospital employees to. She was fairly useless as far as psychiatrists went, dismissing a lot of patient concerns so she could get them back to work immediately and absolve the hospital of any liability. She offered Band-Aids rather than solutions, and she was a little too quick to fire with her prescription pad. Fortunately, this had benefited me when I was trying to convince her to give me more refills on the prescriptions I needed so I could avoid going back. I had originally been assigned to see her when I was first suspended from the hospital. She was the counsellor who was being contracted to determine whether I was fit to continue to work or not. Strike that, she was the counsellor who was being paid to determine that I was indeed not fit to return to work. A counsellor with independent interests is not the one I wanted assigned to me back then, and it wasn't the one I wanted now.

When I had yelled out her name, the staff outside of the room began peering in uneasily. A security guard walking by on his regular route slowed down, watching me from the corner of his eye. He quickly glanced over in my direction and quickly looked away when he saw me noticing. I rolled my eyes and held my hands up in the air in an apologetic gesture.

"Sorry, I didn't mean to raise my voice," I said through clenched teeth, barely masking my anger. "I just thought they'd be assigning me to one of the new counsellors that they hired after they fired me. I didn't think that they'd be hiring you specifically to take my place."

"They haven't hired me actually. I'm still considered independently contracted by them."

"Are you fucking kidding me," I muttered under my breath.

"I can see that this makes you frustrated. I assure you though, my interests lie in your recovery."

"My recovery? You mean your interests don't lie in your own personal gain since the independently contracted counsellors the hospital hires make double the amount than the in-house counsellors make? Even though the other counsellors manage entire caseloads whereas you are only assigned to single clients and nothing more? And speaking of which, can you tell me why Crista, a girl who I had

212

nearly helped into a full recovery, is still here? I saw her walking the halls the other day and was told I'm not allowed to speak to her, and yet those who are speaking to her have obviously not been doing their jobs correctly as she's still here. Can none of those counsellors, or you for that matter, help that girl out? She had improved dramatically when I was counselling her, so how is she still here and not in the residency program yet?"

"I'm afraid I can't discuss other patients—"

"You can't discuss other patients with me, I know. But why is she still here? I'm telling you, let me chat with her. Not counsel, but let me talk to her and I can help her. I can—"

"That's not an option, I'm afraid," she said, interrupting me. I was stunned at her interruption; we were always taught never to cut off a client mid-sentence as that was a sure fire way of harming your rapport. Well, she just proved that lesson was true.

I leaned back in my chair and crossed my arms like an angry student refusing to participate in class. She stared back at me vacantly; it was clear she was trying to give nothing away, refusing to react to my agitated state. She held her silence for a few more seconds and I leaned back and scoffed.

"Silence?"

"I'm sorry?" she asked with the same vacant expression.

"You're using silence on me, correct? Leave an awkward tension in the room that forces the client to feel obligated and pressured into talking so they can fill the void left by the silence. I mean that's what you're doing, right?"

She smiled at me, if that's what you can call it, her mouth didn't curl at the edges but rather it remained a straight line that looked painted on. It was an unsettling smile and a sight I had forgotten I hated.

"I can tell that you're frustrated with me, and certainly if you're feeling frustrated and not willing to talk today, then we can certainly reschedule for a time that you feel is more appropriate."

I rolled my eyes at her and sighed. "There's no point in rescheduling. Let's just do this now and get it over with. So what then? Are we talking about my depression? My breakdown when I lost my license and my job? My alcoholism?"

"Talk to me about the day Gwen died."

Pain flared in my mouth as I clenched my jaw and my teeth began grinding together; it was all I could do from not bursting out in anger at her statement.

213

"Why? Aren't I supposed to be the one who picks what we talk about?" I finally got out.

"Normally, yes. But would you say that it's safe to assume that that's where the issues began? The very same issues you had just listed moments earlier?"

"I suppose they did, didn't they?" My foot was tapping rapidly on the floor and my head was beginning to hurt from my grinding teeth.

"Tell me about that day," she repeated.

"I've already talked about it. We talked about it in our first session, and the session afterwards and the session after that! What else is there to say? I fucked up. I failed to notice her deteriorating mental health and I placed myself in an unsafe environment with her. She was in an agitated state which I failed to calm her down from, so she smashed a glass, attacked me with it and then stabbed herself in the neck as I watched helplessly from the floor." I spoke rapidly and a number of my words were strung and slurred together. I had repeated this story countless times and yet was being forced to repeat it again so I didn't bother adding the usual pauses and details that I normally gave her.

"You've left out numerous details you told me about before," she said with a slight tilt in her head. It was a minor gesture but for some irrational reason it angered me.

"Well, you know those details, so why ask?"

"There are some points in there I wanted to explore further."

"Like what?" I said in a challenging tone.

"The details that as you stated have made their way into your dreams, dreams that you mentioned were recurring until we prescribed you the sleeping pills. One detail in particular stands out for me, you standing in the pool of blood as Gwen lies on the floor. That is a point that I feel is essential to our discussion and your recovery. Can you think of any reason why this might be the case?"

I finally let my anger show on my face as I became openly frustrated with her questioning. She was asking incredibly leading questions and it was evident that she wanted very specific information that she was unwilling to simply come out and ask for. I hated her for making me relive a conversation I dreaded having just so she could get to her long winded point.

I threw my hands up in frustration and shook my head from side to side.

"I have no idea. Why don't you tell me? You've already given me about a million leading questions so why don't you just ask exactly what you want to ask."

She didn't respond; she simply capped the lid back on her pen and closed her notepad which I imagine was covered in notes about my lack of cooperation. She placed the book gently in her lap and smiled at me.

"I acknowledge how frustrating this is for you and how discussing Gwen's death once again can further that frustration. I do feel, however, that accepting her death and accepting what happened that day is essential to your overall recovery process."

"I haven't accepted it? Tell me how I haven't accepted it."

I threw back at her. A part of me knew that she was right, and that she was asking me the exact questions that I needed to be asked. Had it been any other counsellor, I imagine, I would have been completely and entirely open. But with her, I was reluctant to divulge anything.

I had hated her when we first met as it was incredibly apparent that she didn't have my best interests at heart. But the thing that I hated most about her was that she was simply a bad counsellor. She had grown lazy in her years of providing drive-thru counselling for employees that belonged to various companies who only covered their employees for a limited amount of sessions, so they could get them back to work ASAP. She had forgotten what real clients with real problems were like; instead, she dealt with employees who were feeling burnt out from too much paperwork or had grown frustrated from a lack of a promotion. She wasn't dealing with clients suffering from severe depression, PTSD or with long histories of self-harm.

I found her to be an older version of my old classmate Jasmyn, the one who made empty statements about wanting to help people without actually wanting to help people. I would have hated her had we simply been colleagues, but the fact that they assigned her to me as an actual counsellor made me feel absolutely infuriated.

"Well, Jack, I don't mean to be blunt but you're here, aren't you? Checked into the hospital for severe depression and suicidal risk. That to me says that you haven't been able to fully accept what happened that day and that it's still affecting you."

"Well, then I suppose it is, isn't it?" I said as I leaned back in my chair, arms crossed and head turned towards the door.

"I can see you're growing more frustrated as we speak. Why don't we look at carrying on tomorrow? How does that sound?"

I scoffed loudly before turning back to her. "Fine," I said and with that one word, it was clear our session was over. She looked towards the glass and waved over the orderly who had been waiting on the other side of the glass.

Our session had only lasted a few minutes, but when it was over, I felt as though I had just run a marathon. It had been so taxing, keeping my guard up against her so I wouldn't get caught in any of her counselling traps, but it wasn't nearly as exhausting as maintaining that level of anger. I was happy to be leaving her presence and I welcomed the orderly's company.

As we walked back to my room in silence, we passed by the set of rooms that I had walked Crista back to after numerous sessions. These were the rooms I wasn't supposed to walk her back to when I was her counsellor, and the rooms I was supposed to stay away from now as a patient. I slowed my feet slightly and glanced out of the corner of my eye towards her room; I couldn't see her and cursed under my breath. I picked up the pace and caught back up with the orderly who hadn't noticed my slight delay.

Suddenly, a deafening crash exploded in a nearby room. My heart jolted with an unexpected bolt of electricity that left me feeling alert and alarmed. I looked around for the source of the noise but saw nothing out of place. That was when staff flew past me towards one of the supply closets. I realized that a supply room could be the only place that the noise could have come from as they had the tall heavy steel shelves that, if they were to ever topple over, could cause a significant amount of damage.

The shelves were heavy, sharp edged and nearly impossible for anyone to move. And yet it had sounded as though someone had just knocked one over. Suddenly, a cry of pain rang out from the room and a group staff began pushing against the door. The shelf that had been knocked over had been partially blocking entrance into the room and the staff were struggling to open it. The orderly I had been with turned to me and hesitated. It was apparent he wanted to rush and help but he hadn't had time to assess whether I was a flight risk yet. I looked towards the door, and tilted my head up towards it to try and indicate to him that he should go and help. He nodded at me and took off. I stood in place, behaving myself and showing him that I was trustworthy. That's when I heard the voice cry out in pain again and I realized where I knew that voice.

"Crista!" I shouted and without wasting another second I took off as quickly as my feet could carry me in the traction-less hospital slippers I had been given. A few steps into my sprint and I nearly wiped out as my slipper caught a piece of smooth tile; luckily I caught myself on the edge of the nurse's counter, preventing what would have been a nasty fall. I kicked my slippers off and took off once again towards the room. I arrived at the scene and without hesitating I threw myself at the door, grabbing the knob with one hand and driving my shoulder as hard as I could against it. The door began opening slowly and the door budging open gave me the motivation to keep pushing despite the burning strain that began coursing through my muscles. At last the door was open wide enough for a small person to be able to fit through and with that a short, slim nurse slipped past me. I caught a glimpse of her blonde hair and noticed it was Melissa, the nurse who had been infatuated with me, and who I had begun to develop an interest in before my dismissal. She was in the room and the sound of her throwing items throughout the room was unsettling as it made us all realize that Crista might not have only been knocked over but she may be buried.

Seconds later, the pressure on the door was released and I realized she had been tossing items aside to help us gain entry into the room. Luckily, Crista wasn't buried but she certainly wasn't in good shape. I sprinted over to her and saw that bruises were already forming on her pale skin from the impact of the shelf, and that her forehead was bleeding profusely. Medical staff came rushing in and were pulling me away in order to have room to assist her. I was slapping their hands away as I tried reaching for her—I was an inch away when her eyes fluttered open. We locked eyes and she reached for my hand.

Two of her fingers were broken and there was some deep bruising on her forearm from where I imagine she tried to catch the shelf from falling. I reached for her hand and held it gently, trying not to hurt her broken bones.

She pulled me towards her as tears filled her eyes. "Jack," she whispered as loudly as she could, which was not very loud.

"Jack. It was her. She's not dead. Jane isn't dead!" I tried to speak but no words came out of my mouth and before I had a chance to come up with any response, her eyes fell closed again. The staff finally succeeded in pulling me away and before I had time to absorb what she had said, I was being thrown out of the room. Two orderlies were waiting for me on the other side of the door and before I had a chance to speak or protest, they held me by the arms, firmly but not roughly, and they lead me back to my room.

Back in my room, I sank down onto my bed and began cursing into my pillow. Tears of frustration poured out of me as I began punching the mattress as hard as I could. I was cursing myself for not warning her, I was cursing myself for not helping her and I was cursing myself for not making sure she was kept safe.

Her sister was back. Jane was here. And she had just tried to kill Crista.

Chapter 34
December 2016 – Jack

It was 2AM and I wasn't even remotely sleepy. Normally, the anti-depressants they prescribed me would have me under a heavy sleep by now, but adrenaline was somehow still coursing through my veins, leaving me unable to sleep.

I had to see Crista. I had to make sure she was okay, but also I had to see how I could keep her safe.

When I couldn't fall asleep, I gave up and took to pacing back and forth in my room, trying to figure out a way that I could slip out of my room and into hers. I knew that she would have been taken to the emergency care wing to receive treatment for her injuries, but since she was a patient with an existing bed, they would send her back to her room. It was the hospital's policy that if a patient already has a room assigned to them that they be transferred back to that room rather than taking up a bed in the ER.

My only question was how do I get there? Patients are certainly allowed to leave their room if necessary, it's not a prison. However, the security in the Psychiatric Ward was always heightened compared to other wings of the hospital, and freely moving around was near impossible. I thought of the layout of the hallways that I was walking back and forth on a daily basis and couldn't believe that I had never bothered learning their layout. Since most of our counselling rooms were already assigned, I always just walked to the room with my blinders on, ignoring the layout of the hallways. I regretted this entirely now. All I had to work with was my unreliable memory that was going to have to tell me if there were any blind spots or corners I could hide in when the security guards were off rotation. Unfortunately, everywhere my brain could think of left me in plain sight and completely exposed.

This section of the hospital was built specifically for intensive psychiatric care and so the original architects ensured that no blind spots existed so that the patients could be kept under watch at all times. As a counsellor, I understood the constant monitoring as several of the patients had suicidal and self-harm tendencies. As a patient, I found it demeaning and overbearing, but mostly I found it incredibly frustrating as it left me with no escape plan.

I peered out of my room and took a quick scan of the hallway. I sighed in defeat as I found two nurses at their regular station, two security guards posted near the emergency exit and an orderly who was escorting another patient through the halls. At 2AM, you would expect the hallways to be silent, but instead it was its usual beehive of activity, leaving me trapped. Or so I thought, before I saw Melissa's golden blonde hair pouring down the back of a pair of light green scrubs. It was a sight that I normally would have avoided to prevent myself from having any awkward encounters, but today I wasn't nervous. Today I knew that this was my only chance out of here.

I went back to my bed and called the nurse button. Hoping and praying that it was her and not the other nurse who responded. I heard the ping of my call button sound off in the distance and my palms became increasingly sweaty as I awaited Melissa's arrival.

The door opened fully from the partial crack I had left it at, and I breathed a sigh of relief as Melissa stepped into my room. I had worried that perhaps my being in here may make her uncomfortable or that she would request to not have to treat me. However, the eager look in her eyes told me that she didn't care whether I was staff or a patient. A crush was a crush to her. I suppose it also helped that in terms of patients, Melissa had to deal with in the mental health ward, I was a nice break.

"Hey, Jack. How are you doing? Everything alright?" she said in an incredibly sweet and tender tone that said to me, 'I actually care about how you're doing'. It was sweet and made me smile; unfortunately, it also caused me to feel guilty for what I was about to do.

"Hey, Melissa. I'm so sorry to bother you. I know it's late and you're tired and probably busy filling out paperwork and stuff—" I was doing my best to appear apologetic and apprehensive about having to bother her. She quickly waved me away.

"Please. I'm bored to tears out there. Between you and I, the nurse they put me on with tonight is so incredibly dull. I'm more than happy to come in here and help you out." She smiled sweetly at me. "So what can I do for you?"

I maintained the timid tone that I knew would work on her if I laid it on thick enough. "Well, I was wondering, and if you can't and say no that's completely okay, but I was wondering if maybe if it wasn't too much trouble you could let me go for a walk? I know we're not supposed to leave our rooms at night but I'm starting to go a little bit stir crazy here and I just feel like a walk through the halls might do me some good. Change of scenery and that stuff, you know? But again, feel free to say no, I totally get it."

She bit at the corner of her lip and pushed her hair behind her ear as she thought about it. Her face held a look of concern, but I could see that she was trying to work out how she could let me roam the halls free. It's the look of a parent who doesn't want to say no to your request but isn't sure if it's possible.

"I don't know, Jack. I mean I totally get it and I'd be happy to. But Nurse Shelly might say no and I don't want you to get in trouble of any kind."

I waved her away immediately and began apologizing profusely. "Of course, of course! I'm so sorry I asked! I didn't mean to make things uncomfortable!"

She shook her head and began apologizing back to me, "Oh no, of course not! You didn't make me uncomfortable. I'd like to, I just don't know. Well actually—" Her voice went up an octave as she began formulating an idea in her head.

Success.

"Actually maybe we can? She's going to do her rounds in a few minutes. Why don't I come let you know when she does. We're taking care of the entire floor tonight so it'll take her about 40 minutes. Is that enough time for you to walk around?" Her eyes were pleading for me to tell her it was enough. She wanted validation of some sort from me, she wanted me to thank her and tell her how helpful she was. So I obliged.

"Yes! That's more than enough time. Oh my God, you're amazing! You just became my favourite nurse," I said with the smile that I used only when I needed to be charming. Judging by the smirk that spread across her face, I'd say it worked. Her face was turning slightly red and she turned away from me.

"Oh stop!" She walked back to the door then stopped, as if reading my mind. "And don't worry, I'll tell the security guards to follow Shelly at a distance in case she needs any help with the patients. That should free you up." She winked at me as she left my room.

Our encounter had left a smile on my face. In another life, I thought to myself, maybe we would have been a good couple. But there was always that part of me that still thought that maybe, just maybe I would find a way to win Amy back.

I shook thoughts of Amy out of my head as I returned to my task at hand. I was going to walk through the halls and find Crista's room where I would try to quietly slip in. Once there, I needed to find out everything that happened, and figure out a way to keep her safe.

I had mapped out what I thought was the best route to her room when a gentle tapping came at my door. I sprinted towards it and opened it a crack to see Melissa waiting on the other side of me. Her lips had a shine that hadn't been there moments before. Did she put on lip gloss?

I wondered.

"Hey! Coast is clear. 40 minutes, maybe a little bit less and definitely not more," she whispered to me. I opened my door completely and stepped out, turning towards the hallway leading to the other set of rooms before stopping myself. I turned back and gave Melissa a light squeeze on her arm.

"Thank you." It was genuine and I truly meant it. She blushed and turned away. With that I walked as quickly as I could without making it seem obvious that I was trying to race against time. I followed the route exactly as I had mapped out in my head, until I turned the last corner and froze in place.

The older nurse, Bernice, who had grown to hate me over the past few months, was standing directly outside of Crista's room. And she looked as though she was planted there for the remainder of the evening. Presumably to ensure that Crista remained undisturbed while she recovered. Or perhaps it was to ensure that she wasn't attacked again.

I began cursing as my mind raced with trying to formulate an idea on the spot. I felt my face getting hot as my frustration at a lack of an idea grew. I worked out every possible idea I could to try and move the nurse, when suddenly I heard a loud ping come from the nurse's station. The older nurse sighed loudly and waddled her way over the station. She looked at the source of the ping and then sighed again as she began making her way over the room that had called. I saw her turn a corner and enter a room. Somehow, I had an unexpected moment of luck that I would never question, but definitely be thankful for. I thought about being thankful later; at the moment I was running as quickly and as stealthily as I could towards Crista's room. I opened the door as quickly as I could and moved my way into the room, closing the door behind me while the knob of the door was still turned in an attempt to silently latch the door. I ducked down, so in case the nurse came back she wouldn't be able to see me in the window that looked into the room. I waited a few seconds before tip toeing over to Crista's bedside where I could hear the gentle sound of her breathing.

Two of her fingers on her left hand were splinted together and she had bandages over her arms where the falling debris had cut and bruised her. On her forehead lay a large bandage which no doubt was covering the stitches they had sewn into her to stop the gash that she had received from the shelf. I reached for her uninjured hand, and held it gently in between mine.

She moaned as she stirred awake, like a child being woken up on an early school day. Not yet ready for the day to start, and moaning in protest for a few more minutes of sleep. But I held onto her hand and moments later, her eyes fluttered open and what was a momentary look of confusion, turned into one of pure joy.

"Jack!"

She yelled then covered her mouth as I brought a finger to my lips, shushing her.

"What are you doing here?" she whisper yelled as she threw her arms around me. It felt strange hugging a client back, but I suppose at this point she was no longer a client. I gave her a small squeeze back, in an attempt to not further injure any potential internal injuries she may have sustained.

"I came here to make sure you were okay! I'm so sorry."

Her arms wrapped themselves tighter around my neck. And I felt my neck getting wet with her tears as she buried her face into me.

"Please, don't be sorry. You were the only one helping me. I miss you. God, I missed you." She finally detached herself from me and smiled as she wiped away the tears. I handed her a box of tissues that was beside her bed. She laughed and said, "Forever the counsellor, right?" I laughed and nodded.

"Crista," I said as the brief moment of laughter died down, in a much more serious tone. She recognized the tone, and her face grew as grim as my voice. "How? How did she get in?" I asked.

"I don't know. But she did. And she almost did what she promised she would. I thought I was safe!" Her voice was still in a whisper but it was getting louder. I wanted to shush her again but I knew she wasn't shouting on purpose.

"Tell me what happened."

"I don't know, I was walking back from my session with my new counsellor and that's when a nurse had called me over. The orderly walking me was on his phone, not paying attention so he

223

was oblivious when I heard the nurse call again. I turned and looked towards the supply closet where she was standing. Her hands were on her hips and she looked angry with me. She waved me over, so I went to her but not before looking back over at my orderly. He kept walking and didn't even see me leave his side. I turned back towards the nurse and she entered the supply closet, holding the door open for me.

I was so confused but I didn't know what was happening. The nurses hardly ever spoke to me so I thought maybe this was important. I followed her. She waited for me to come into the room at which point she closed the door behind her. When we were face to face, she pulled off her surgical mask and her nursing cap.

It was her.

I tried screaming but she covered my mouth with both hands, crushing my mouth and nose, making it nearly impossible to breathe. She was wearing the same synthetic gloves all the nurses wore and it took me a moment to realize that her hands weren't moving off of my face, but rather the pressure they were placing on my face was growing stronger and tighter. The material of the glove made the perfect seal, and I couldn't breathe. She continued pressing harder on my face and I could see the veins in her arms protruding as her muscles tensed. That's when I realized that she wasn't trying to quiet me, she was trying to kill me.

Chapter 35
December 2016 – Crista

I tried pushing her away, but she was so much stronger than me. She pressed me against the shelf and I felt a bolt from one of the shelves drive itself into my back. I cried out in pain but it was muffled in her hands. My eyes filled with tears, my face tingled as it slowly began feeling numb and my chest twisted in pain as my lungs fought for air.

I felt the strength from my legs give out, causing me to drop straight down to the ground. My unexpected drop was so sudden that Jane lost her grip on my face. As my body crumbled, I felt the sweet rush of air into my lungs, before the impact of my fall pushed it out all out of me. Jane reached for my again but I threw my arms around my head and curled into a ball. It was the way you defend yourself against a bear, but in that moment, it was all I could instinctively think to do.

Jane growled in anger as she tried wrestling my arms away from my head so she could get back at my face and neck, but the harder she pulled, the tighter I curled into my ball. Finally her frustration made her lose all control and she began kicking me in the ribs with the tip of her shoe as hard as she could. I wanted to scream out in pain, I wanted to move my arms and protect my sides but I knew that the moment I did, she would lunge for my neck again. So I held on and bit down in pain with each kick until finally they stopped.

I heard her breathing heavily as she regained her composure and I knew that this was my moment to make a break for it. So I let out a small and weak whimper so she would mistake me for being in worse pain than I was. I peeked up from my knees and saw that she had turned slightly away from me, facing the shelves to see if there were any tools to help her in her efforts.

I sprang to my feet and threw my shoulder into her chest as hard as I could. She stumbled back and I heard her clatter against the shelf which had stood behind her. I had made it to the door and even had my hand on the door handle when a sharp burn erupted from the top of my scalp.

Something tore at my head and whipped me around and I saw that she had a handful of my hair. I moved with her hand as she twisted me around in an effort to minimize the pain, pain that was so intense I was beginning to see coloured spots as my vision blurred.

She whipped me into the shelf and a loud crash echoed out the room. My only relief was that the banging of the shelf would draw someone's attention who hopefully would come to rescue me. Jane realized the same it seemed and, as a result, lost all desire to remain quiet. She stood over me as I lay against the shelf and she began stomping down on top of me as hard as she could. My arms were bruised and bleeding as they protected my head, and for every kick to the ribs, legs or stomach, I nearly gave up protecting my head. But instincts told me that this was the only thing saving my life, so I kept my arms up.

Finally, when we heard voices shouting outside the room, I heard Jane back away from me. Through my arms I saw that she had walked over to the shelf on the opposite wall, and she was pulling on it as hard as she could. I screamed at the top of my lungs as I knew that the weight of the shelf would surely kill me.

After a few strong pulls, she achieved her goal, and I screamed louder than I had before as the tall steel shelf came down on top of me. I braced myself for impact and covered my head as best I could when I heard the shelf get caught on the way down. While the shelf itself hadn't fallen on me, everything that it was holding certainly did. Something hard and metallic landed on my hand, crushing my fingers, while something else penetrated the shield my arms had made, scrapping across my head and slicing it open. The shelf had luckily not toppled directly on top of me, but it still did a fair bit of damage, leaving me near broken and shattered.

That's when the door began banging and I realized that help had come too late. Jane stood over me, smiling and wiping the sweat from her forehead. Before the door opened, she smiled then placed her surgical mask and nursing cap back on her face. I could hear voices shouting on the other side and I prayed that not only would they save me, but that they would see her as the imposter that she was. I prayed that they'd realize she was my attacker. But before they could get the door open, she spoke quickly to me.

"All I did was try to love you. In my own way. But now? Now, I'm going to make sure that no one ever gets the fucking chance to love you ever again. Do you understand? I'm going to kill everything you love, make you watch and then I'll kill you. You fucking pathetic bitch." She spit out the last worst and spit flew from her mouth all over me.

That's when the door burst open, and moments after that you came running in to save me. During the commotion of everyone running into the room, I never let my eyes leave hers. She slipped in between the concerned nurses and began acting accordingly, she was shouting and panicking with the rest of them and helping the staff who brought in the stretcher.

I thought I was starting to hallucinate when I saw you. My sweet Jack, my caretaker, my friend. I knew you'd believe me so I tried to tell you. But I was fading out of consciousness and found it hard to focus. I tried telling you that Jane was alive, and if I could have pointed, I would've. But you stayed with me and wouldn't turn around. I loved you and hated you at the same time. You were saving me but not the way I wanted you to. And before I could tell you just what you needed to hear, I blacked out.

I blacked out and let her escape. And now she's here. Here at the one place I thought I was safe. She's here and she's going to kill me.

She's at the hospital and she's going to kill me.

Chapter 36
December 2016 – Jack

"Jack. She's going to kill me." Crista cried as she wrapped her arms around my neck again. She repeated the same thing over and over again as she buried her face into my shoulder. I rubbed her back and told her it would be okay but her sobs wouldn't stop.

"I'm so sorry," I said finally. My voice was shaky and I felt a lump form in my throat as my eyes unexpectedly filled with tears. I was holding back my desire to let them out when she pulled away from me and looked me in the eyes.

"Why are you sorry? You've been so helpful, you're the only one who's helped me at all!" She tried smiling through her tears but I could tell it wasn't real. It was her way of trying to comfort me, almost as if she was trying to become the emotionally stable one instead of me. But as I spoke, her smile faded almost instantly and the look of fear returned.

"No, I haven't been helpful," I said. "I thought you'd be safe here. I asked the nurses if you were safe in here and they promised me you were, but you weren't and I should have made sure!"

She was wiping away tears when she suddenly stopped sobbing and raised an eyebrow.

"Why were you making sure I was safe?"

The lump in my throat returned and suddenly I felt my chest grow cold. In my brief moment of guilt and vulnerability, I had made a grand error in judgement. She spoke again, only this time with a little more sternness in her voice.

"Jack. Why were you making sure I was safe?"

I began to stammer and I couldn't get my words out. Normally I was so quick on my feet, but that was only when I knew I was going to be questioned on a lie. When I could anticipate it.

When I was caught unexpectedly, I became a nervous wreck.

"Jack!" She snapped me out of my stammer. "Did you know? Did you know that Jane was still alive?"

"Look, Crista, I—" I wiped at the sweat on my forehead. "I wasn't sure, I thought maybe. But you were doing really well. I didn't want to make you regress by revealing that she was alive. I thought maybe—"

"You didn't want me to regress! Jesus, Jack, isn't that what you did to Gwen? It's the exact same fucking thing and you just did it to me!" she began to scream. I turned towards her door to see if her voice had called over the nurse. I pressed my finger to my lips again in a failed attempt to silence her. She smacked my hand away from my face and sat up.

"You knew that my sister was alive. My sister who is a murderer, my sister who I tried to kill and who would very much like to get revenge on me. You knew she was alive and you didn't say anything? You didn't fucking say anything! You knew! You fucking knew!" I held my hands up in an attempt to plead with her and she began using her unbroken hand to smack at me.

"You fucking knew! You fucking knew!" She screamed again and again as she continued to wail on me with her open palm. I tried grabbing her wrists in an attempt to stop her when I felt the strength in her arms. She was furious and she wasn't as frail as she looked. I was having trouble handling her when suddenly I heard the door burst open.

I cursed and backed away as I saw two orderlies rush her side with Bernice beside them. I tried to rush out of the room before they had a chance to address my being there but stopped when I saw the security guard standing in the doorway. His large frame blocked me in.

I cursed again and turned back to Crista who was screaming at me and fighting off the staff. I tried calling out to her, but her screams drowned my voice out.

"Crista! I'm sorry! I'm sorry!" I tried to plead but she didn't hear. She simply continued swinging her arms and fighting off the staff. My thoughts turned to Jane, and what Crista had said about constantly being overpowered by her. How could anyone overpower this girl I thought as three staff members struggled in handling her violent outburst?

I tried shouting over her still but my voice was swallowed by her screams. Finally the nurse turned back to me and the guard, shouting, "Get him out of here! Now!"

With that the guard placed his hand on my upper arm firmly, not roughly, but he was certainly not giving me any choice in where

I moved. He led me out of the room and walked me back to my room where he dropped me off without saying a word.

I dropped against the wall as soon as he shut the door, tears spilling from my eyes. I wiped away at them with white knuckled fists as I pounded on the floor in frustration.

"Another one! I can't believe I fucked up another one!" I muttered to myself through a clenched jaw. I thought of Gwen and how I had let her down. I had tried saving her but I pushed her past where she was ready to go, and it ended up being too much for her. Now I had done the same with Crista and she too had ended off worse than when she first came in. I had failed in helping them both and now there was surely no way I'd ever get the chance to help her ever again. They were going to keep me under heavy surveillance which would eliminate any chance I would have of seeing her again. I began shaking with fear at the thought of what was going to happen to her.

"You can't save everyone, Jack." Amy's voice rang through my head.

She had told me this the countless times that she found me pouring over Gwen's old case notes. And even though I dismissed her advice every single time, I knew that she was right. I couldn't save everyone, I couldn't even save myself. Here I was in the psych ward after having been diagnosed as severely depressed and a high risk for suicide.

I had tried so hard to save everyone that came through my door that in the end, I'm the one who ended up broken. I'm the one who ended up in need of saving. I wanted to save Crista, I did. But I couldn't. Not in the state I was in, and certainly not in the environment I was in. A patient would never be allowed to treat another patient.

But a Social Worker, even one not associated with the hospital, certainly could.

I turned to the smooth, unmarked and clearly untouched telephone that hung on the wall beside my bed. With the age of cell phones most of the landline phones the hospital had installed in the rooms years ago went untouched and were in near perfect physical condition. I grabbed it off the wall and checked to make sure that it was capable of more than just internal calls. The dial tone that only came on when you were making external calls buzzed into my ear and I nearly jumped with joy.

My fingers flew over the buttons and I dialed the only phone number that I ever committed to memory.

Chapter 37
December 2016 – Jack

"Hello?" The voice on the other end of the phone said. The phone, while it was unmarked and in pristine condition, didn't actually operate very well. It made the other end difficult to hear, as if the person speaking to me was doing so at the end of very long and tunnel that echoed every time you spoke.

"Ames," I said into the phone. Unsure if she would be able to hear me through the phone's muffled speaker. There was a pause before the sound of an audible sigh came through. "Jack. You know when I ignored your calls, it wasn't so then you could start calling me on random phone numbers to trick me into talking with you. I don't have time for this right now."

"Please!" Amy I pleaded on the phone, immediately regretting how needy that had come out. There was a pause on the phone and I could hear her faintly breathing in the background.

"I'm sorry, but I don't have anyone else to call. Ames, I think I fucked up again, and I think I've put one of my clients in danger just like before. It's my fault she's in danger and I don't know what to do." My voice was trembling, I was on the verge of breaking down into tears and I was failing at keeping it hidden in my voice.

After a slight pause I heard, "Tell me what's happening."

I explained the situation fully. How my client had endured years of abuse at the hands of her sister and that she had not only been the victim of her violence but had witnessed it on numerous occasions. I told her how Crista had attempted to kill Jane, only to fail and how now Jane had somehow managed to sneak into the hospital and attack her back. I then confessed how I was there as a patient and not as an employee which is why my hands were so tied. She was silent the entire time on the other end of the phone, but I could tell that she was actively listening. What comforted me is that she let me speak without once cutting in or disregarding any of my concerns. She listened to my entire story and when I was finally done, she gave me a few seconds longer in case I had any last details to get out. When she realized I had nothing left to say, she spoke.

"Jesus, Jack. You didn't tell anyone about this? You didn't tell a single other person that your client's life was at risk? Even if she was delusional, you still tell someone. And how many times did you find people wandering halls that they weren't supposed to be in? Security isn't exactly top notch in that place. And now you say she's been attacked? This needed to be addressed immediately, but now you're a patient there which has basically makes your entire story less credible. Anything you tell them will just look like a plea to get back in contact with her; it's way too fantastic for them to simply accept at face value."

"I know that! I know, I just—" I went silent for a few seconds as I choked back my tears of frustration. "I just don't know what to do. Help me, Ames. Please."

"What do you want me to do, Jack?"

"Come see me. Help me talk to them. To Katelyn or the board or whoever! I'll be more credible with you here with me. I promise that's all I want; if you do that I'll leave you alone."

"Jack," she said in a tone that I had grown to recognize. Her voice always took on this tone whenever she was delivering bad news to me.

Jack. I'm seeing someone.
Jack. I filed for divorce.
Jack. I can't see you anymore.
"Jack, I'm not going there. I can't help you."

"Why not?" I felt a building pressure in my chest that was close to eruption. The frustration I had tried to keep dormant was now spilling over into my voice, causing me to speak harshly at her. I wanted to apologize, but I was too far gone in my agitated state.

"You know why."

"Ames! This is more important than that!"

"No, Jack. It isn't. You know why."

My eyes burned and finally I rubbed at them with the back of my hands, trying to force the tears and anger down. But the moment I had touched them, it broke down whatever walls I had put up to keep them at bay, forcing the wall to crumble and spill out the tears I had forcefully choked back until now.

"Ames. She needs help. She needs our help."

232

"Gwen needed our help, Jack. This girl needs physical protection, and that's not something you or I could do. Talk to Katelyn, then move on. This isn't your job anymore."

"It is my job! And it would be a hell of a lot easier if you helped me!"

"Jack. I can't. You know why."

"For fuck's sakes, Amy!" I slammed the receiver back onto the base that was attached to the wall and turned around to see two orderlies standing in the doorway. Katelyn was with them. "Katelyn! Thank God! Just the person I needed to see! Look my patient Crista—"

"Who were you talking to, Jack?" Katelyn said, cutting me off. The two orderlies blocked her path to me and kept her well protected—in my highly agitated state I didn't blame them. I realized how I looked and walked back to my bed, to show them that I was cooperative and that I was non-threatening. They moved into the room but still formed a human barrier in front of Katelyn.

"Who were you talking to, Jack?" she asked again. Her tone told me that her question was more of a command, and that I had no choice in whether I answered or not.

"I was talking to Amy. I thought maybe she could hel—"

"To Amy?" Katelyn asked again.

"Yes! I was talking to Amy, trying to see if she could come in and help Crista. There's a lot I didn't tell you from our counselling sessions that I need to tell you now if you'll listen."

"Jack," Katelyn said, in the same tone that Amy had used moments earlier. She gently moved the orderlies aside and came face to face with me. She reached for my hands and held them tenderly in her hands. "Do you still not know what happened that day?"

"What? On the day Gwen died? What does that have to do with this? Listen to me, Crista is in danger. The situation is a whole lot worse than I let you believe! Please, she was almost killed today and I know why!"

"Tell me what happened that day?" Katelyn said, less in a commanding tone and more in a warm motherly tone. It was a tone I was not used to hearing from her, a woman who was normally so authoritative and rigid. It completely threw me off and for a few seconds, made me forget all about Crista.

"Why do you keep asking about that? Why does everyone keep asking me about that day?"

"Tell me what happened that day. Tell me what happened to Amy?"

I was starting to shake with frustration and felt my face start to heat up. I felt an anxiety attack coming again, I felt my skin prickling from the sudden breakout of profuse sweating. "Tell you what happened to Amy? I don't know, she left me! After what happened to Gwen. I spiralled and she tried to save me but it was too much and she left me." My hands were still shaking and I felt Katelyn grip onto them firmly, trying to ground me as it was clear that she felt their shaking.

"Jack. No she didn't."

I tilted my head to the side and I raised an eyebrow at her, trying to study her face. Her face gave nothing away, and I noticed that this was causing my hands to shake more than they had been before.

"Katelyn," I said. "What the fuck is going on? Why are you asking me all of this?"

"I need you to remember what happened."

"To Gwen?" I said in a shaky voice.

"To Amy."

"Look, I just got off the phone with her! Whatever happened that caused her to leave isn't important right now!"

"No, you didn't."

I pulled my hands away from her and backed up until I felt the bedframe painfully hit the back of my legs, causing me to fall backwards onto the bed in an awkward seated position. My movements had been sudden and had caused the orderlies to jump towards us. Katelyn raised her hands to stop them, keeping them behind her. I felt sick, and my head had been plunged into a bucket of ice water. I felt the anxiety slowly rising and I knew that if it got any worse, I was going to have one of the worst panic attacks I had ever experienced. I gripped onto the sheets of my bed until my knuckles were white, and I tried to steady myself as I shook uncontrollably. "What the fuck are you talking about?" I hissed through my teeth. "I just got off the phone with her just now! Call her right now! She'll tell you!"

"No, she won't, Jack. She can't."

"Why not?" I shouted at her.

"You know why." Amy's words out of Katelyn's mouth.

I was starting to hyperventilate but still felt as though I wasn't receiving enough air. I was pulling at the collar of my shirt and had stood back up on my feet where I began to pace back and forth. Katelyn backed away and allowed me the space I needed to regain control, but no matter how much I paced, I still felt breathless. I began to feel lightheaded and backed myself into the corner of the room where I leaned back and sat down against the wall.

Katelyn approached me and bent down so her face was level with mine. She reached for my hands again and I let her take them.

"Jack. You know why."

"I don't! I don't know why!" Spit flew from my mouth and my face was soaked with tears and sweat.

"You know why." Amy's words repeated out of her mouth. I shook my head in an attempt to physically toss all thoughts from my head. Suddenly, Amy's voice cut into my head once again.

"You know why."

"No, I don't," I responded to the voice of Amy that was ringing through my mind.

"Yes, Jack. You do."

I shook my head and suddenly Amy's face flashed through my mind. The image was of Amy's face, smiling at me. I clutched the sides of my hair and began shaking violently.

"There! You have it now!"

Amy's face flashed again, and when I looked down, I was standing in a pool of blood. Gwen was standing a few feet away from me pushing the glass into the side of her neck, blood pouring from her wound as her face turned ghost white. The blood was soaking into the carpet at her feet, which was still a few feet away from me. Yet there was a pool of blood at my feet.

Wasn't this my blood?

"No. Not YOUR blood."

My brain flashed back to the sight of the pool of blood, and to the body lying beside it.

The dead body. Amy's body.

That was when the world turned black and I fainted.

XI

From the pages of the Middlesex Community News

Obituaries

Middlesex Community News
Tuesday, November 24, 2015
Amy Katherine Ryan-Fletcher

A long-time resident of Middlesex County, Amy attended St. Martin's Catholic Elementary School and Middlesex District Catholic Collegiate Secondary School before she attended the University of Toronto where she obtained her Bachelor of Psychology, Bachelor of Social Work and Master's in Social Work.

Amy was a devoted member of the University of Toronto faculty where she instructed, conducted research and continued her studies in the field of Social Work. She was in the process of obtaining her PhD and had started her own private practice which had become one of the leading practices in the Middlesex region.

She was one of the best things to happen to this department, her co-workers at the University of Toronto stated. She brought something completely new to the table and her passion was unquestionable. There will be no replacing Amy.

Amy was a loving wife to Jack Fletcher for the past 3 years. The two had met while both attending the University of Toronto, where Jack also studied Social Work.

Members of the community are being invited to visit the Ashford Funeral Home in Middlesex County where Amy will be remembered by friends and family.

If you wish to honour Amy's memory, a donation can be made to the charity that Amy had been supporting and volunteering for since high school—The Middlesex Women's Shelter. All proceeds go towards women leaving abusive relationships and who are looking to start new lives.

The Ryan family thanks you for your support, your wishes and your prayers.

Chapter 38
November 2015 – Jack

Amy was leaning back on the leather stool we had purchased specifically to match the bar we had built in our rec room. She was leaning back, propped up on her elbow and swirling her finger around the rim of her wine glass. Her thick framed glasses were low on her nose but she hadn't noticed and hadn't yet bothered to adjust them. It was the only imperfection I could see at the moment, but it was an imperfection that I had loved. It was a flaw that wasn't even a flaw, because I loved nothing more than seeing her grab the sides of the frame and sliding them back up her face.

It was a move that slightly reminded me of the way Superman would adjust his glasses in the comics. Everyone else pushed their glasses up on the nose piece, making a scrunched up face as they did so, but I always noticed how Superman adjusted his frames by grabbing a full lens and almost lifting them back into place. It was clear to me that Superman did so because he didn't actually need the glasses, so he never took on the habits of those who actually needed them. It was the one flaw in his disguise that I had noticed immediately as a child.

Amy had this same tick, this same habit. And it always made me think that she was just like Superman. She didn't really need the glasses but rather she wore them to try and mask her superiority over us regular humans. She was so perfect that she had to disguise her perfections. I was staring at her face, studying it and loving every single line on it. She would frequently catch me staring, and she would tell me how she didn't know it was possible for me to stare at her like it was the first time I was seeing her.

I had gotten lost in her face once again, which had resulted in my not listening to a single word that she had said—it took her a few minutes before she finally noticed. She swatted playfully at my arm and hit me out of my hypnotic state. I shook the thoughts of Superman and Amy adjusting their glasses out of my head and tuned back into the conversation.

"What did I just say?" she asked as she took another tiny sip from her wine.

I hesitated and squinted as I studied her face. I could tell she was hiding a smirk and that she wasn't actually annoyed with me, so I playfully answered, "You were saying how handsome I was and how you want nothing more than to take me upstairs." She laughed and took another sip of her wine.

"Oh absolutely, great job! I find it especially sexy when my husband doesn't listen to a word I have to say. It just drives me absolutely wild," she said as she leaned into me. I could smell the wine on her breath and I felt the uncontrollable urge to kiss her. That was until I felt the hand on my chest pushing me away.

"What I said, before I was accosted by my husband who can't keep his hands to himself was, Katelyn called me. She said you had suggested they offer me a contract for independent counsellors to assess the clients looking to be released from the housing complex. She said she thought it was an amazing idea and that they could work around my schedule."

I took a long deep drink from the red wine she had poured me. She always kept a bottle in the house just for me because she knew how much I hated the white stuff. I drank before saying anything the way politicians do when they need to collect their thoughts before responding. Unfortunately, she knew this technique all too well. After I took a drink, I still hadn't spoken or responded to her statement. I was trying to remain silent so she would continue without me having to ask her what her answer was.

"You can't use the silence technique when it's apparent you have a question you're wanting to ask. I can see it written all over your face, so don't try and use counselling techniques to the very person who taught them to you." I almost spit my wine across the bar as I began laughing. She had read through my façade with ease and between being my teacher and my wife, she had learned to read me better than anyone.

"Well! I was waiting for you to tell me what your answer was, but since you insist on holding out that last detail until I actually ask, I'll ask. So I hate to pressure you, but did you take it?"

She laughed mockingly at me and leaned back again. "You? You think you could pressure me? It's funny that you think you call the shots around here," she said as she smirked.

"Can we at least pretend that I do?" I asked in a fake pleading voice.

"Absolutely not," she said as she finished the last sip of wine in her glass before tipping the bottle and refilling it, nearly to the brim. She was on her way to getting to a fun level of drunk, which meant that we would be having drunk, passionate sex later. I struggled to contain my desire for her. But I could tell by the fact that she was still leaning away from me that she wanted to continue our discussion and that she wasn't ready to move this party upstairs just yet.

"Well then?" I asked. "Are you going to take it?"

"Hmmmmmm, I don't know!" she said as she dragged each word out as long as she could. I grinned as I realized that her playfulness meant that she was going to take it.

"Oh, don't give me that!" I said as I leaned into her. She wrapped her arms around my neck and pressed her forehead against mine.

"Of course I'm going to take it. And thank you for suggesting it. Doing this is going to open a lot of doors for me. Between the university and the hospital, it won't be long before my private practice really takes off. This is going to help me make even more connections and maybe before we know it, we can counsel clients in the way we've always wanted to, without corporate stipulations. We can really do it. Thank you, Jack." She kissed me gently. Her lips stayed on mine, but she didn't press in hard. She simply let the kiss hang on the edges of my lips.

It was perfect and it made me love her even more.

"You're going to be amazing. I know it." I kissed her with the same tenderness she had kissed me with. When we pulled away from each other, we paused and made eye contact. Without hesitating this time, I plunged in and kissed her deeply, my hands pulling her face into mine. She pressed her body against mine and kissed me harder than I had thought possible.

We hadn't bothered going upstairs—we couldn't wait another moment. We had made love right there on top of the bar and had laughed uncontrollably when it was over as we saw the spilled wine all over the floor. But we didn't care. We had each other.

***

The week after our wine filled discussion, Amy had begun working with the hospital as an independently contracted counsellor, coming in to numerous appointments with various counsellors. The counsellor would give Amy an idea of the client's history, their counselling sessions and what their plan for release was. Once this discussion was finished, Amy would go into the room with the client and independently assess the situation to see if what the counsellor had said lined up with what she was able to assess.

It was unbelievable seeing Amy in action; you could counsel a client for months and build a solid rapport, Amy would build a better rapport in a single hour. She assisted us in releasing numerous patients that we had all deemed appropriate for release and argued with us on a few others who she believed weren't ready yet. On my best day I couldn't out-argue her, and from what I saw, no one else could either. I had loved her personally and respected her professionally, but after seeing her actually work with clients, I grew to adore her personally and idol her professionally.

The staff had grown to love her as well, despite her sometimes cold and hard demeanour. They knew that it was her way of distancing herself from the trauma of our clients so she would avoid burnout. They also knew how much she truly did care about the clients and how she really did have their best interests at heart.

Her work with the hospital was already being recognized by the university and they were already lining up a grant to offer her to complete a PhD so they could hire her full-time in the department and even look at making her one of the department heads.

Everything was moving along perfectly for her.

And then I brought her Gwen's file and asked her to assess if my client was ready to be released.

Chapter 39
November 2015 – Jack

We were scheduled to meet in my office that morning. I was prepping Gwen's file for Amy and was a little presumptuous in preparing Gwen's release papers. Amy had been meeting with Katelyn about the renewal of her contract as the hospital was already keen on extending and upgrading her existing contract based on feedback from staff, clients and management. Amy arrived at my office door and was looking as beautiful as I had ever seen her. She was wearing a dark red shade of lipstick which matched her auburn hair perfectly. She had a long dark skirt on, which didn't exactly hug her hips but it showed a slight hint of her curves. She wore a white shirt underneath a charcoal blazer which matched her skirt. I stayed on the other side of my desk as I knew I would be tempted to grab her and kiss her if I moved any closer.

"So? Tell me about Gwen."

We sat down, and I focused on the file as I spoke, avoiding looking at my wife's perfect image. I explained to Amy about how Gwen has been steadily medicated to treat her paranoid schizophrenia and has developed numerous coping strategies to combat her previous coping strategies of drugs, drinking and self-harm. I explained how well Gwen maintained her apartment and that she has taken up cooking along with numerous household chores that she often neglected before she was checked in with us.

When Amy asked how Gwen's been doing as she prepares to be released, I hesitated. Amy caught it immediately and called me out on it; I didn't think it was a huge deal but I knew that my reluctance to talk about it showed that it was in fact a big deal.

"Gwen's actually incredibly eager to leave," I said. "Because. Well, because she's told me that the apartments are haunted and that they've been frightening her."

"Jack. Jesus Christ"

"No, but see! This is exactly what her concern was! That mentioning ghosts or anything of the like would have everyone believe that she had relapsed again but she hasn't. I check her medication, I monitor her behaviour and it's all fine! It's just this one thing."

Amy pushed her fingers under her glasses and rubbed at her eyes. She took a deep breath and calmed herself before she spoke.

"You understand how difficult this is going to make the release, right? This isn't going to be easy, because even if, let's say, what she's saying is true—which I don't think it is since ghosts aren't real—what will I write on her release forms? Patient is lucid, healthy and cleared to be released so long as an exorcism is done on her new apartment beforehand?" She pushed her hair back and kept her hands on top of her head.

"Actually an exorcism is when you're possessed. What you're referring to is a house cleansing."

"Jack."

Her tone told me she wasn't looking for a sarcastic response from me and she wanted to deal with this situation seriously.

"Look, I know it sounds crazy, but please just talk to her. Other than that one thing, I stake my reputation on the fact that she's of sound mind. And who knows, maybe there are really ghosts there and we're just being overly critical."

She raised a questioning eyebrow at me, and I knew that my plea was failing. I really had believed Gwen to be of sound mind, minus the one detail of her adamantly believing the fact that her apartment was haunted. I had forgotten that my wife never believed in anything of the sort so this was really going to make this difficult for me.

"Well, if you're so sure that she's ready to be released, then let's go see her. Shall we?" She reached her hand towards me and I laced my fingers through hers. She pulled her hand away and reached for the file I had been holding in the other hand. I turned red and began fumbling to hand the file over. She laughed as she flipped through the pages.

"How embarrassing for you." She laughed. And with that we left to meet Gwen.

When we arrived at Gwen's apartment, we both entered together. Gwen was there waiting for us on her chair. She looked upset and it was evident that she had been crying. The lights down the hallway which lead to her room were turned off and she was facing away from them, a glass of water in one hand and a cigarette in the other. Her pack of cigarettes sat in front of her and her hands shook uncontrollably as she brought the cigarette to her lips. Amy and I both stopped in the doorway and Gwen turned towards us.

"I saw him again."

I moved forward but Amy stopped me and nodded towards the door so I would back away. She moved towards the chair facing Gwen with her pen and paper in hand and sat on the very edge of the chair so she could lean closer towards Gwen. It was her move when she wanted to make the conversation feel more personal, more intimate. It often worked whenever she needed clients to open up more than usual.

"It's a him?" Amy asked. Gwen nodded and leaned forward as she began rocking back and forth. She hadn't even acknowledged that she didn't know Amy; she was in too agitated of a state to care or notice anything going on around her.

"He talks to me while I sleep. I can't always tell what he's saying but sometimes I can. He whispers to me and I can't get him to stop. I—he tells me things. Bad things. He"—she sobbed violently as she tried to continue—"he tells me to hurt people. And I don't want to! I don't like hurting people! I know I did when I went off my meds, and I know everyone is scared of me and thinks I'm going to do it again but I won't. I don't want to!"

"Who is it telling you to hurt?"

"People I know." She paused and looked down at the ground. "You."

"Do you want to hurt me?"

"No!"

"Gwen. I have to ask, and I need you to be honest with me. Do you have a plan to hurt any of these people? The people the voice is telling you to hurt?"

"No! I just told you no! I don't want to hurt anyone! But I can't get him to stop! All I want is for him to stop! My meds won't even help because it's not a voice like the other ones.

This one is real, and I know it's a ghost, but no one believes me!"

"Gwen, I believe you. But I need you to tell me what you need from me? What can we do to keep you safe from harming yourself or anyone around you?" Amy said.

"Gwen?" Amy asked again.

"Let me leave here."

"We're working on that. But we have to make sure you're ready to live on your own, risk free, before we let that happen. Now you're making good progress, Gwen, but we still have work to do."

There was a small whisper that came out of Gwen that was nearly inaudible.

"Gwen? Did you say something?" Amy asked.

"I said"—Gwen looked up and made eye contact with Amy—"I said then kill me."

Amy leaned further towards Gwen and placed her hand gently over hers. I could see her give Gwen's hand a small squeeze at which point Gwen began sobbing uncontrollably.

"Gwen. I'd like to place a call to have some staff from the hospital come over. Would you feel better spending the night out of this apartment? Away from the voice?" Gwen nodded.

Amy turned towards me and said, "Hey, Jack, would you mind?"

I nodded towards her and felt my pocket for my phone. Making sure it was in there. It was and I breathed a sigh of relief as I exited to the hallway. I rushed to the end of the hall to avoid Gwen being able to hear me and I immediately dialled the hospital, asking for the orderlies who serviced the living complex.

"Hey, it's Jack. Would you be able to send two staff over to the living complex ASAP? To apartment 3A? Yeah, it's Gwen, I think we're going to have to re-administer her to the hospital. Yeah, we do feel she's at immediate risk of harming herself or someone else. Okay. Okay. Thank you, I'll see you guys in a minute."

I hit the end call button and walked back to the room when I heard a crash and a scream. My heart sank and I felt a burning in the pit of my stomach. My phone screamed in my hand, and Amy's ringtone blared from the small speaker.

'Hey, Jude, don't make it bad…'

I sprinted back on shaky legs as Amy's song continued playing on my phone.

'You have found her, now go and get her.'

I burst through the door at full speed. The glass of water that had been sitting in front of Gwen was shattered, and the largest shard was in her hand. She was standing in front of her chair, looking down at Amy. Gwen's eyes looked up at me and before the glass entered the side of her neck, she mouthed, 'I'm sorry'. She drove the shard into her neck, and when she pulled it out, a deep shade of red blood poured from the wound. She collapsed to the ground as her eyes were staring at the ceiling, the life slowly faded from her.

I looked down and saw a pool of blood beneath me. I was in shock and trying to figure out how Gwen's blood, which was very clearly soaking into the carpet in front of the arm chair, could have pooled beneath me. Amy's whimpers broke me from my shock and I turned to see her lying a few feet from the blood. I rushed towards her and saw that the entire front of her once-white shirt was soaking wet with dark thick blood.

My shock wore off immediately and I ripped off my button up shirt that Amy had given me for a birthday present the year before. It was my favourite shirt.

I balled it up and pressed it against the wound I could see on her chest. She cried out in pain but I ignored it and pressed harder, knowing that I would need to keep as much pressure on it as possible.

"Amy! Amy! Oh Jesus Christ no!"

She continued to cry and struggled to speak. Blood coming from her mouth and it bubbled at the corner her lips.

"No you can't! You can't leave me! Amy, please!"

"Tried—" she forced out, she coughed violently and more blood came up and out of her mouth. "Tried to stop her." I looked at the room and noticed how the coffee table had been flipped and the arm chairs were moved out of position. Amy had tried to stop Gwen in her suicide attempt and had given her own life for her efforts.

"Don't speak! It's going to be okay!" I fumbled through my pocket and grabbed my phone to call the emergency line they gave us if a patient is in medical distress; it was the quickest way I knew to get someone to come and save her.

My hands were drenched in Amy's blood and my phone slipped out of my hands, smashing against the ground with an audible crack. The song from her ringtone still came out of the shattered device.

'...nah nah nah nah! Hey Jude!'

I fumbled with the phone and hit ignore call so I could make an outgoing call. With slippery fingers I was finally able to get a solid grip on the device. I saw that the screen wouldn't respond to my wet fingers. I wiped them against my pants as well as I could and tried calling again.

"Fucking hell! Come on!" I screamed. Just then, the two orderlies who had come to help Gwen back to the hospital arrived. I shouted at them to call the emergency number and let them know that one of the workers has been critically wounded.

As they moved quickly, I turned back to Amy. Her face a deathly grey, and her eyes were slowly losing focus. Her breathing had become raspy and she was becoming more and more limp in my arms. I shook her slightly to try to shake her back to her senses but it was no use. She was slowly fading further and further away from me.

"Please, Ames, no. Please stay with me. Stay with me!" I said as my tears dripped onto Amy's face. Tears were also running down her face as she continued struggling to breathe; I wiped them away for her and left red streaks on her cheeks from my blood stained hands.

"Jack," she said between raspy breaths. She reached for my face and cupped it gently in her hands. It was the same way she held my face after the first time we made love. She told me that the shape of my face was perfect for the shape of her hand, and that's how she knew that we were a perfect match. Our bodies fit perfectly together. We fit perfectly together.

I reached for her hand to hold it against mine and before I could touch it, it dropped. Her head fell back and her bright green eyes that I had fallen in love with from the first second I saw her, lost the bright life they once held. I buried my face into her neck and screamed out every ounce of agony that I was feeling. I screamed and sobbed until my throat was raw and no sounds came out.

I felt a pair of hands pulling at my shoulders but I swatted them away. They were joined by more sets of hands, but no matter how hard they pulled at me, I wouldn't let Amy go. I held her to my chest and kept my face in her neck asking her to come back to me.

Finally, a stronger set of hands latched onto my shoulder and I was too powerless to fight them off. I was pulled off of her and I saw from the medical staff's lack of urgency that they knew exactly what I knew. The hands that had pulled me off finally let me go, but I didn't move. I stayed on the floor, watching and wailing as the staff shook their heads at each other and checked their watches. Time of death.

"Jack! I'm sorry! I'm so sorry!" Katelyn's voice rang in my ears as I felt her arms closed around me. Nothing she was saying was registering; all I could focus on was Amy's face being covered by a white sheet. Even in death she was more beautiful than any woman I had ever seen.

The room was filled with people in almost no time, but I didn't take notice of who any of them were. My eyes were fixed on the outline of Amy's body which lay under the white sheet. Her blood was already starting to soak through. My cries had finally stopped and my expression had turned vacant. Katelyn tried helping me to my feet but my body wouldn't move. I didn't want to move.

I wanted to stay in that exact spot and not move ever again. I had no point in ever moving again.

My wife was dead.

My love was dead.

My Amy was dead.

Chapter 40
December 2016 – Jack

"So you remember?" Dr. Hamilton asked as rested her pen and notebook on her lap. Not taking any notes at all.

"Yes."

"Do you think your wife Amy is still alive?"

"No"

"And the incidents that you once described to me that occurred afterwards. Your drinking, your suicide attempt, her leaving you? Do you still believe those are real?"

"No. I—" I inhaled in a few quick bursts as I was choking back tears. "I think I created those. I think I fabricated the whole thing to try and forget what happened."

"Can you tell me what did go on during the year that you were away from work? What was going on during the months before you started coming and seeing me?"

"I don't know. I made myself believe so hard that all of those things with Amy had actually happened that I don't even know what I did do."

"When do you remember hearing from Amy most recently?"

"It was the day before I had Crista assigned to me. I had come into work incredibly hungover that day and I was working on my computer when—"

"When what, Jack?"

I inhaled long and slowly. "When 'Hey Jude' came on my iPod."

"The song that was playing when Amy died?" she stated matter-of-factly.

I nodded.

"That's okay, Jack. We can spend time trying different exercises to try and trigger your memory so you can remember how you've actually spent the past year of your life rather than this world of hallucination you've built. There are also numerous things you can do to try and—"

"No," I said abruptly. "I don't want to remember anything from that time. I don't want to remember any of it. I just want—" my voice trailed off. "I just want to forget everything."

"Well, Jack, sometimes when we accept the terrible things that have happened to us, it helps to empower us. By embracing our past, we develop the ability to move forward."

"Move forward? My wife was murdered, because I put her at risk. I put her in a room with a patient who was very obviously not ready to be released and she murdered her. THEN, I created an entire fabrication about how my wife had turned hateful, dismissive and vulgar. I tarnished my dead wife's memory all because I was feeling sorry for myself. I thought terrible thoughts about her, I resented her and I grew to hate her. A woman who loved me and who I killed. So yes, if it's all the same to you, I'd like to forget about the past few months. I don't want to remember the time when I selfishly turned my wife into a monster she never was!" I stopped and suddenly my stomach felt sick. Several images began flashing through my brain and I completely tuned out whatever response Dr. Hamilton had said towards my little rant.

I created an entire fabrication about my wife.
I created an entire fabrication.
The entire thing was a fabrication.

Oh Jesus, I thought. The words kept repeating over and over in my head. *A monster she never was. A monster she never was. A monster she never was.*

"I have to go. Can I please return to my room?" I said without any waver in my voice.

The confidence and the urgency of my voice appeared to have caught Dr. Hamilton off guard. "Jack, we've only just begun today's session and it appears as though you've made a breakthrough, I think—"

"Please, Dr. Hamilton. I will answer every single question you have tomorrow. But for right now can I please go back to my room? Now." It was a command. I had never spoken to her so forcefully.

She sighed loudly and she wore a look of annoyance and frustration on her face.

"Well, I suppose I can't force you to stay." She waved the orderly stationed outside the room for me, and I quickly shot to my feet to go meet him.

I was near jogging back to my room, and I could hear the orderly breathing heavily as he kept up with me. It was evident that I was following the exact route I was meant to follow back to my room. Had I deviated in any way, I know he would have stopped me or thought I was trying to escape. But instead he just protested in silence until we finally arrived to my room. I thanked him and rushed to the phone that was hanging on my wall.

I began panicking, worried that I wouldn't recall the officer's number that had been assigned to Crista's case. I knew the numbers but couldn't recall the sequence, so I began trying various combinations and getting wrong number after wrong number. My hands were shaking now as I grew more frustrated with each failed call, until I finally heard—"Detective Sullivan."

"Detective! It's Jack Fletcher. From Middlesex County Hospital. I'm the social worker assigned to Crista Sunderland." I realized that the detective may have no idea that I had lost my license and that I had not been assigned to Crista for months. Everything I needed to do relied on him being absent minded to that fact.

"Mr. Fletcher, did no one from our precinct contact you?"

"No, I'm afraid I haven't heard anything from your department for quite some time." The truth, however, is that his precinct may very well have contacted Katelyn or whoever the new social worker was on Crista's case but I had to gamble and hope he didn't know that. Luckily, for me, it appeared as though he had no idea that I wasn't in charge of her case anymore, so I spoke on. "Have you had any new information surface or have you developed any new leads?" I asked eagerly.

"Well, I'll tell you what the officer I placed in charge of contacting you was supposed to tell you. We spent weeks searching for any evidence of the sister that was apparently occupying the house with Ms. Sunderland. But we couldn't turn anything up, no IDs, no prints, and not even any evidence of another person living there. We tried to rummage through all of the wreckage to try and see just who else was in the house when she burnt it down but so far we've found nothing. With no body and no evidence of murder then, realistically, all she's going to get is an arson charge when she's deemed mentally capable of standing trial. We were incredibly confused, so we looked into the lease and found that it had been in her mother's name before being signed over to Crista. There wasn't any other tenant listed as living there."

"Is it possible that Crista simply inherited the house herself and just had Jane living there?"

"I thought that originally; however, a few weeks after our investigation started, I had a thought. All of this time we were looking for Jane, Crista's missing sister. But none of this time had we been looking into Crista. So we did. So we took the lease that had Crista's name on it and used it to conduct a background search. We found all sorts of documents in her name, driver's license, employers, school history and everything we needed. Including her family history."

He grunted and I could hear him tapping at his keyboard in the background. "One second, let me pull it back up, I believe we have it here. Yes here it is. Before I go on, what exactly does your office have access to over there?"

"Medical records, birth records, former psych evals. That sort of stuff."

"Do you have access to any information from when she was a minor?" he asked as he continued typing away on his computer.

"Unfortunately no. Those records are sealed and held with the office of the Public Trustee. They can't confirm or deny whether a client has a record with them, and even if we put in a request of information, there's no guarantee they'll release anything helpful."

"Well, what I'm about to tell you I didn't tell the officer to tell your office. This is between you and I. Understood?"

"Of course." I was starting to sweat and I could feel beads of sweat running down my back. I knew he had exactly what I was looking for, but I couldn't appear too eager to grab the information, I had to remain calm and composed.

"Okay then. Well then let me explain, Crista was born in '92 along her twin sister Jane. Nothing written for name of father. It appears as though her and her twin sister were raised by her single mother as we have no record of the mother ever remarrying. Probably on account of her never recovering from her depression and spending a lengthy period in the Thamesville Community Home for Psychiatric Care."

"Her mother spent time in psychiatric care?"

"That's right. She spent a few years there actually, on account of her suffering from a severe depression."

"I had no idea her mother had a history of mental health issues. That would explain part of what I've been able to find." My heart became heavier in my chest, and I began feeling each individual beat thumping louder and louder. I didn't need him to finish his explanation, I knew exactly where this was going. "When was it? When was her mother admitted to the Psychiatric Home?"

"Well, you see. She was admitted in the summer of 2000. Right around when her daughter was found drowned in the river at the Thamesville Park."

My heart beat was now echoing in my ears and I felt my legs lose all strength. I was silent for a few seconds as I absorbed what he was saying. Until finally I found the courage to ask.

"Her daughter Jane?"

There was a long pause.

"Yes."

He dragged the word out as his attention was back to reading the file notes. "It looks like she drowned in the Thamesville River, the one that runs through Mitches Park. It says that she and Crista were playing at the park and the mother had left them unattended. Crista is the one who reported that Jane had fallen into the water. When the mother and other people at the park arrived at the river, Jane was already dead.

"All this time we had been searching for a ghost. Had we had access to this information, we would have been able to determine immediately that there was never anyone else at the house and that Crista had some sort of mental illness that made her believe that there was. It's kind of Norman Bates-ish, isn't it?"

I had tuned out the last of what he said and my mind had returned to Crista. The world suddenly lost focus and my heart gave one last heavy beat that drowned out every other sound around me.

Jane drowned the dog.
Jane drowned Taylor. Jane drowned Troy.
Jane killed my mother.
"Your sister died that day in the park."
"Get rid of her. You need to make your sister go away."

"Hello? Mr. Fletcher?"

"I'm sorry, Detective. I think I may have to call you back. There's something I have to check with her before I can confirm anything for you."

"Are you sure everything's okay?"

"Yes. Yes everything is fine. I just have to check one thing."

His voice had turned suspicious and it was clear that he knew I wasn't letting on as much as I knew. "Okay. You call me back when you know something, okay?"

"Of course, Detective. Thank you for your help." And with that, I hung up the phone.

I ran to the doorway of my room and called at the first nurse I could see.

"Yes, Mr. Fletcher, what can I do for you?"

"Call Katelyn Thomas' office! Tell her it's Jack, and it's an emergency. If she's not there, call her direct cell. Please it's an emergency."

The nurse nodded and turned with no urgency at all. I wanted to scream at her to move, but I had to remain calm. The only way to get anyone to listen to me was to remain as calm and rational as possible.

I had to tell someone that the patient in our care wasn't a victim of years of abuse. She was the victim of years of mental illness.

A mental illness that caused her to believe her sister was still alive.

A mental illness that caused her to create an entire fake life.

A mental illness that caused her to maybe kill?

Chapter 41
December 2016 – Jack

Minutes later, Katelyn arrived; however, to me it had felt like hours. I didn't know where Crista was and what my time frame was, all I knew was that I either had hours to fix this, or minutes.

"Jack? Is everything alright?"

"I have to tell you so much but we don't have a lot of time. It's about Crista, I misdiagnosed her. She doesn't have PTSD, she has dissociative identity disorder!"

"Jack, I've told you that you can't work on her file anymore and that we won't talk about this anymore."

"This will be the last of it, I promise! But please just listen—"

"No, Jack, I don't want to listen. Not only is dissociative identity disorder one of the hardest things to identify and diagnose, but you also haven't treated her for months. What's makes you believe—"

I began spewing out words rapidly. I told her of our conversations about Jane and the years of abuse Crista suffered at her hands. I described the murders Crista had told me about, and that every time she tried to escape her, Jane found her. I then told her about my conversation with Detective Sullivan and the information he told me about the day Jane died.

By the end of my several minutes long rant, I was sweating profusely and my mouth was bone dry. I was panting as I realized I had barely taken any breaths during my long winded explanation.

Katelyn didn't dismiss it or talk down to me again. She simply kept her face still as she tried to process all of the information I had just thrown her way.

"And what makes you so sure of this diagnosis then?"

"Because of me," I said. She raised an eyebrow. "After what happened with Amy, I built a fake identity for her to try and normalize my guilt. I made her into a monster who was terrible to me so I would grow to hate her, it was my brain's way of trying to change the emotion to something other than guilt. I used to think that Amy was the one who made me take my medication or that Amy was the one who would calm me down from my anxiety attacks and that Amy was the one who stopped my suicide attempt. But the truth is, I did all of those things myself. I sorted out my own medication, I calmed myself down from my anxiety attacks and I stopped my suicide attempt by myself. Those things all still did happen, only Amy didn't do them. I did them. I did all of that by myself but I built an entire fake person to the point that I have crystal clear memories of these interactions with her." I let the words hang between us, and Katelyn's eyes finally met mine and the astonishment in her eyes told me that she didn't need me to finish.

"So you think that she built two personalities that were so disconnected and detached from one another that she truthfully has no idea that her sister is dead?

"That's right. Which means that even though Jane isn't a real person—"

"She still committed those murders...." she said in a whisper, as if she didn't want to actually speak the words, let alone let anyone else hear them.

"I have to go check where she is," Katelyn said as she sprinted to leave the room.

"Wait! Katelyn! She'll talk to me! Please let me go with you!"

Katelyn was too flustered to argue so she nodded and turned back to run towards the phone at the nurse's station. I ran beside her so I could listen in on the conversation, Katelyn leaned towards me so I could hear as well.

"Hi, it's Katelyn. Can you tell me where Crista Sunderland is at the moment; there's something that I need to speak with her about." There was a long pause on the other end of the line that was causing Katelyn and me to get more and more anxious.

"You do? She's not? Wait, say that again?" Katelyn said. The voice on the phone was too low for me to hear and I had to pull away so I could try to read Katelyn's expression instead. Her eyes went wide and she quickly slammed the phone down.

"What?" I asked. "Where is she?"

"She was complaining about aches and pains from her accident. So one of the nurses took her the physiotherapy pool in the rehabilitation wing."

"The pool," I repeated in a daze. Katelyn and I knew exactly what this meant and without speaking another word, we took off running.

XII

Records from Parkwood Treatment Centre for Psychiatric Care
Patient: Stephanie Sunderland
Counsellor: Dr. Cynthia Vasquez
Date of Admission: August 1, 2000
Today's Date: November 22, 2000
Note: Appointment

Client attended her appointment for her three month assessment. Upon entering the room, the client had appeared as though they had recently been crying as her eyes were red, puffy and she had streaks down her face. I asked the client if she was okay and if she would prefer to move this appointment to a different day. Client stated that no she wanted to do it today and she apologized for crying. I assured her that it was no problem and that she was allowed to cry if she needed. She thanked me and then sat quietly as she waited for me to speak.

I asked the client how she has been doing for the past three months since she was admitted to our institution and she began to once again cry. I handed the client a box of tissues and a plastic cup of water while she composed herself.

During her last appointment, we discussed the death of her husband before her two daughters were born. Client stated that her husband Christopher had always wanted children and she was ecstatic to tell him about the pregnancy. But before the letter could be mailed out to him, she received the phone call that his unit's vehicle was hit with an IED and that he had died instantly. He had been on short-term leave for his father's funeral when the two of them had conceived, and he only had a few more months of duty before he was to return home permanently. Client stated that she had buried her depression during that time in order to be a good mother for her twins who were on their way.

However, when her daughter Jane had died, the client could no longer bury the depression she had been experiencing for years. Afterwards, the client stated that she's been feeling more depressed than ever, since last week was her children's birthday. She then corrected herself and said 'child', at which point she broke down again.

When asked how she's been coping with the death of her daughter Jane, she struggled to speak. When she was finally able to, she stated that she has not been good at all and that spending time away from Crista has made things worse. When Crista was brought to the institution to visit her mother last month, Crista had been speaking about Jane as if she were still alive. She would point to the air beside herself and she'd respond as in conversation with someone who wasn't present. This was incredibly upsetting for the client and she wanted someone to speak to her daughter about her hallucinations. Staff assured her that this was most likely a coping mechanism and that she had turned her sister into an imaginary friend of sorts, to try and cope with the death. Client stated that she wasn't satisfied with this and that she wanted her daughter to be spoken to.

I asked her if she felt comfortable speaking about the day her daughter drowned in the river, but she had said that no she wasn't ready yet.

She simply kept repeating that she wanted someone to speak to her daughter because she was worried about her. I assured her that we'd look into it; however, that became all she could focus on. At this time I do not feel it appropriate to release the client from the facility as she is still experiencing symptoms of severe depression and she is still unable to completely speak about the day her daughter Crista found her other daughter Jane floating in the Thames River.

When we were ready to end our session for the day, the client asked me to wait. When I asked her what was wrong, she stated that she wanted to tell me something horrible but she was afraid of saying it out loud. I told her that this was a safe space and she could tell me whatever it was that she needed to say.

The Client continued to cry as she spoke and took a full minute to compose herself. When she finally appeared ready to speak, she turned to me and stated:

"I sometimes wonder if Crista was the one who drowned Jane."

Client then went silent and would not speak despite me prompting her to follow up on that statement numerous times.

Chapter 42
December 2016 – Jack

We were panting and out of breath as we had run through the entire length of the hospital. The rehabilitation wing was on the opposite end of the hospital from the psych ward and there was no quick way to reach it. Katelyn had stopped us only momentarily so she could call security and have them rush over, hoping they would get to the scene before we could. However, their office was located next to ours as we were the ones with the most frequent incidents. They never even patrolled the rehabilitation wing.

We didn't bother to wait after she made the call; we just kept running and knocking over anything and anyone who got in our way. Finally, we reached to the main entrance of the rehabilitation pool.

Katelyn swiped her staff card and the green light above the door turned on. She turned the knob and pushed but stopped when she realized it wasn't moving. I moved beside her and pushed as well, but was met with the same resistance. At that moment we both realized Crista had blocked the door.

Katelyn turned the knob again and this time we both drove our shoulders into the door even harder, trying to move it together. It inched the tiniest bit and we thought we had found success but after it refused to budge anymore, we realized that this was as far as it was going. After a minute of trying, we both stopped to catch our breath and to give our shoulders a break from the constant ramming into the door.

"It's stuck! What do we do?" Katelyn yelled between gasping breaths.

I was bent over at the waist, trying to catch my breath as beads of sweat dripped from my face, forming a small pool under me. Had I not been bent over, I never would have noticed the coloured line on the ground that indicated the fire escape route. I suddenly remembered that each hallway of the hospital kept a map of the hospital posted to indicate the fire escape closest to your current location. I had an idea.

"Katelyn. Give me your card."

"What?" she said as she was still gasping for breath.

"You can wait for security! I can't, they'll just take me back to my room. But if I go into the intensive care unit through the second floor, then I can get to the rehabilitation wing from there and then into the pool from the back entrance!" She saw that my eyes were resting on the map that was mounted on the wall. She moved towards it and studied the plan I had just given her, nodding when she realized I was right. Without any further words, she handed me her card. I grabbed it and sprinted off towards the stairwell—I didn't have time for the elevator.

I was in a completely foreign area of the hospital and didn't know where I was going at all. My only hope was that I had studied the map enough so my body would take over without letting my brain overthink where to go.

When I reached the second floor through the stairwell, I burst through the doors; I turned left, then right, then left again before sprinting down a long corridor. It was quiet and nearly abandoned as most of the patients were asleep. I came around a sharp turn and found the stairwell I was searching for. However, my hospital slippers betrayed me and flew out from under me as the lack of grip on the bottom of the shoe met the freshly mopped floor.

My feet were up in the air for what seemed like minutes until I landed at an awkward angle on my left shoulder which snapped so loudly I was convinced I had waken the entire floor.

Pain flared along my collar bone and all the way down my arm. I growled in pain and clutched my shoulder, trying not to move it, while at the same time trying to get up. I moved slowly as every single movement made the two ends of the broken bone grind together. It felt like someone was crushing glass in my arm and then lighting the shards on fire.

I clenched my jaw and tried to stifle my cries as I made my way back to my feet. When I finally found my footing, I couldn't help but notice the colourful spots that were dancing in front of my eyes, making it harder to see. I tried my best to ignore them, pushing through the door and gingerly walking down the stairwell that led to the back entrance of the pool.

Each step down the stairs was agony, and I frequently wanted to stop and take a break. But I kept telling myself that they can fix me afterwards; this was more important right now. With that thought I pushed through the door at the bottom of the stairs and saw the glass wall that surrounded the pool. The entire lobby around the pool was abandoned as all of the physiotherapists had already gone home. The pool was only kept open after hours for patients who were required to do their physio exercises several times a day every day, even during the hours where there were no physiotherapists around. As long as they were supervised by medical staff, they were allowed to access the pool. It was also open to any other patients who were recovering from any other injuries and whose mobility was limited. The pool wasn't just necessarily limited to patients receiving physiotherapy. It was also open to patients recovering from injuries from the emergency ward, the intensive care ward and—

The psych ward.

Right now, one of those patients was in the pool.

And she was drowning a nurse.

Chapter 43
December 2016 – Jack

I moved as quickly as I could, moving my shoulder as little as possible. If I moved it suddenly or too quickly, then the spots would come back and blur my vision, making me stop to reorient myself. And I couldn't afford to waste any more time; the nurse in the water was starting to lose strength, her flailing limbs were starting to move less and less.

I opened the door to the small pool deck surrounding the water and jumped into the water as far as I could to try and avoid swimming which would have been nearly impossible with one arm. The water was much shallower than I expected and the unexpected impact of the shallow water that only reached my waist caused an unexpected jolt of pain throughout my body. A blinding flash of pain tore through my shoulder as my feet had come down hard on the tiled floor. I screamed out in agony and steadied myself as the colourful spots returned, filling my vision and disorienting me. For a few seconds I couldn't move or see.

When my vision finally cleared and I could focus on something other than my broken collar bone, I saw that Crista had let the nurse go and that she was facing me. She looked towards my shoulder and then at my face.

"Crista," I pleaded. "It's me. It's Jack."

"Jack," she said as she smiled the smile I had grown so fond of just a few months ago. I reached for her hand which still had its splint to protect her broken fingers with my good arm and she let me hold it, smiling at me. I smiled back.

She backed away slowly, still holding my hand until her arm was fully extended. Then the smile disappeared and even with her broken fingers, she yanked me towards her with our hand still locked into place. She wound back with her free hand and swung a fist as hard as she could at my shoulder. I howled in pain and ripped my hand from her grip. My body instinctively turned towards my sore shoulder and before I realized my mistake, she was behind me.

"Crista! Wait no!" And then the world went silent. My head was below the water before I had a chance to take a breath, I inhaled just a second too late and breathed in a lungful of water through my nose. The water burned as it made its way down my sinuses and into my chest, distracting me from the fact that I needed to fight her off and stand upright. That was when I realized that the things that had betrayed me only a few minutes earlier were betraying me again. The hospital slippers, they were smooth and flat on the bottom with zero traction, they had caused me to wipe out at the top of the stairwell and at the moment they were causing my feet to slip out from under me.

My feet continuously slid against the pool's tiled floor; perhaps if it had been deeper, this wouldn't have been an issue but this pool was awkwardly shallow. I didn't have the room under me to plant my feet properly which would have allowed me to stand. My fingertips could touch the bottom of the pool, but with only one arm I didn't have enough strength to push myself up or push her off. The impact of her punch as she pulled me towards her had left me dizzy and in shock. My body was slowly betraying me as I struggled to find air.

Her hands were incredibly strong and the weaker I became, the stronger they felt. Finally, my feet stopped kicking and my arms stopped fighting.

"It's okay, Jack."

I let out the last bit of air that I had in my lungs and waited for the world to turn black.

"It's okay. I'm here."

In those last moments I thought of Amy. I thought of her hair, I thought of her lips, I thought of her eyes and I thought of her laugh. I thought of the first time we met, I thought of the first time we made love, I thought of the first time I said I love you, and I thought of holding her in my arms as she was released by death.

"It's okay, Jack. Calm down. Think. Think of me."

I thought of her reaching for my face and cupping it in her delicate hands. I thought of how she had fought off Gwen to stay alive until her very last breath.

"Yes. You've got it."

She fought until her very last breath.

"Yes, Jack! Do it!"

My eyes shot open and I found that I still had some strength left in my already burned out muscles. It wasn't much but it was enough. My legs began to flail behind me; only now they weren't fighting to stand, instead they were kicking off the hospital issued slippers that were hanging off my feet. The left slipper came off quickly, and the right one took an extra kick but it came off seconds after. I placed my bare feet on the bottom of the tiled pool, this time actually finding some purchase; with that I tightened my muscles and planted myself as hard as I could.

"Yes, Jack! You've got it!"

I kicked off the bottom as hard as my legs would let me and found that it was just enough to throw her off of me. I gasped desperately for air and stumbled as my body swayed back and forth. My lungs burned and my stomach was already turning from the amount of water I had either swallowed or inhaled. I was panting heavily and trying to force myself to take deep breathes was a struggle, but I knew I would need all the air I could get if she submerged me again.

Crista had fallen back into the water, but her scramble to her feet only lasted a few seconds, and my battle to refill my lungs had given her enough time to prepare for another attack. Even though I was ready this time, I would have to act quickly as the look in her eyes told me that she wasn't holding anything back. She was meaning to kill me.

She lunged at me, but this time her movements were sluggish and it was clear that she was exhausted from holding me under for so long. I backed away quickly and felt her fingertips graze my chest as I narrowly escaped her attack. She screamed and took a swing at my shoulder again. This time I was ready for her and I side stepped the punch which left her overbalanced, causing her to miss me entirely.

Her feet slipped out from under her, and she fell in the water directly in front of me. Her feet and arms immediately began to flail as she searched for purchase on the slippery pool floor. I used the temporary distraction to hook my good arm through the crooks of her elbows, locking her arms in place behind her. Enough of my hand was free that I could use it to grab onto my shirt. I grabbed a handful of the soaking wet clothe and twisted my wrist to lock her in place as best I could.

She thrashed violently and threw her head back in an attempt to smash my face with the back of her skull. I had to turn my face away to avoid my nose getting broken but winced with each attempted headbutt as it jarred my injured shoulder. The harder she flailed, the harder I gripped onto my shirt, keeping her in place.

The muscles in my arm that I was using to lock her in place began to burn and I could feel my grip getting weaker as the strength drained from my fingers. I was moments from having to let go when I saw Katelyn and the security team through the glass walls surrounding the pool.

I breathed a sigh of relief until I saw that Katelyn wasn't looking at me and Crista, rather she was looking at the shape that was floating in the water.

The nurse.

I had completely forgotten about her and saw that she was lying face down with her long blonde hair floating around her. Her arms hung lifeless at her side, her feet were slowly starting to sink towards the bottom of the water.

I turned my attention back to Crista who was still thrashing against me, then back to the nurse. Cursing, I tossed Crista aside and ran as quickly as I could move through the water, swimming not an option at this point as my shoulder was throbbing worse than ever. I reached her in what felt like minutes, but must have only been seconds, and flipped her over with my good arm which now burned almost as much as my damaged one. I dragged her to the side of the pool as quickly as I could and lifted her awkwardly onto the pool deck, making sure I didn't let her head smack against the hard tiled floor. I threw one leg over the side of the pool, and pulled myself up with one arm in an awkward attempt at a roll.

I came over to the nurse and moved the hair out of her face.

It was Melissa.

Without another second of waiting, I tilted her head back, pinched her nose and pulled her chin down. I exhaled slowly and deeply into her mouth trying to prevent myself from breathing too hard too fast.

Suddenly, a hand wrapped itself around my ankle and pulled me back. My knees slipped out from under me and I felt the world spin as my chin clunked the tiled floor of the pool deck. The room spun as I tasted blood in my mouth, and slowly I felt myself being pulled into the water.

Crista roared behind me as her nails dug into my skin, and I knew I wouldn't be able to fight her off this time. The door to the pool was then thrown open and the two security staff members rushed the pool and grabbed Crista off of me. She began to twist away from their hands and clawed at them.

As she screeched with fury at them, I climbed back out of the pool and came back beside Melissa who was so blue and lifeless.

266

I always remembered from my First Aid courses that breathing too quickly into someone's mouth during CPR can sometimes make the air go to the stomach and not the lungs where it's needed. This causes their stomach to fill with air and almost always ends in the victim throwing up. I couldn't afford to make that mistake with her as it had already been minutes that she had gone without oxygen. I had to be careful to send the air to the right place if I had any chance of saving her.

After breathing into her mouth, I straightened up on my knees, interlocked my fingers and got ready for compressions. I felt my teeth grinding as I bit back the screams I wanted to let out at the blinding pain of my shoulder. I landmarked where to do the compressions and began pumping away. My muscles were exhausted from my fight with Crista and I myself had nearly drowned only moments before; I felt ready to pass out. I ignored the pain and continued pumping on her chest as best I could. My lower back and knees began to scream with fatigue and stiffness as I continued switching back and forth between compressions and breaths.

I had developed tunnel vision, as my intent to rescue her became so intense that I was blind to what was happening around me. Katelyn was calling for medical staff as we had an unconscious, unresponsive patient at the rehabilitation pool. The security team were still struggling with holding Crista and Katelyn was staying here with me, waiting for the med team.

I continued pumping away for what felt like hours, even though I knew it had only been a few minutes until finally I heard the sound of a crash cart and stretcher banging against the pool's walls. I breathed a sigh of relief. The sounds of the staff shouting instructions to each other was heaven to my ears, and when the first staff member knelt down across from me to take over CPR, I smiled before collapsing from the physical exhaustion.

I looked over and saw that the security team were holding Crista in place and walking her out of the pool. Before she stepped out of the water, she turned back to me with tears in her eyes.

She mouthed my name and I knew that Crista was awake in her body again.

I mouthed her name back to her and smiled.

Then everything went black.

Epilogue
September 2017 – Jack

Hi, you've reached the voicemail of Amy Ryan. I'm not available at the moment but if you leave me a detailed voicemail with your name and number I will return your call as soon as I can. Thank you.

"Hey, Ames. It's me. I got released a few months ago. Did you know that? Probably not, you're probably up there talking to all of your idols, the psychiatrists and social workers who wrote all of the textbooks that you refused to throw away even though they were ancient and eight editions behind. If only you had taken those textbooks with you, you'd be able to have them all signed!

"You're probably the only person I know who would get your textbooks signed and wouldn't be ashamed of it. It's one of the million things that I loved about you.

"So listen, I have to say goodbye. The psychiatrist told me that part of my release from the hospital and part of my release from you is dependent on me finally saying goodbye to your old phone that I've been paying for, for the past two years. I hadn't even paid attention to the credit card statements that told me I was paying for both yours and mine phone plans. I had never bothered cancelling it after you died, can you believe that?

"Maybe it was subconscious, maybe it was on purpose, I have no idea. But it was the only real sound of your voice I had.

"It's funny to me, how our parents always had videos and tapes of everything they did. Weddings, birthdays, parties and just videos of them around the house. And yet our generation, who has a perfect quality video recorder in our front pocket, never bother taking or saving videos of the same thing. I couldn't believe how I had not a single video of you and me together on my phone. The only thing I had that still let me hear your voice was your answering machine. And I would curse it every time I heard it. But now, I can't even wait for the four rings to hear you speak. I just want to hear it the second I call, I want to hear it again and again. I want to hear you again.

"But I have to stop. Dr. Hamilton said that I can't fully commit to any new relationships until I commit to saying goodbye to you. This includes my relationship with Melissa, the nurse who I had been running away from for the past few months. Dr. Hamilton told me that if I wanted to learn to care for her the way I once did for you, that I have to accept your death which means saying goodbye the things that won't let me move on.

"Mine and Melissa's relationship all started on that night. The night Crista tried to kill us both.

"After they took us both to emerge, they were able to resuscitate us both. I guess I had gone into severe shock from a combination of my broken collar bone and the exhaustion from the fight I had with Crista that was topped off with the CPR I gave to Melissa.

"It took them a while to bring her back to life, and even when they did, she didn't regain consciousness for a while.

"When I woke up in the hospital bed, I swore I saw you beside me. Holding my hand. I was so completely and entirely sure that it was you that I brought your hand to my face. It felt the same it always did, the cup of your hand fitting perfectly along my jaw. Perfectly fitting for each other.

"I kissed it, and then you were gone. In your place was Katelyn, a little bewildered by the kiss on the hand but she forgave me on account of the plethora of drugs I was on.

"When I finally woke up, I saw that Melissa was in the bed beside me, and from that day forward, we were spending all day together. Recovering together, healing together and fixing each other. She's since left the hospital and took a job at a retirement home, where there isn't any single nearby body of water.

"Me, you ask? Why I took a job at the university. They even gave me your old office. Not as a professor though, they said that it would be far too public and too much negative attention on the university if they hired me. Rather, my job is to help build, evaluate and continuously assess the Social Work Program, organizing guest speakers and helping the university complete publications and reports on supporting clients with mental health.

"And yes I know, that sounds too good to be true, right? Well it happened after I submitted an article to the Canadian Psychology Association about Dissociative Identity Disorder and the validity of the diagnosis. It got a lot of people's attention and helped repair my near broken reputation in the social services community. So much so, that the university was willing to overlook my terminated license and they hired me on full time in a scholarly capacity rather than in a counselling one.

"Things have been okay here for me. Not perfect, but they're getting better. And Crista, well they took her out of the hospital and put her in a full-time treatment centre, designed particularly for violent patients with mental health issues. The last I heard she still believes that it was her sister who attacked me. She has a very vivid memory of being on the other side of the glass, watching helplessly as Jane attacked Melissa and I. She still claims that Jane pushed the shelf on her even though it was flush against the wall, and her broken hand was lying under the exact spot where she had pulled it on top of herself.

"I asked Katelyn about the deaths that Crista had told me about in our sessions. From what she could find in news reports, incident reports and old records, the death of Jane, Taylor and Troy were all true. It appears as though the day at the park they were in fact playing with the dog, and the dog had fallen into the water. Jane had tried rescuing it, but Crista had walked onto the scene and had misconstrued what happened, thinking Jane was drowning it.

"So she pushed Jane away from the dog, not realizing she had pushed her sister into the water. She went into a state of shock afterwards and early assessments discussed that she truly believed her sister was still alive. It was her way of coping with the guilt of what she had done. The psychiatrists all believed it was just a phase of her recovery; however, she never came out of it. She always spoke of her sister as if she was right there beside her. People felt so bad for her that she had lost her twin that they never bothered saying anything, they simply let her keep believing her sister was still alive. When she was invited to parties or to a friend's house, she always asked if Jane was also invited. Everyone thought her mind was too broken to be able to commit the crimes that she was always surrounded by. No one even bothered accusing her of drowning Taylor or Troy even though they mirrored what happened to her sister.

"They never put the pieces together and each death was treated as an isolated event. But after years of splitting between personalities, she finally decided she wanted to try and kill one, so he burned her house down thinking Jane was inside. During her treatment, however, she began to feel more and more vulnerable, and anytime she felt weak or vulnerable, her stronger personality would take over. Jane would take over.

270

"Crista turned Jane into a murderer and a monster. Rather than the innocent 8-year-old girl she was when she died. She recreated their history, fabricated incidents and placed her at the scene of every murder. She was so wrapped up in this illusion by the end that she had re-written old memories to the point where she completely erased everything that actually happened. It wasn't that she was actively trying to convince herself that all of these things happened. It was that she actually believed all of these events with her sister occurred in the exact way she had written them.

"I wanted to visit her, but Dr. Hamilton told me that was a bad idea. She said that while it might be closure for me, the guilt of the incident might cause Crista to react poorly and potentially revert back to her Jane personality. I accepted that and for once wasn't stubborn.

"So instead I mailed Crista an Arctic Monkey's T-shirt along with a note that said:

They're not as bad as I thought they'd be…

Your friend, Jack with K

"I received a letter from her psychiatrist telling me that Crista with a C thanked me for the shirt and for giving her band a chance. However, her psychiatrist feels as though part of her recovery will require us to no longer be in contact.

"That was the last I heard from her.

"And I guess, this will be the last I hear from you. I'm cancelling your phone plan right after I leave you this message. But I kind of don't want to stop talking to you. I never want to forget you. I love you. LoveD you.

"I'm sorry about everything. I've forgiven myself, after months and months of therapy.

"I've finally learned to forgive myself. But I'm still sorry and I hope you forgive me. I hope that you didn't hate me in the end even though you have every right to.

"I hope that you know how much I loved you, and that you were the thing I loved most in this world.

"I guess that's all I have to say.

"I love you, Ames. I love you so much.

"I miss you.

"Goodbye."

If you are satisfied with your message, please hit pound.

I smiled as I hit the pound key.